KU-367-650

GAME TO MISS COWAN

GAME TO MISS COWAN

*A charming story of wartime love,
from an ever-popular author*

It is the summer of 1939 – the last, glorious
summer before the war. In Craigton, a small
Scottish seaside resort, Lisa Cowan falls in
love with a handsome pilot. During the
following years, Lisa and her family suffer
their share of hardship and tragedy. By the
time the war ends Lisa has grown into a
wiser and sadder woman, yet vulnerable still
to love...

GAME TO MISS COWAN

Frances Paige

Stockton Borough Public Libraries 4/02

00 41472624

Severn House Large Print
London & New York

This first large print edition published in Great Britain 2002 by
SEVERN HOUSE LARGE PRINT BOOKS LTD of
9-15, High Street, Sutton, Surrey, SM1 1DF.
First world regular print edition published 2001 by
Severn House Publishers, London and New York.
This first large print edition published in the USA 2002 by
SEVERN HOUSE PUBLISHERS INC., of
595 Madison Avenue, New York, NY 10022

Copyright © 2001 by Frances Paige

All rights reserved.
The moral right of the author has been asserted.

British Library Cataloguing in Publication Data

Paige, Frances
   Game to Miss Cowan. - Large print ed.
   1. World War, 1939-1945 - Social aspects - Scotland -
       Fiction
   2. Scotland - Social life and customs - 20th century - Fiction
   3. Love stories
   4. Large type books
   I. Title
   823.9'14 [F]

   ISBN 0-7278-7130-7

Except where actual historical events and characters are being
described for the storyline of this novel, all situations in this
publication are fictitious and any resemblance to living persons is
purely coincidental.

Printed and bound in Great Britain by
MPG Books Ltd, Bodmin, Cornwall.

One

You can't disown the past, Lisa thought, many years later, and the longer you live the more gilt-edged it becomes. Like a Tiffany vase. Like a fairy tale. Craigton, that little summer resort on the Firth of Clyde, certainly had the necessary story-book ingredients. The villagers, the yearly invasion from the big bad city, Glasgow, the castle (not a king's castle but owned by a shipping magnate), it was all idyllic, that particular, special time before the Giant came. Before the War.

That was the summer when Lisa Cowan was there with her family as usual, at nineteen still unsophisticated, as many gently nurtured girls were at that time, dark-haired, white-skinned – a pearliness, even, which you could imagine as dewy with the freshness of youth. Her eyes could still widen, kitten-like, when she was being teased, but they were intelligent, grey like her mother's, sometimes darkening to cobalt, wide-set, expressive eyes.

Being a modern fairy tale, in those rented villas at Craigton there were tennis rackets, golf clubs and fishing lines cluttering their entrance porches, wellington boots, raincoats, walking sticks, croquet mallets, knitting bags, folding prams, bicycles, a whole way of life transported for that precious month of summer, not forgetting baskets for collecting wild raspberries and, if it were late summer, blackberries.

Ragtime music from the wind-up gramophones floated on the summer air from the open windows. Those were the days of wine and roses, when the laughter was careless but tinged with sadness because it was August 1939 and Hitler was beginning to jack-boot over Europe...

On a warm day towards the end of August, Lisa Cowan stood at the end of the pier waiting for the afternoon steamer. Waiting for Beryl Craig. Another of Mother's ideas, but you could see the point – or could you? All the same, she had been obviously upset about the death of Beryl's father.

'Lionel Craig's dead,' she had said, raising her head from the letter, her face white, her eyes clouded. 'It's from his wife.'

Father had said he was sorry to hear it, but had gone on eating; that afternoon Lisa had come across her mother crouched on the window-seat halfway up the staircase, and when she'd looked up her face had been distorted with weeping, her eyes eating up her face.

'Is it Mr Craig, Mum?' she had said, puzzled. Her mother was the least demonstrative of women. Besides, they had only known the Craigs slightly during the time the Cowans had lived in the Glebe, the house in Kilmacolm, a village near Glasgow, which had been left to Mother on her parents' death.

Lisa tried again. 'I lost touch with Beryl Craig ages ago. Probably when I started travelling to Hutchy.' It was the school train journeys to Glasgow for Lisa and Tommy, her brother, coupled with the fact that Mother had also inherited Grandfather's business, an art dealership there, that had decided Mother to move back to the city. It must have suited Father too, as his office was in Glassford Street, but Lisa didn't remember that being discussed. She thought of adding, 'And I never liked her much anyhow,' but, remembering Beryl's stereotyped gold-and-pink prettiness, she thought it might sound like jealousy. Which it had been. At the time. Later she had become more discriminating.

Her mother's head was still bowed. Lisa stroked her bent back. 'He was a painter, wasn't he? Cheer up, Mum,' and thought immediately, What a crass thing to say. You were always being warned about false cheerfulness when someone was upset...

Her mother's back moved; there was a little pause as if she was gathering herself together, and then she was looking up apologetically at Lisa. The half-smile was more like a grimace; her eyes were bruised-looking. 'I'm being stupid,' she had said; 'I'd known him for such a long time, you see. Things ... get to you sometimes.' She was on her feet now. 'Water under the bridge...' And then a little laugh. 'I've had an idea!' It wasn't convincing, the sudden cheerfulness. Far from it. She looked gaunt, suddenly old. 'Perhaps Beryl would like to join us here for a holiday?'

She looked so pitiful that Lisa had stifled any protests. She knew her mother. That self-control. That iron determination. It was useless to protest...

She turned away from the sun-dazzle on the water, her eyes resting on the row of boys fishing off the pier, their legs dangling over its wooden side. She noticed one of them was Tommy, but, apart from a glance, he ignored her. Sisters had to be kept in their place. All the same, somebody should warn them of the danger, but that Dowthie, the piermaster, was too intent on the fat tips he got from the fathers when they

10

arrived with weekend cases and bags of delicacies from the Italian grocer in St Enoch Square.

Glasgow, and Craigton for the summer, suited Father better than the Glebe. It had always been Mother's house, Grandfather's business. He looked much happier nowadays, or, at least, content. You could never say he looked deliriously happy, he wasn't that type, but he was his own man in the Holland Street flat where they now lived, and he had made friends with the other male commuters on the steamer at the weekends. Tommy, who came out with quite sharp remarks occasionally, said that Dad hadn't liked being a kept man.

'There's the boat, Lisa!' he called, deigning to recognise her.

'You watch you don't fall in!' she cautioned him, worried about the nonchalant way he swivelled round. The water was deep there. She shrugged as she turned away to watch the steamer advancing towards them like a stately dowager. Its shape reminded her of Miss Mawson, her former headmistress at Hutcheson's: the same jutting bust – well, prow.

She saw Beryl waving from the deck and was nearly bowled over by the rush of young fishermen eager to catch the mooring rope thrown by a deckhand. But Mr Dowthie was already there.

'Out o' ma way, boys!' he was shouting, officious now that his moment had arrived. 'Stand away frae the gangway!'

Beryl Craig was first, tripping down neatly in a white belted mackintosh, the collar turned up (*à la* Marlene Dietrich); she still had the same golden curls and pink cheeks; her lipstick had been generously applied. 'Here I am! Just made it!' And as she grew nearer she shrieked, 'Long time no see!' and, rushing at Lisa, gave her a great hug. 'You haven't changed!' And immediately, 'How d'you like my shoes? A sale in that dear shop in Sauchiehall Street! Real snake-skin!' The passengers were brought to a halt behind her as she waved a smartly shod foot. And shouldn't she be wearing black?

'Lovely! Come on, I'll take your bag. Daddy's waiting with the car.' The whole holiday, she thought, as they walked towards the end of the pier. She had planned to have a 'thinking' time, about life and her future. Should she scrub the Art School and volunteer for one of the women's services? Tommy had assured her that war was imminent now that Germany was preparing to invade Poland. At fourteen he was more *au fait* with developments than her father, and Mother, who generally took an intelligent interest in world affairs, had become 'different' somehow, since Mr Craig's death.

On the other hand, apropos her future, perhaps it would be better to equip herself so that she could help her mother in the Sauchiehall Street premises of Alexander Lyle and Son, the family business. She had difficulty in employing staff nowadays, she'd said, the young ones were leaving her to volunteer. Sometimes Lisa thought she was like the non-existent 'Son' of the title. She certainly had inherited Grandfather's artistic flair.

One good thing that she had forgotten about Beryl was how she talked, and talked. Her snakeskin shoes clattered expensively on the wooden boarding of the pier, her chattering was non-stop. It saved Lisa making conversation. If she hadn't been lumbered with Beryl her plan had been to cut out tennis this year and go in for a Proust-like seclusion instead, occasionally taking contemplative solitary walks in the gentle hills above the shore road.

'Yoo-hoo!' Now Beryl was shouting and waving as she saw Lisa's father in his Vauxhall. 'Here I am, Mr Cowan! Up to time!' Lisa saw the masculine look of approval before it changed to conventional sympathy. Men, even fathers, were all susceptible to Beryl's feminine charms.

'Well done, Beryl!' He had jumped out from behind the wheel and was shaking hands with her. 'You two girls get in the back. I'll stow away the stuff.' Father could always be relied upon to play his part.

'Are you sure you can manage, Mr Cowan?' How often Glasgow people said that, and Beryl was certainly one for clichés. 'Can you manage?' shop assistants said, giving you a tiny parcel with a loop for your finger. 'Are you sure you can manage?' Beryl hopped in with a flash of snakeskin and sat back smugly, tightening even tighter the belt of her mackintosh. 'Plenty of room, Lisa!' Lisa hopped.

'I see you've brought your tennis racket. I wondered...'

'Yes, Mummy said I had to try and enjoy myself...' Her face fell into sad lines. 'Life must go on...'

'That's the sensible way to look at it,' Lisa's father said from his place behind the wheel.

'He's right, Beryl.' Lisa wondered how *she* would feel in Beryl's place, and warmed to the girl. 'We'll try and make it a good holiday for you.'

'Mummy thought I'd be better with some young company, Mr Cowan. She's gone to Granny's.'

'Quite right. Well, we'll do what we can.' He revved up the engine.

'Didn't you *want* me to bring my racket, Lisa?' Beryl's voice was plaintive.

'Yes, of course. It's just that I'd grown ...

14

well, a little beyond the club here. It tends to be parents and families ... but there's no saying this year ... There's Joe's Café, look. It's quite spruced up this year. Morning coffees, and that sort of thing.' She felt a wave of sympathy for the girl. It must be terrible, your father dying. Hers always seemed immortal, and there was Mr Craig, possibly the same age ... Her parents still played tennis, seemed young yet, well, age-less...

The road curved in front of them, following the stony shore-line where as children they had built fires and made smoky tea with the holiday crowd. It had been fun. And Tommy had skiffed a stone and hit her leg, which had bled profusely and frightened the life out of him.

One thing was sure: she must put away her plans about coming to terms with the fact that soon war was going to swamp everyone like an avalanche, and concentrate on this girl who had lost her father. It was what Mother wanted.

They bumped over the rough, hilly road leading to their rented villa, and Dad turned into the gravel drive leading to it, and there was Mother emerging from the wooden porch with its scalloped roof-edging like a cuckoo clock to welcome the visitor.

'Here we are!' Father said, stopping, and Mother was opening the door on Beryl's side. They always seemed to work as a team. She was helping the girl out.

'I'm glad you were able to come, Beryl.' She put her arms round Beryl and kissed her. How pale she was. 'Come along in and we'll have a nice cup of tea. Lisa, help Dad.' You could tell she had been crying. Her eyes were dark-ringed. 'It was good of your mother to spare you at this sad time,' she was saying.

Lisa smiled at her father as she helped him with the luggage. 'I don't know if she wanted this, but she's doing her stuff.'

'As usual,' her father said.

The two girls were quiet as they walked up the hill to the tennis club the following morning. Everything will be different after this holiday, Lisa was thinking. Even Beryl must feel the shadow looming over them. Tommy had spread the *Glasgow Herald* over the table after breakfast, hunting for the latest news. 'On the brink,' he had said. Mother and Father hadn't spoken, Beryl had looked uninterested. Perhaps personal grief blotted out everything else.

How often she had toiled up this hill as a schoolgirl. She could remember the feel of small pebbles through the thin soles of her white sandshoes. The fields looked golden glimpsed through gaps in the hedge, the trees ink-black, there was the occasional haystack. Monet had painted them at all times of the day. They had done the Impressionists at school before she left, but maybe she should give up artistic metaphors now and call a spade a spade, recognise the ugliness but the necessity of war.

She turned back to check the wide expanse of the Firth, blue today, a few white sails. Tommy was keen to have a dinghy. A blackbird which seemed to have climbed the hill with them let out a raucous call, piercing yet sweet. 'Maybe it's a good idea, tennis,' she said to Beryl, who turned a sad face to her. Lisa put a comforting arm round her. 'It will take your mind off ... things. And there might be new people...'

'Mummy insisted I should come.' Beryl seemed prepared to be consoled. 'And she bought a new racket for me.'

'We'll DOB.' She spoke brightly. 'That's what that brother of mine used to say when he was a Cub. Saluting.'

'You're lucky to have a brother.'

'Oh, they're a mixed blessing.' She had been pleased with Tommy, who'd held out a fishy hand when he'd come back from the pier yesterday. 'Glad you came, Beryl. Sorry about your father.' Gruffly, but not bad for fourteen.

'You first,' she said as they reached the wicket gate. As she followed Beryl she saw that the Allans were sitting in deck-chairs on the veranda of the pavilion. They were all right, Mr and Mrs Allan, although he was inclined to think he owned the club. Jane Allan waved when she saw Lisa and called, 'Are your parents not coming?'

She walked with Beryl towards the wooden steps. 'Not today, Mrs Allan.' And, when they were at the top, 'This is Beryl Craig who's staying with us. Mr and Mrs Allan, Beryl.'

'Glad to meet you, Miss Craig.' Cubby Allan's eyes always lit up at the prospect of a new member. 'We like to see new faces here, especially pretty ones.' Beryl smiled, pleased.

'We've a guest here as well,' Jane Allan said. 'Neil McLean. That's him umpiring just now. Sit down, girls. And there's an old friend of yours here, Lisa, Bruce Semple. He's in the clubhouse making tea. Neil's parents have taken the steamer round the Kyles today since it was fine.'

Lisa wasn't listening. Her eyes were on the young man perched high on the umpire seat. He was dark, his hair fell over his forehead, the cuffs of his white shirt-sleeves fell over his wrists, his long white flannelled legs were curled round the metal legs of the seat. Everything about him looked loose, like a happenstance, and yet elegant, as a loose but well-made suit is elegant.

As if he was aware of her scrutiny, he

turned and looked directly at Lisa. He smiled, and the smile pierced her, dazzled her, and she was lost immediately. Her face went red. She turned away in confusion as Bruce Semple came out of the clubhouse carrying a tray of cups, and she thought, He's as different as night from day, stocky, fair-haired, ordinary. Last year she had thought she was in love with him.

'Lisa!' he said, 'I knew you'd be bound to come. Once you heard *I* was here, eh?'

'Well, you know you're irresistible.' She laughed loudly, falsely. 'This is an old schoolfriend, Beryl Craig, primary school, actually. Your fame has spread.'

'Howdy, Beryl!' Bruce said, and burst into song, '"A'm jus' an ole cowhand ... From the Rio Grande ..."' Last year she would have thought that funny. Beryl giggled. 'Have a cup of tea, Beryl. Thank goodness Lisa's brought someone decent along at last.'

'I'm glad you're pleased.' Beryl's eyes were sparkling. 'I knew there was a club, so I brought my tennis racket, just in case...'

'Game to Miss Christie and partner!' It was Neil McLean's voice, and as Lisa turned she saw him shin down from his perch and go towards the players to con-gratulate them. In a minute or two he was bounding up the stairs to the pavilion.

'Stint over, Neil? Well done!' Cubby Allan

19

joined him.

'Thank you.' His eyes were on Lisa. 'How about someone introducing me?'

'Trust you,' Bruce said. 'Thinks he's Lothario. Lisa is an old pal of mine. Miss Lisa Cowan, Mr Neil McLean,' he swept off an imaginary hat, 'and she's brought along her friend, Missy Beryl, who's jus' come ridin' by.'

'Beryl Craig,' Lisa said. Strange how you changed your mind about people ... She couldn't imagine this Neil McLean behaving so childishly. He was altogether different from Bruce. Where Bruce was ruddy, he had an olive-skinned complexion, so smooth that it looked as if it had been poured over his cheekbones, and his eyebrows were dark.

'All the girls fall for Neil,' Bruce said. 'He's in the Air Force. It's the uniform, of course.'

'Are you?' Lisa asked. 'Are you really?'

'Voluntary Reserve. I'm based outside Oxford.'

'Oxford!' Beryl said, her eyes round. 'I'd love to go to Oxford. Dreaming spires and all that.'

'And munitions factories before long.' Neil McLean smiled kindly on her. 'But there's still the river.' He turned to Lisa and his smile had changed, become intimate. She drew an imaginary hand down her face to smooth out the immediate response, a kind of tremulousness which she couldn't understand. She turned her glance to the other two.

Bruce was obviously smitten. Most men, she felt, would fall for Beryl. Mother had once said that Beryl's mother, Grace, had been known in Kilmacolm as a flirt. She and Beryl shared a blonde, blue-eyed prettiness, and perhaps, Lisa thought, a capacity for making men feel good. There was a kind of wide-eyed admiration which she supposed they fell for.

Jane Allan called from her deck-chair: 'Why don't you four bag that court while it's free? Neil would probably like a game now.'

'Sure,' he said.

'You'd like a game, wouldn't you, Beryl?' Lisa asked. She kept her eyes away from Neil.

'Oh, yes! Ready, willing and able. I'm game for a game.' She laughed prettily at her own wit. 'Shall I go first?'

She went tripping down the steps, her legs plump and shapely beneath her short skirt. Bruce had got rid of his tray on a table, picked up the racket lying there and was close behind her.

'Ready, Lisa?' Neil McLean turned to her. A racket seemed to have grown in his hand. There was a copy of a painting in their gallery at Lyle's of Byron, the poet. The resemblance was there, the same brooding, sad look in spite of Neil's quick smile, the same dark hair falling over his forehead.

'Ready,' she said. The tremulousness was there again.

Two

She and Neil must have played well,
because at the end, which came quickly, she
heard Cubby Allan's voice from the umpire
seat: 'Game to Miss Cowan and partner!
Game, set and match.'

The spin of the racket had paired her with
Neil, and from the beginning they were a
unit, as if controlled by one brain. Every
nerve in her body seemed tightened; she
had never been more light-footed.

Because of his height he had a long-reach-
ing, smashing serve, and she complemented
its power by being reliable and keen-eyed at
the net. She heard a ripple of applause from
time to time, and saw that there were more
people on the veranda than before...

Neil remained cool, though there was the
odd joking remark when they passed each
other, and when it was over she scarcely felt
tired.

'What got into you?' Beryl said to her as
they met at the net to shake hands. 'You

were all over the place.'

Lisa shook her head, smiling, looking at Neil.

'We were like two peas in a pod,' he said. 'I had to do my damnedest to keep up with her.' His eyes were admiring.

She noticed Bruce was unusually silent. It was unlike him.

They split into two couples from then on, Beryl and Bruce playing more tennis than they did. If Grace Craig had wanted her daughter to be diverted, Lisa thought, she would be more than satisfied. They were soul-mates, and Beryl was obviously happy. Her flirtatiousness had gone, as if there was no need to use it now that she had met Bruce. He was soft-eyed when he looked at her. Already they seemed an ideal couple.

She and Neil were different in temperament. She knew she was sociable; he was polite, amusing, but reserved, as if he didn't want to become closely involved; and yet she was drawn to him as she had never been to anyone before. There had been various young men in her life, but there had always been a feeling that they were temporary, part of her sexual progress.

Neil was introspective; sometimes he was withdrawn and scarcely spoke, at other times he was brilliantly funny, clowning to amuse her, but always the sight of him gladdened her in a particular way.

He was very handsome, of course, with a natural elegance, but she had always said she didn't like handsome men. Bruce was a prototype, athletic, stockily built with a pleasant, laughing face, amiable, not imaginative.

Neil was an enigma. Sometimes he talked incessantly, mostly about flying, never about his parents or home; other times he fell into silences. She found herself watching him for changes of mood, obsessed by his quicksilver temperament and taking a peculiar pleasure in his dark good looks. Put simply, she was captivated and didn't understand herself. In only one thing was he consistent, and that was in his obsession with flying. 'The air is my preferred element,' he said once, and she found herself feeling jealous of this obsession of his, already wishing that she came first in his life.

'Aren't you ever afraid?' she asked him. 'You could be in danger sooner than you think.'

He shook his head. 'It can't come soon enough. Flying's been my life. I joined the Volunteer Reserves when I was eighteen.'

'You're so different from me. I fear the War coming. There should be a different way.'

'Ah, but it gives you a chance to prove yourself. That's the thing that matters most to me in my life, to prove myself.' She was left with a feeling of dismay at his attitude, that she didn't count in his scheme of things. He would be gone in a few days and she would never see him again. The thought was unbearable, a physical pain.

In this frame of mind she felt that Craigton had never looked more serene, more beautiful. It was like a soothing balm. There was nothing dramatic in this small coastal village, which had been chosen by her mother as a convenient weekend retreat for Father, and a place where she could move for two months during the school holidays. Since her parents had died, leaving her the Kilmacolm house, she'd always had a peculiar reluctance to spend much time there. Lisa had wondered if it had been anything to do with Lionel Craig, especially since she had seen the effect his death had had on Mother.

But here in Craigton, for everyone, there was nothing but pleasant memories. Tommy loved fishing and knew the village boys; until this year Lisa had been an ardent tennis player; her mother seemed more relaxed; and Father, always amenable, took the weekly boat from Craigendoran or sometimes the ferry across the Firth to the Craigton pier, the whole journey taking little more than an hour.

Craigton's familiarity increased its charm for Lisa. She enjoyed showing her favourite walks to Neil, the short cuts to the High

Road, the untouched territory above that, a strange limestone country of mossy ground inhabited only by sheep where one's feet released the smell of thyme. Lower down there was Middle Wood, the lush dells where the blackberries were thickest, and dark woods where raspberries gleamed ruby red.

Once, when they were sitting in the dimness of the wood, she tried to tell him something of her background.

'Mother inherited an art dealer's business from her parents, and their house at Kilmacolm. You'll know it possibly. In Renfrewshire. But she likes our flat in Holland Street for convenience. She has a good staff, but she's getting worried that the younger ones might be called up. All through my schooldays in Glasgow, I haunted Lyle's after four o'clock, fascinated by it. She told me she did the same. It must have been the smells, paint and glue in the work-room, then there was the front with the gallery, and the great files of prints I was allowed to look through if my hands were clean. The whole atmosphere ... the shop window generally only had one painting on an easel, draped with velvet. There was never any rush or bustle. Just quiet and respectful. And I've been wondering if...'

He interrupted her. 'But you're going to the Art School first, aren't you?' He had his arm round her as they sat.

'I *was*, but...'

He hugged her against him. 'Training is what matters. The War will end. *You're* all right. Shh!' He was looking at a red squirrel climbing a nearby tree and they stayed very quiet, his arm still round her. She waited for him to kiss her, but he didn't.

'Yes, but sometimes I see her looking very tired – ever since Beryl's father died, strangely enough. It worries me. Dad would never go into the business. He's an account-ant. I'm sure he'd help her if he could, but he's a moron when it comes to art.'

He laughed. 'What an intellectual snob you are! And *you* aren't a moron when it comes to art?' He mimicked her.

'No, I'm like her. She took us to galleries when we were quite small and I loved them. Dad would take us to pantomimes.'

'That's art too.' He laughed again. 'All the same I think you should start your studies in September. See how things go.'

'Or join up?' She met his eyes. 'Men aren't the only people who can fight for their country. I might even become a WAAF, be posted beside you.' She was watching his face. 'I expect they'll have women too.'

'Haven't noticed. I can't see past Spitfires, or Whitley bombers.'

'I wonder you noticed *me*.'

'You're acting like Beryl. Of course I

noticed you.' His eyes were on her, dark, serious. 'If I could choose, you're the girl I'd want to live with, to be close to for the rest of my life.' His voice was calm, and she laughed incredulously.

'I thought it was one-sided!'

'Far from it. We could live together ... if it were possible.' He bent his head and kissed her on the mouth, like a seal between them, chastely, as if he were on hallowed ground. She could have wept. Instead she was suddenly deeply, darkly angry.

'I'm cold!' she said peevishly, and shook herself free. 'I thought you said we should walk up to the High Road to see the lights.' She had told him that it was one of the things she liked best, tracing the car-lights on the opposite shore. She had imagined them looking from a hollow in the hillside, close in the darkness.

'You're annoyed,' he said. 'Did you want me to roll you in the grass?'

'Don't be stupid!' She got up. He would have seen the desire in her eyes. So what? she thought.

She was introduced to his parents at the tennis club, which only added to the puzzle. His father was amiable, an accountant like her own father, and the two men chatted together. His mother was withdrawn, haughty, unfashionable, and her eyes followed Neil. Lisa's mother commented on it at the supper table. 'Is Neil McLean a mother's boy? She seems devoted to him.'

'I don't like her much,' Tommy put in. 'She looks down her nose – when she's not looking at Neil. His father seems OK.'

'Nobody asked for your opinion,' Lisa said.

'Bruce says he can't get very far with Neil,' Beryl said. 'You know how funny Bruce is, but Neil doesn't laugh at his jokes.'

'No wonder!' Tommy said.

'Tommy!' James Cowan looked up. 'Beryl's a guest. I liked Mr McLean. Very friendly. He plays golf at Hagg's Castle. He's invited me for a game when we get back.'

'Did you see them together?' Tommy said, sniggering. 'She's tall and skinny, he's short and fat. Mutt and Jeff!'

'That's enough. Supposing we leave the McLeans for the time being,' Jean Cowan said. 'Anyone for more shepherd's pie?' She touched her forehead as if she were wearied by the conversation and turned to Beryl. 'See what a nice friendly family we are, Beryl. Never a cross word.'

'Oh, Mum and I are the same, go at each other with knives. She's got a temper. She tried it on with Dad when he was alive but he just smiled.' Lisa saw her mother's eyes widen almost as if she had been struck, and then she was on her feet. 'Just remembered something...' She went quickly out of the room.

'Hope I didn't say anything out of place,' Beryl said, 'but it's true.' She bent her head to her plate. Neil had said Beryl had no imagination. He was right.

They had their last walk together the following evening. Neil was due back at Oxford and had to catch an early steamer the next day for Glasgow.

'I've conveniently brought a raincoat,' he said, 'so that I can spread it on the ground like Sir Walter Raleigh. I noticed you didn't like the log.'

'It wasn't the log.' She was on edge. 'But in any case, we're out for a walk. We don't have to stop.'

'But we do. We must be comfortable when we're saying goodbye. We'll be like the Babes in the Wood except that we're luckier than they were, living in such exciting times...' She was going to reply but he put his hand on her arm. 'Here's just the place.' It was a mossy clearing dotted with the pink of sacrifage. He spread the coat and said, smiling, 'Will this suit Madame?'

She had been oddly uneasy, but her good temper came back. He was going away. She mustn't be peevish. 'You're daft,' she said, laughing, and sat down, then stretched out full-length and rested her head on her folded arms. She felt his light breathing on her face and the weight of his body. 'Here, this is a bit sudden!' She tried to smile.

'Not to worry. I just wanted to see what it was like in the seduction pose. Did I frighten you?' He kissed her gently, his lips soft, a clean, innocent kiss.

She met his dark eyes, and shook her head, frustrated. 'Neil, I can't understand you. Kiss me again.'

It was the same kind of kiss, but its very innocence aroused her. A slow, deep thrill went through her. She tried to subdue it, not to move. They lay silently with their mouths together. Her heart was beating loudly. He must hear it.

'Love is … painful … difficult. I can't…' He put his face against hers, and she felt his cheek wet. She bit her lip, her own eyes filling. 'There will be leaves.' His voice was low. 'I'd rather see you than go home, much rather … and I'll write. Maybe I'll be better at writing…'

She didn't understand his sadness, couldn't cope with his strangeness. Was it some trouble with his parents? Or innocence? But he was three years older than her. Or the coming war? But that should have made him *more* demonstrative rather than less. 'Yes, we'll write,' she said. 'And we'll see each other. Don't worry. We'll be happy.'

'Yes, that's it.' His voice became cheerful.

'And you'll be my lucky charm when I'm away.' He suddenly rolled off her, jumped to his feet and held out his hands. 'Come on, I'm being a fool.' They stood together for a moment and she wondered if she should ask him what was worrying him. No, he'd tell her when he was ready.

She smiled at him. 'I thought we were out for a walk?'

They went slowly downhill, his arm round her, and once again they were at ease; he was boyishly funny, almost like Tommy and he acted as if he hadn't a care in the world. Was she too sensitive? She laughed with him, and told herself she would never have liked an ordinary man anyhow, but her heart was screwed up with doubt, and a searing kind of love.

His farewell kiss at her gate was passionate. It left her shaking and in tears. 'Sorry,' he said. 'Oh, sorry, Lisa. I'm hopeless. I never get it right.' He touched her cheek gently. 'Think of me.' Before she could reply he had turned and left her. The pain was acute, a mixture of frustration, anger and love.

Beryl, she found when she went in, was in a different mood – as she put it, 'in the seventh heaven of delight', but her eyes were tender. Hers was a straightforward kind of love with no problems. Lisa was envious.

'We're going to get married just as soon as

we can make plans. But he wants me to have my domestic-science training first. Says it's essential for a farmer's wife. His parents will clear out to a cottage and give us the farm, and can you believe it, Lisa, the best bit of it? He's in a reserved occupation! He won't have to go away and fight! Oh, I'm so glad your mother asked me here and I met Bruce.'

Lisa listened and made pleased and encouraging comments. She couldn't have borne to speak about Neil.

Three

1939–40

It seemed that the Cowans' return to Glasgow was a signal for Hitler to start moving. At the beginning of September he did what everyone had been waiting for with trepidation, crossed the Polish border. The War had truly begun.

Tommy, in their comfortable flat in Holland Street, soon had his room papered with maps. Jean Cowan said she had ceased to worry, for the time being, about losing staff: business was at a standstill. There was a feeling that the whole country was drawing breath, taking stock. James Cowan said they must gird their loins. He was having to work late because the young ones on his staff were rushing to enlist. He had done the same in the last war.

Lisa decided the sensible thing to do after all was to enrol at the Art School, since she had an allocated place there. Secretly she was looking forward to it, and her desire to join up had temporarily gone. She hadn't heard from Neil and it would take her mind off him.

She enjoyed the School, its freedom after Hutcheson's, the excitement of meeting new people, joining societies; she liked the curriculum, which satisfied her need to know more about art and that world which had interested her almost as soon as she could read. She had only a mediocre aptitude for drawing and painting: her talent lay in her appreciation and perception; as her mother said, she had a good eye. She would have made a good teacher had that appealed to her.

She studied at home, she went to various museums and art galleries in student groups and was asked out by various young men. Sometimes she accepted, but their ordinariness, as she thought of it, only reminded her all the more of Neil and his strange, puzzling quality.

At first she pictured his life, the excitement of flying, but when she read of the fatalities at the Kiel Canal she agonised that he might be involved. As time wore on, however, she managed to convince herself that no news was good news.

He had wanted to be involved, he had said he had to 'prove himself'. Why was that so necessary? She would get annoyed at herself for worrying about him, then her annoyance would be overtaken by a shudder of fear when she read statistics of the short life expectancy of a war pilot.

In bed at night she would visualise his features, the easy elegance of his walk, the brooding dark eyes, the impish smile when he was teasing her. He was her yardstick, and when she turned down invitations from congenial male students she was angry with herself for having become obsessed by someone who was obviously not truly interested in her.

Tommy was having a fine time. His school had been taken over by the Army and classes were reduced to one or two days a week. Teachers were joining up. He tinkered endlessly with the wireless he was trying to make, and lounged about the house except when as a prefect he was given the job of visiting young evacuees in the country. Jean gave him errands to run on his bicycle. She didn't seem to worry about his idleness, and Lisa would remind herself that she had never been a fussy mother.

She, too, 'did her bit', going to soldiers' canteens in the evenings, taking a short nursing training and spending weekends at a hospital for chronic tubercular patients, standing in for nurses who had volunteered. She enjoyed being there, and the teasing she got from the young male patients. 'A want a boattle, Lisa!' one would call, 'but ye'll hiv to help me,' or, throwing back the bed-clothes, 'Can a no' staun in for yer boy-friend?' She would laugh to herself as she made her way home after a stint, and think that it must be hard for them, lying there month after month realising their useless-ness.

But nothing shifted Neil from her mind, which kept going back to Craigton and the few days she had known him. He couldn't be as innocent as he had seemed, she would think. He was twenty-two, for God's sake. She would compare him with the young men she met at the Art School, their pseudo-sophistication, their sexual aware-ness. They played the usual game. Neil didn't seem to know there *was* one. But then she would remember his passionate farewell kiss which had left her in tears ... Frus-tration made her sleepless. But then with Christmas came the long-awaited letter.

Dear Lisa,
It has been impossible to write earlier, but you are still first in my mind and in my heart.

I'm getting a short leave before an important mission, but will have to spend Christmas Day with my parents. If you could meet me at Central Station at six o'clock that evening we could have a few hours together before I catch the train back. It would be wonderful. No time to write more. Please don't disappoint me. All my love, Neil.

The Cowans generally spent Christmas at The Glebe, which was looked after in their absence by Margaret Currie, a former maid of Lisa's grandmother. She had been approached, since the house was large, to take in evacuees, and Jean had agreed. Margaret and her husband, Alec, were childless, and they had said they were willing to look after them.

James Cowan had wanted the family to move to Kilmacolm when the War started because he was convinced that living in cities was dangerous, but Jean had vetoed it. She had to be near the business; Tommy and Lisa must be near their schools. In his usual amiable fashion he had given in. Sometimes Lisa was surprised at her father's constant amiability, almost a blandness. She had never seen her parents quarrel. It wasn't her idea of marriage, but maybe that was how it became. Where's the passion? she would think. Did every marriage reach a status quo?

'I have to meet Neil McLean at six,' she told them when they were having their Christmas dinner. 'Do you remember him?'

'The brooding young man?' Jean said.

'He's a pilot. You'd be brooding too!' she flared.

Her mother smiled at her. 'Sorry. A brave lad.'

'Where should we be without them?' Her husband backed her up.

'Remember and pump him,' Tommy said. 'Get as much detail as you can. Find out about his missions...'

'Careless talk costs lives, little boy.' She got up from the table. 'I shan't be late. He's catching a train back tonight.' She tried to look calm, speak calmly. She saw her mother's look, *that* look, typical.

Three months, she thought, as she made her way to the usual meeting-place in the station, the Shell, a First World War relic. He'd see her there easily.

She had only waited a few minutes when she saw him coming towards her, his tall figure made more distinctive by the Air Force uniform, the long, blue-grey greatcoat. No one could possibly look more elegant.

'Lisa!' he said, taking both her hands as he reached her. 'Even more beautiful!'

'Hey! Aren't you going to kiss me?' She tried to smile but it went crooked.

'Of course.' He put his arms round her, his face against hers, she felt his mouth on her cheek. Just the same ... he couldn't be shy at the Shell! Kissing had become public since the War, especially here, the place for arrivals and departures.

'When is your train?' She released herself, saying the first thing that came into her mind.

'Do you want rid of me already?' Now it was the impish smile she loved and she was immediately happy, complete. 'Nine o'clock, since you ask. I thought we might walk about the streets in the blackout. I just want to feel you near. Then we'll come back here and have something to eat.'

'All right.' Anything suited her. 'You look good, Neil, but thinner.'

'Oh, they feed you well, especially the mammoth breakfasts after a raid, but it's a fraught existence, as you can imagine. You look so ... wholesome.'

'That makes me sound like a dairy-maid.' Somehow the remark made her think of Beryl. 'Remember Beryl? She's learning to bake scones and things and pluck chickens and game, getting ready to be a farmer's wife for Bruce Semple. They're very happy.'

'So are we.'

'Are we?' She looked up at his thin, pale face and drew a breath. 'So we are. Let's walk.'

'OK.' They made for the steps leading to Union Street. 'I should have said "beautiful" instead of wholesome,' he said.

41

'Second thoughts? But you'd said that already.'

'You'll grow in beauty, that's the difference.'

'Thanks.' She looked at him. 'But you're teasing again.'

He shook his head. In the dim light of the blackout he said, 'Take my arm and keep close so that I know you're there. I've dreamt of this ... Isn't it mysterious? Different from a floodlit runway. Even the traffic seems subdued, quieter than I remember ... waiting. Put your hand in my pocket if it's cold. That's the only thing I suffer from, the cold. But I've fur boots and fur gloves. There's hardly room for me in the cockpit.' They turned towards Argyle Street.

A miserable Glasgow drizzle started falling, and she clung closely and put the side of her face against his shoulder. It was the kind of cold that dug into your bones. I should like to be in bed with him, she thought, lie against his long lean length... 'Tell me more about your life,' she said.

'Torpor, then great bursts of activity, elation, sometimes getting roaring drunk ... it's an odd kind of life. The public-school boys held off at first, but they were quick learners. It's all right now. They're great chaps. They don't show fear. The difference is, I don't feel it. Tell me about *your* life.'

'It's good. Suits me. I'm going into art

history, studying painters, their lives as well as their work. The Glasgow Boys. The Glasgow Girls. The School makes them come to life, they haunt it. And we go further back, of course, Italian painters, Spanish ... Yes, it suits me. I'm eternally curious.'

There was a pause.

'And how are your parents?' he said politely.

'Fine. Mother seems better now that she's got the business to run.'

'How's your brother?'

He sounds old-fashioned, she thought. It must be his parents. That mother...

'Being Tommy. Directing the War from his bedroom. He would have come along with me if I'd let him, so that he could pump you.'

'Yes?' He sounded amused. 'Who is he like?'

'Like?'

'Your mother or your father?'

'Strangely enough, neither. Tommy is ... Tommy. I'm like my mother, the same eyes and colouring, and I think I have the same temperament. Not like my father's. He goes on from day to day, imperturbable. I'd say, "Still waters run deep," but I don't think it applies in his case.' She couldn't restrain herself. 'You're so polite, Neil!'

'I'm nervous. Can't get over the joy of

meeting you. I'm not good at chit-chat with girls.'

'Don't worry. As long as you're here.' She pressed close to him.

They had reached Argyle Street and they turned right and went into the cavern under the railway bridge. It was colder than ever, her bones were aching with it. 'I don't fancy this much longer, do you?' she said, shivering.

'No. I liked the thought of just you and me in the darkness, isolated, but things never work out as you expect. All I feel is sad ... sad...'

'I'm sorry I make you sad.'

'Oh, it isn't you!' He turned towards her. 'You're ... joyous!'

Joyous, she thought. That's a strange one.

They walked round the corner into the narrow river of Hope Street and up towards the station entrance. There were a few taxis parked, and Lisa saw the glowing tip of a cigarette in one of them. Was that an offence, she thought, a security risk? She was glad to go into the hotel with Neil because of the cold, but all thought of food had left her.

In the lounge he said, 'Shall we have a sherry first and plan what we'll eat?'

'I'd like the sherry, thanks, but I'm not very hungry. How about you?'

'The same. I had a huge lunch at home.'

44

'How are your parents?' She laughed. 'And *I'm* not nervous!' She remembered his mother, how her eyes had followed him at the tennis club. She would make anyone nervous.

'Mother weeps when she sees me. I don't know whether it's because she's glad I've come back ... or she wishes that I hadn't.'

'You're cynical. How about your father?'

'He whacks me on the back, gives me a drink and tells me lousy jokes. The atmosphere is...' He shrugged. 'I don't make them happy, the opposite, and all I long for is to be up there, free as a bird...' His eyes shone for a minute. 'And I don't think they're happy together, either.'

'I sometimes think that of my parents.'

'Maybe it's because both fathers are accountants.' He smiled with the sudden impish smile she liked, and she thought, That's the Neil I want. 'Let's have some sandwiches and then you won't say to your parents that I didn't give you anything to eat.'

'They don't ask for a blow-by-blow account.'

The sandwiches and coffee came, and they talked about Craigton and meeting there and he said, 'I'm going to tell you something. That was the happiest week in my whole life. I treasure it. I'll never be happier.'

'It could go on being happy.'

'Do you think so?' His dark eyes, brooding, were on her. 'You're what ... might have been.'

'The War's getting you down. It was the happiest week in my life too, but I don't have your feeling of impending doom. Oh, I understand why, but I hope you haven't a ... death wish?' She looked at him.

'Me?' He smiled at her and shook is head. 'I'm living the life I wanted, the only one, the only suitable one. I don't want to come down, go back ... When I'm up there I'm in heaven ... I know that sounds stupid as I say it, but it's truly ... celestial, which, when you come to think of it, is heavenly. I'm like that French guy, St Exupéry.'

She didn't know of him. 'Or Icarus?'

'Who was that?' He leant towards her and kissed her lightly. 'You're trying to outdo me with literary allusions.'

'Well, you tell me first. Who was St Exupéry?'

'Some day, in the life I'd like, but will never have, I'll give you a present of *Le Petit Prince...*'

'You do have a death wish.'

'No, I'm pulling your leg. I love to see your expression changing, your eyes going a deeper grey...' He remained like that, charming, playful, until he looked at his watch and said, 'God, do you realise it? I've

46

only twenty minutes to catch my train!' She had dismissed trains from her mind, or they had dismissed themselves, or perhaps she had been so entranced that she'd thought, What the hell, Hitler can wait...

'What if you miss it?'

'Can't afford to. I'd be court-martialled. Come on.' He paid the bill, hurried her out of the hotel, took her hand and hurried her even more through the crowds.

'Your luggage?' she said, breathless.

'Just this holdall.'

They reached the platform barrier and she watched him put his hand in his inside pocket, checking his pass, presumably, then he turned to her, putting down the holdall. He was breathing easily.

'No flap,' she felt like saying. 'That's it, as far as you're concerned. Over.' Her heart was twisting inside her, she was sweating with misery.

'It was too quick,' she said. 'Oh, Neil, it was too quick.'

'You can't come beyond here.' He put his arms round her, his eyes met hers, dark, mirroring her misery. 'Do you know my heart is breaking?' He held her closely. 'Breaking...' She felt his mouth on her cheek. After a second or two she pulled away to look at his face. It was white, pinched, his eyes were haunted. 'You were my last chance,' he said.

47

There were other couples near them. The attendant at the barrier said importantly, 'Train leaving in two minutes!'

The tears ran down her face. She couldn't see anything for tears, except the white face, the misery in it.

'You'll write?'

He smiled. 'I'm no great shakes at it, but yes, I'll write.' He bent to get his holdall, slung the strap over his shoulder, then kissed her long and hard on the mouth. 'Good, eh?' he said.

She tried to smile, then stood on the same spot watching him as he walked away, elegant; he stood out in his elegance. At the barrier he turned and waved, and she waved back then turned and blundered into someone behind her because of the tears.

She was composed by the time she got home. 'Well,' Tommy said, 'did you pump him?'

'No,' she said, 'I didn't.'

Her mother was knitting. She was a bad knitter and only did it because women had been asked to knit and she had a stern sense of duty. She looked up at Lisa. It was an understanding look. She said, 'Tut-tut,' because she had dropped a stitch.

Her father was reading and he looked at Lisa over the top of his newspaper.

'You look cold,' he said kindly. 'Go and make yourself a cup of cocoa or something.'

'I know a boy who calls it coco-*a*,' Tommy said.

'We've run out of milk,' her mother dismissed this.

'Anyone for watery coco-*a*, then?' Lisa said. She looked at the three of them and thought, Well, at least I've got a decent sort of family, I think...

'War,' her mother said, bungling another stitch, 'all the unhappiness it brings. How is that young man standing it?'

'He loves it,' Lisa said. 'He bloody loves it!' She saw her father's newspaper shake as she left the room.

Four

'Fancy meeting you here, Miss Smith!'
James Cowan said. It was an old joke, dating
from the first time he'd met her here in Miss
Cranston's tea-room in Argyle Street.

He sat down opposite her and put a hand
over hers. 'I was very sorry to hear about
your mother, Betty. A sad loss.'

'Thanks, James, and for your letter. It
meant a lot to me.' She put a handkerchief
to her eyes. She had a 'Betty' face; plump,
pleasant rather than pretty, marcel-waved
dark hair which received its weekly wash
and set from Marguerite round the corner
from their office in Glassford Street.

He said earnestly, 'You have no need to
reproach yourself, Betty. Not many girls
would have sacrificed themselves to their
mothers as you've done. At least you will
have no cause for regret.'

'Thanks for the "girl".' Her smile was
watery. 'I feel worn out with all the arrangements. I must look about a hundred.'

'No, you don't.' He stroked her hand, a baby hand, he thought, with dimpled knuckles. 'Let's see that nice smile.' She had a dimple in her left cheek as well.

Those daily lunches had begun when Jean had first been off colour and he had offered to eat in town to save her more work. She was punctilious about his lunches and hurried back from Lyle's daily to prepare them. Her very determination to continue this practice had meant a further distancing between them, he had thought, and eating in front of her pale face as she played with her food a further embarrassment. 'Are you sure, James?' she had said when he had made the suggestion to eat out, but he could see the relief in her eyes.

'Well, Betty, what are you having?' He released her hand with a little pat.

'Do you know, I fancy a pie and chips. I haven't been eating much lately – well, you can imagine, there's so much to do. What about you?'

'I'll have the same. Now I want to ask you, my dear: is there anything I can do to help? I know there are tasks where a man can be of more use. A woman on her own can be a bit ... helpless.' Not Jean, he thought, but this wee thing was different. She needed someone to support her. He gave the order to Maggie, their waitress. 'That'll set you up a bit,' he said, 'stick to your ribs.' She managed a girlish giggle in spite of her grief.

'You'll stay in your flat?' he asked while they waited.

'Oh, yes. Mother left it to me, and it's a main-door one in Byres Road. She and my father bought it years ago. Next to the tram stop. Couldn't be handier. I can get any-where, really, and of course it's fine for shops.'

'Well, I'm glad you felt able to come back. You were missed in the office. Those young-sters are enlisting one by one, and lady clerks are at a premium, especially one of your calibre. Don't think of leaving us!' he added playfully.

'Oh, I'd never do that! I have some loyalty to the firm. And to be quite frank, James, I'd miss you. Your friendship has meant a great deal to me. Listen to me!' The dimple on her cheek was entrancing, he thought. It was the first thing he'd noticed on their first lunch together.

Maggie – he always thought of her as 'their waitress' – appeared with their laden plates. 'There you are!' she said, putting them down. 'I've put gravy on the pies because I know that's how you like them. The aipple tairt's really nice the day. Will you have that to follow?'

'Betty?' He looked at her.

'Well, I don't know ... I have to watch my figure.' The dimple played hide and seek.

'Nothing wrong with her figure, is there, Maggie?'

'Wrang? Aw a can say is a wish a had yin like it. Two aipple tairts, then?'

Those lunches were very satisfying, in more ways than one, he thought, as he dug his fork into the pie and watched the gravy oozing out. They made him feel, well, important, unlike at home where in some subtle way he felt out of step, out of place. It wasn't their fault. Lisa was a good girl, kindly, and Tommy was always polite to him, although sometimes there was a bit of the devil in his eyes at the same time. It all stemmed from Jean, who he imagined looked at him as if he were a stranger, not her husband. But he mustn't think of himself when this wee thing needed cheering up.

'Churchill's talking about some kind of reserve, a kind of home army, just as a back-up, so to speak,' he said. 'Like the Voluntary Reserve pilots who mind the barrage balloons. There's only armbands as yet. If he does, I think I'll join. I'd like to do my bit.'

'You did more than your bit in the last war from all accounts, James.' She was tucking into her pie. It did him good to see her.

'No, I'd like to. Sets a good example in the office.' He didn't say it would also give him an excuse to be out of the house in the evenings. He couldn't bear to look at Jean sometimes, so unlike the girl he had known, the young girl he had proposed to. It all stemmed from Lionel Craig. He'd cast a constant shadow over their marriage. 'HP Sauce?' he asked, holding up the bottle.

'No, thanks, the gravy's lovely.' She speared a chip, munched it down. She was a good eater. 'I'll take you up on that offer, James. I was just thinking...' she speared another chip, dispatched it neatly, 'there's one or two things about the house that I'm going to change, and I could do with some help there, a new sofa perhaps, just some-one who could place it where I want it. I'd like to give the room a new look ... Not that I want to obliterate Mother, but just to make it look a little more like mine.'

'And not like an old woman's place. I know what you mean. They leave their imprint; I remember my own mother – fashions change. What you want is a little nest for a bachelor girl.'

'Oh, James! You like to pull my leg. An old maid's more like it. But I'll get new curtains, and nice cushions, and those artificial flowers, generally brighten the place up a bit. I'm really quite looking forward to it.'

'Well, anything I can help you with, just say the word. Lisa's always so busy, and where Tommy gets to is nobody's business; and Jean – well, she's grown fond of her bed in the evenings, now that she's not so well.'

'Oh, I'm that sorry for you, James. So much to contend with, and manager of the office and everything.' Her eyes were Irish blue and full of sympathy. 'I don't know how you stay so cheerful...'

The old feeling of being on the outside was back. Sometimes he even felt Jean deserved her bad luck, but that wasn't fair. He wasn't like that, really. He mustn't be bitter, but he *had* tried his best.

She had a good appetite, Betty. He liked to see that in a woman. Supper-time at home was sometimes to be dreaded, Lisa making conversation, Tommy bolting his food and going out with his friends, Jean drinking endless cups of tea. It was Lisa who held things together. She was a good girl, and not a very happy one either. He could see that.

'This lass of mine, Lisa,' he said. 'Since we came back from Craigton she's been different. I think it's a young man. There was this family, the MacLeans. The father was all right but the mother was odd. Ill-matched. I could have got on with him ... we had things in common – work, golf – but her...! And as for the son, well, I could never make out whether he'd fallen for Lisa or not. Air Force pilot. A striking-looking young man, I must say, film-star looks. But there's no doubt she fell for him.'

'Well, you've said it all, James. The poor girl's worrying about him all the time. Do you know what I read once? That their average life expectancy was a fortnight! It's a tricky position for young girls nowadays. They're throwing their caps over the windmill right, left and centre because they're thinking a dead man's no use to them, better now than never. Maybe he's asked her already, to, you know...'

He was quite surprised.

'I never thought of anything like that, Betty, but now that you mention it, it's an explanation ... Oh, if only my family would talk the way *we* do, about all sorts of things, free and open, easy, confiding in each other ... A man, a father and a husband needs that.'

'Of course he does! I can't understand people *not* talking, but then I'm a chatterbox, I know it. That's where I'm going to miss Mother. She was good at listening to all my little stories when I got back from the office. And she knew all their names. "How's Mr Cowan?" she would say. "You should bring him home to see me!" The dimple went in and out. "Oh, Mother!" I'd say to her, "Mr Cowan's the boss! I couldn't ask him! Besides he's a married man."'

'But you could ask me now,' he said, taking her hand. Her lips were shiny from the chip fat.

'What are you suggesting, Mr Cowan?' she said. Her smile was roguish.

'Well, you did say there were little jobs I could do for you.' He watched the dimple. 'I'm quite handy about the house.'

'Handy about the house, are you?' She looked up at Maggie, who was hovering above her. The smile was still there.

'Finished, Miss Smith?'

'Yes, thanks. It was lovely.'

'Well, here's your next course.' The 'aipple tairts' descended on their deep plates. 'And I've brought a fine wee jug o' cream. Dig in and don't ask where a got it from.'

Five

June 1940

There was only one war for Lisa, the one in the air, and she followed the operations of the RAF in every newspaper she could lay her hands on. She had a brief note from Neil saying that he had been moved nearer London (she thought of Uxbridge), because it was 'hotting up'. 'Don't expect to hear much from me,' he wrote. 'It's impossible to divide my loyalties.'

She had enough pride not to bother him with letters. Her days and evenings were full; she schooled herself not to think of him in bed, nor relive those few magical days they had spent together in Craigton. There was always someone at the Art School to fill the gap, young men she had much in common with, but they weren't Neil.

She met Beryl by chance one evening when she was serving at the Forces Canteen in Hope Street. 'Long time no see,' she said.

'Could we meet up for coffee later?' Beryl looked even prettier than she had at Craigton, and later, when they had done their stint, she didn't need any encouragement to launch forth about Bruce.

'I'm sorry I haven't been in touch, Lisa, but life's hectic. Any weekend I'm free I take the train to Dumfries. Bruce's parents seem to have accepted me. His mother says she's so pleased that he's chosen wisely...' She slanted her eyes, her mouth smug. 'But there's no monkey business. I'm determined to go to the altar as pure as the driven snow. All the same, we're getting ... desperate. Well, you know what I mean. A lot of the girls are going the whole way. You should hear how they talk at the Do School! What about *your* place?'

'Oh, well, art students always were a Bohemian lot.' Lisa spoke airily.

'The thing is, Bruce is running the farm now and he's taken on some Land Girls. I know one of them is determined to get her claws into him.'

'Oh, I think you can trust Bruce.'

'Yes, I'm sure I can.' Her smile was smug again, and Lisa thought, I preferred the old Beryl, the flirtatious one.

'Does he ever mention Neil?' She hadn't meant to say that.

'No, they didn't hit it off. Too cynical, he said. Well, you know my Bruce, open,

59

friendly, everyone likes him ... he said there was something ... mysterious about Neil McLean.' She had thought she might confide in Beryl about Neil, but she gave up the idea there and then.

'How's your mother?' she asked.

'Fine. In fact, blooming. She's been helping at a recruitment office and she's met a man! Can you imagine?'

Lisa could. 'Really?'

'Well, I expect she was lonely, and I've to be out so much at the School, and weekends at Dumfries, and you can't blame her, can you? Seeing me so happy, I mean...'

'No, you can't blame her.' Like mother, like daughter. 'I think I must be going, Beryl. The trams stop earlier now at nights, and I don't like to walk alone in the blackout.'

'I don't blame you. Lisa, before you go, could I book you to be my bridesmaid? After all, we're childhood friends, and your mother and my parents coming from Kilmacolm, and that...'

'When will it be?'

'As soon as poss, maybe at the end of the year.'

'Is it to be a dressed-up affair? I don't know if...' The idea didn't appeal. Surely I'm not *jealous*? she thought.

'Oh, yes, it's got to be. They're well known, the Semples, in their part of the

60

woods. People will expect it. So will their parents. Besides, Bruce says he's dying to see me in white...'

Why not naked? Yes, she must be jealous. Nevertheless, she made up her mind.

'You'll have to count me out, Beryl. I really don't have the time...' No, she wouldn't say that she thought big weddings were inappropriate at this time. 'I think I may be joining the WAAF pretty soon.'

'But you're at the Art School!'

'It can wait. Haven't you noticed there's a war on?' She laughed to take the sting out of her words. Besides, it wasn't a lie. She had lain in bed last night and thought that the only way to ditch this obsession of hers was to get involved. Any women's service would do, but she liked the WAAF uniform, and it brought her closer to Neil. 'Tommy's worked it out that after all the cities in the south have been bombed it will be Glasgow's turn. I want to be in there when it happens.'

Beryl looked at her with horror. 'What an idea! Well, there's no accounting for tastes. Thank goodness I'll be living in the country, I hope.'

On her way home she felt good. She climbed to the top deck of the tram, which stopped and started, and swayed through the busy street she knew so well. She was a city girl, in spite of Kilmacolm where she had spent her youth, in spite of their yearly visits to Craigton for the sea air ... She remembered going there with her pail and spade although there was no sand, and later as a schoolgirl with plaits and tennis racket, and those family times at the tennis club with her parents and their friends' children, all typical of the belief in the Glasgow-born middle class that 'sea air' was beneficial, and the custom of establishing one's family at the coast for the summer was the thing to do. Did those weekend fathers have a fine time when their wives and children were away?

But, yes, she was a Glaswegian in spite of Kilmacolm and Craigton. She had been educated in Glasgow, she was at the Art School there, she knew every inch of this artery she was on, the big stores, Copland & Lye's, Pettigrew and Stephen's, the same but different, a distinction which only the true Glaswegian knew. She saw the long queue snaking from La Scala cinema and wished she was part of it, just to be one of the crowd. And Daly's, for special-occasion clothes, and the Linen Shop for wedding presents, and Tréron's (Mother knew the owner there, Walter Wilson, in his tailcoat, so dapper), then the art shops further up, the furriers, Jean Dougal MacDonald – she remembered her mother's sable cape for state occasions. Now her stop ... she ran downstairs quickly and rang the bell. 'Cut it fine, hen,' the conductress said, big rear in her bottle-green skirt, big bust bisected by the leather strap of her money bag. Doing her bit...

Yes, her mind was clear. Much as she enjoyed the Art School, it was too much of an escape hatch. She could resume her course when it was all over. She walked round the corner towards Holland Street, remembering that last walk in the city with Neil at Christmas. She had pressed close to him and he'd said, 'You're ... joyous.' She liked that. She wasn't built for sadness. That's what she would be from now on, joyous.

When she went into the flat she knew Tommy was having a bath by the snorts, grunts and blowing coming from the bathroom. She stopped outside the door and shouted over the splashing.

'Stop acting like a whale! Where's Dad and Mum?'

'He's at the LDV meeting. He's a changed man since they gave him that tin hat. Quite jovial. He's gone to see about outdoor shelters when the bombs start dropping. What did I tell you?' Tommy, the oracle.

'Lisa!' It was her mother's voice coming from the sitting-room.

She went in and saw the dim figure sitting at the oriel window. She was immediately uneasy. 'Trying to save electricity?'

'I forgot to put it on.' Her mother's voice was flat.

Lisa sat down on the chair opposite her. 'I met Beryl Craig tonight at the canteen. She was telling me about the Land Girls on Bruce's farm, but she says he spurns them. Would you like me to draw the curtains and put the light on?'

'No.'

Lisa's uneasiness increased.

'Mother,' she said, 'I'm thinking about joining the WAAF. I don't feel I'm doing enough. Studying art when there's a war on seems ... self-indulgent.'

'I see your point. Why the WAAF?'

Their eyes met, her mother's gaze held her, then she said, 'Never mind. Is there something wrong?'

'You could say that. Lisa, don't get upset when I tell you this. I went to see the doctor recently about a lump on my breast. It turned out to be malignant.'

'Oh, Mum!' She put her hand on her mother's arm. 'Why have you been so secretive? I could have gone with you, you should have told me...'

'Two worrying was enough. Dad knows. I go into the Western tomorrow.'

'Tomorrow!'

'It's not the end of the world. I haven't told Tommy. At his age it's ... difficult.

Growing up, I mean. Your father couldn't face it. Would you tell him?'

'Oh!' She bit her lip. 'If you want me to.'

'Make a joke of it. Tell him that Granny's dressmaker in Hillhead – I used to go with her as a wee girl – used to stick pins in her bust. Handy. It took me ages to puzzle out what it was.'

'You're the limit!' she spluttered. 'And fancy Granny not explaining! OK, I'll tell him, but I don't think I'll tell him about the dressmaker.'

'Breasts weren't mentioned then. Now they're all the go.'

'Oh, Mum!' she said again. She was near to tears. 'The worry you've had! I thought it was because of ... Mr Craig.'

There was silence.

'Did you really think that! Lionel...' Her voice seemed to caress the syllables. 'It's funny, though. First him and then me.'

'Mrs Craig has met someone else, Beryl says. Quick, wasn't it?'

'Not quick for Grace.'

There was a pause.

'You're tired. Come on!' Lisa helped her mother to her feet. 'Get to bed and I'll bring you a nice cup of tea.'

'Right.' She was standing straight. 'Dad's late. I hope he's having a drink with his mates.'

'Not him. He's planning outdoor shelters

for back yards, Tommy says. Can you imagine, Mum' – she was trying to be cheerful, as if your mother's breast being lopped off was of no account – 'Mrs Docherty crowding in with that cheap perfume of hers?'

'And maybe half a dozen of her followers!' They laughed, thinking of their jaunty neighbour, treating it as if it was a great joke.

Later, when Lisa was in the kitchen washing up, Tommy came in wearing his teddy-bear dressing-gown, which he'd grown out of. 'Good bath, that! You've no idea how dirty you get working in that allotment.' It was an idea thought up by his headmaster in the school grounds. 'And the sweat!'

'Spare me the horrid details. Just be glad you're digging for victory. What was the spoil today?'

'A cabbage and some potatoes. Is Dad in?'

'Yes, I heard him. But he went straight to their room.'

'He's quiet these days, have you noticed? But then he's never a barrel of laughs.'

'He's worried about Mother.'

'Mother? What's wrong?'

She drew in her breath. 'She's to have a mastectomy.'

'What's that?' She saw the look of fear spread over his face.

'It's when a lump appears, and they find it

is malignant, and they have to ... take the breast off.' It was like a red river coursing over his face, the blood. She turned away so as not to embarrass him. 'It's the best thing to do. The only thing to do, a radical mastectomy. To be on the safe side...' She sounded like a doctor.

'Do you mean ... cut it right off?' He was casual, and yet at the same time breathless.

'Yes, Tommy, but don't worry...' She put out her hand but he pushed back his chair hurriedly and got to his feet.

'I'm going to bed. I wish ... I meant to tell her about the cabbage and the potatoes, but...'

'You'll see her tomorrow and you can tell her then.'

'Yes, that's best. Well, I'll get to bed...' He stopped speaking, gave her an uncertain smile and went off. She sat, tears hovering, biting her lip. It was a pity she had mentioned the WAAF, but now, of course, she would be needed at home. She would have to take her mother's place in the business, visit her in hospital; maybe she'd take her to the Glebe for her convalescence. Margaret Currie had said the evacuees had gone off with their parents for Christmas and hadn't come back because they'd been homesick. There were all kinds of things to think of. And Father, that quiet man wearing the tin hat that pleased him so much.

Tommy was right there.

It was strange, when they talked about mastectomies, that they didn't talk about the effect on husbands or sons ... the husband, apart from his dismay, the sorrow he must feel about his wife being mutilated, the son, especially, if on the edge of puberty, shocked in a peculiarly filial way. No, she decided, she was wanted here.

And how about a daughter, this daughter, with her vivid imagination, the mother on the operating table, the knife, the blood pulsing in beads from the cut, the severing of a piece of flesh, a *shape*, from the main body, the livid residue. She put her hand to her own breast.

The three of them would suffer in their own way, would *imagine*, each would have a different reaction, but it was their mother who had to live with it. But she was the strong one. She would never mention it and would expect them to do the same.

When she went into the hall the house was silent. She had thought she might tap on Tommy's door, but decided against it.

Six

Tommy thought he knew every part of Glasgow now. Maybe when he had time he would write an article about it, how if you knew it well enough you got a feel for it, as if you began to understand its structure and its people, especially its people. The key to it was its tramcars, 'the caurs', whose penny rides took you miles in every direction, as far as the outlying terminuses.

For instance, if you took one to Anniesland, especially in the winter, and saw the Campsie hills capped with snow, you could think of yourself as a Highlander, and imagine that the people who descended every day to the heart of the city to work felt the same. After all, it was the back door to the Highlands. And would their character be affected, would they think of themselves as Celts, not Lowlanders, feel like their kilted ancestors who had taken the same route, brawny, bearded men with a dirk stuck in their stocking-tops?

He liked thinking like that. His imagination got free rein sailing through the streets on top of a tram, far more so than in school with its narrow discipline. Travel broadens the mind, he would remember the saying, and that surely applied even although it was only on the top of a Glasgow tramcar.

In those endless journeys to the far-flung outposts where you sat until the conductor got out and manoeuvred the electric pole on to the return line, you might arrive at, say, Rouken Glen, where you could get out and have a row on the loch if you liked. You would feel strange, as if you'd arrived at a different country, mostly because of the people. Each district was a different country.

Going south to Newlands and Giffnock, you saw the difference between the inhabitants there and the north-west route through Kelvinside. He thought of it as the difference between old money and new money. The South Siders were flashier, their gardens were packed full of flowers rather than plain grass, they had garden gnomes with fishing rods. In Kelvinside there were stately lawns and trees that looked as if they were hundreds of years old.

You imagined the Giffnock people had made their money in trade, in pubs round Eglinton Street or foundries in Bridgeton, whereas the Kelvinsiders were city men, stockbrokers, lawyers, doctors in the Western Infirmary where Mother was.

Further north from Kelvinside there was the spread of housing estates in Anniesland, and he thought the people who got on and off the tramcar there might well be teachers and clerks who aspired to living in Kelvinside, and that passing through it fed their aspirations. They didn't chatter. They read books or newspapers, and always looked anxious.

Due west, through Partick, Scotstoun and Yoker, on your way to Clydebank, the people were rougher, kindlier, liked to pass the time of day. Their talk was still full of the Clydebank bombing, which they would elaborate for your benefit. 'See, ma Aunt Aggie, one minute she was having her tea, the next minute she was sitting in the street.' 'But here, come 'ere, whit aboot the wumman who was stuck on the lavvy seat wi' no hoose roon her?' The women beside the speaker would laugh and nod. 'Aye, a good yin, that.' These were the wives of the men who had built the ships that sailed all round the world. Many of these men had perished, blown to bits; others were back on the job, house or no house.

They were different in the East End, Gallowgate – frightening, some of them, looking at you as if they'd like to steal the shirt off your back, hordes of dirty-nosed children crowding on with their mammy, all on one ticket. 'In the name o' Goad, hoo many mair?' the exasperated conductor would ask. *Ting-ting*! 'There's your ticket, missus, and take some o' they weans on yer knee.' (He'd been given a toy conductor set one Christmas with a ticket machine just like that.) 'The Corporation would be on its beam ends if it was relyin' on you lot.'

And how about Auchenshuggle? He didn't know anything about Auchenshuggle except that the tramcar turned there, a no-place, a distance between two points. And who'd given it its name, Auchenshuggle? Maybe he'd go into the Mitchell and see if they could tell him. They knew everything in the Mitchell.

They were friendly at Bridgeton Cross, the shawlies. 'Look at this fine young man, Maggie. How wid ye like him in yer bed?' A bit embarrassing, though. Look out of the window. Feel the blush round your spots. Pretend you hadn't heard. 'Onything wid be better than ma auld man. Snores and farts aw the night.'

But sometimes in the afternoon, when the pubs were emptying, they were worse than that. 'Gie's a feel, lad!' 'Maw, you're makin' that poor soul blush.' Mother and son, one drunker than the other. The conductor helping them off, turning to Tommy when they were staggering on to the pavement,

72

shaking his head. *Ting-ting.*

But they were even worse in the Gorbals. Every young man who came on, with his hair sleeked to his head, pointed shoes and a gallus air looked like a gangster. He probably concealed a knife. *No Mean City.* But that was ages ago. And then he would console himself by remembering that every young healthy man had already been rounded up to fight Hitler. A racking cough from the man sitting at his side would make him ashamed. He was probably on his way to Hairmyres in East Kilbride, half his lungs gone.

The healthy Gorbals men were reckoned to be the best fighters in the Territorials, someone had told him. Like terriers. 'See, they've to fight to survive in that hole, it's in their blood. They're like terriers with a rat.'

If he wanted a contrast, he would take a tram past his own street and out to the university. Here in the quiet surrounding avenues you could see professors walking about in black gowns that flapped like wings. Once he'd seen a woman, a young professor. Her gown had blown open and he had seen her full breasts outlined by her tight scarlet jersey...

It was back again, the pain he had felt when Lisa had told him. His beautiful mother. He had tried not to visualise it, had dreaded seeing her in hospital in case she would be swathed in bandages, that there might even be a trace of blood seeping out where they crossed ... He knew it was stupid, of course it was stupid, and when he saw her she had on a bed-jacket thing with satin ribbons, and she was smiling.

'Hello, Tommy! I've always meant to ask you: when the school's closed, what do you do with yourself all day?' She looked as beautiful as ever. The bed-jacket matched her eyes. Lisa's touch.

'I just kind of ... mooch about. Go on the trams. It must be the best system in the world. You can go anywhere for miles, and the different colours! You don't even need to read the indicator board, the colours tell you. Whoever worked that out is really clever – not as clever as the decoders in the War, of course, but clever all the same. Colour coding. I've worked out a map of the system and stuck it up in my room.'

'Did you find a space for it?' She was interested.

'Oh, yes. Maps are like books to me. If I had been older that's what I'd like to have been, a decoder. Bring the German planes down. Get to know their movements.' Her smile was to the left of her mouth, teasing him, but interested. She never laughed at him, that was the beauty of it.

'I know it's difficult for you, not getting a proper education with the War. And the rest of us being so busy all the time. Do you ever meet any friends?'

'Oh, yes, we have howffs where we go for coffees, and sometimes we have a twopenny pie, we know the best places.'

'Don't always go for cheapness, especially with mince. My mother never bought it ready-made, thought it was made up of all kinds of leftovers...' She shuddered. 'Have you enough pocket money?'

'Oh, yes.'

'What she did was to ask the butcher for a pound of the best steak, and then she would say, "Mince it, please," keeping her eye on him all the time in case he tricked her. But that was in the days of plenty. I hope Lisa has a good meal ready for you at night.'

'Oh, yes. She makes good soup, with bones as you told her, and I bring her vegetables. Dad sometimes has his evening meal out as well, now that he's in the LDV. But I don't know about the pies she buys. Maybe they're made of minced cats.' He said that to make her laugh, but it wasn't much of a joke. You couldn't see anything with the bed-jacket covering it. What could he say anyhow? 'Did it hurt, much?'

'Do you ever go to the Mitchell? I did a lot of my studying there for my diploma in teaching. I had a miserable wee flat I shared, and I got peace and quiet at the Mitchell.'

'Oh, yes, I go there quite often. Schoolwork, if there's any, and you can stay as long as you like as long as you're quiet. I go through all the newspapers, and I ask for books. Neil Munro ... It's a radical mastectomy you've had, isn't it?' Should he put the emphasis on 'radical', or not?

'*Brave Days*. It's in the house somewhere. I might read it again.'

'I'll bring it next time.'

'No, don't bother. It would be heavy to hold.'

His heart gave a sickening twist, making him shut his eyes. He opened them and smiled.

'You'll miss going to London, with ... everything?'

'Oh, yes. Galleries and shows, mostly, in Old Bond Street. Funnily enough, I always felt a stranger in London. The folks there are ... different. When you come to think of it the Scots and the English are miles apart, it's nothing to do with distance. I feel more at home in Paris...' She looked away. Her face was sad.

'I'd like to see Paris. That place on the hill where the painters lived.'

'Montmartre. Sacré Coeur. Yes, I've been there. The real painters stay indoors, or go into the country. Argenteuil. I never met any – I would have killed to see Picasso – but now, well, most of them are dead. Some of the very young ones might be fighting. I don't know. But you'd like the Left Bank, and the Seine, and the bridges – I loved the bridges. I bought a Sisley once near one, spotted it on a stall. I wish I hadn't sold it, but then he's not one of my favourites.'

'Who is?'

'Matisse. Always Matisse. I never got to the south of France to see the light there. He painted light. I'll never see it now...'

The paleness of her face ... but then she must have lost a lot of blood...

'You and me could have a holiday there after the War.'

'Yes, I'd like that, Tommy.'

'Maybe I would be living in Paris, in a studio on the Left Bank, and you could come, and we could take a train all the way to the south...'

She didn't reply. He saw her head had drooped. Her eyes were closed, but she was saying something. He strained his ears to hear her.

'There's nothing wrong in mooching if you use your eyes...' Her head stayed down, and now he looked properly, since she wouldn't know he was looking, took his time. There were blue veins at the side of her forehead, and her face seemed to be smaller, and pinched, and if he could have died for her he would have done it. They had no right to mutilate her, no right at all. She lifted her head and smiled at him.

'On you go, Tommy. It was great ... talking.' She flapped her hand and it fell as if it were too heavy.

'Right.' They had never kissed, except of course when he was a baby, or small. They were always doing it in the pictures, when they came in and when they went out, and then there were the lovers' kisses, with tongues, which his schoolmates were always boasting about, and how many they'd had.

What would she have said if he told her that he didn't want to see his mates because that was all they talked about, that and smoking, and it made him feel that maybe he was missing something?

'I'll get on, then.' He stood up, feeling that he'd grown since he'd sat down, become more mature. She always had that effect on him. At the door he turned and looked back, but her eyes were closed.

Seven

1941

Jean Cowan was sitting in the pleasant garden of her old home in Kilmacolm, or nine-tenths of her was, she thought. She touched her prosthesis, as she had learnt to call it in the hospital.

Which was more than James had been able to do. He was so fearful of upsetting her. In bed, after kissing her good-night, he had turned away and said, 'I'm not going to bother you, Jean. You just get better.'

'Take me, I am yours,' she had wanted to sing – she was sure it was a hymn – but he would have been horrified. Lionel wouldn't have been horrified. He would have said, 'Well then, let's see the damage.'

Or would he? When someone is dead, it is so easy to invest them with attributes they never had. Tommy she could understand: probably schooled by Lisa. He had come dutifully to the hospital with flowers he boasted he had grown himself in the school allotment, big blowsy marigolds. Tommy, her special, truly beloved son, coping with the thought of a one-breasted mother.

And Lisa, who had taken over the running of Lyle's. Fortunately, Bill Crawford was there to help her, Bill who had come to work with her father when he was a boy because he'd thought he would teach him how to draw.

'He couldn't draw a herring off a plate,' her father had said, but he was neat-fingered and could tackle any picture-framing job. Over the years he had proved his worth. Her father had used him as a stand-in at auctions when he was too busy to go himself, and found that Bill could run rings round the lot of them. No, there were no flies on Bill.

Lisa had dropped most of her classes. 'Call this my hands-on experience,' she had said. Lisa, who had whisked her down here because she thought she needed some fresh air. 'We'll let Margaret Currie cosset you for a week or so. I'll look after the boys.' She had taken to calling them that.

The view from the garden was certainly better than from the oriel window in Holland Street, consisting there of the sun-obscuring flat front of the building opposite. Flats were for busy people who were out and about all day and only needed a comfortable interior environment when they came home. But here the soft Renfrewshire hills, the distant gleaming glimpse of the Gryfe through a belt of trees, were restful to the eyes.

Margaret appeared with a tray laden with the morning cocoa (made with milk) and some freshly baked scones, obviously still warm because the butter had melted and was oozing over them, making them a rich, golden colour.

'Margaret! What a feast!'

'Don't ask me where the butter came from. I've strict instructions from your daughter to feed you up.'

'Sit down. I hope you've brought a cup for yourself. Oh, yes, Lisa's the boss now. Where's Alec this morning?'

'He's gone to help at Baxter's farm. He can't drive the tractors with only having one leg – never got the hang of it – but he's quite useful. Since Dunkirk they're desperately short of labour. Donald, the eldest son, remember, was killed on the beaches. The thing that breaks their heart is that he needn't have gone. He had an exemption. There's still Kenny, but he's only fourteen.'

'About Tommy's age.' She thought of that young man who had come every year to Craigton with his family, Bruce Semple. He was lucky too, being needed on his father's farm. 'You remember Grace McBurnie,

81

Margaret? Who married Lionel Craig?' She was pleased with her calmness.

'Yes. Sad about his death. I believe he smoked like a chimney.' Her face was impassive.

'He did a lot of things he shouldn't have done. Good cocoa. Rich.'

'It's the fresh farm milk. You don't get that in Glasgow. Blue, there. Aye, I remember Grace McBurnie. You went to the local primary school, the two of you, but then you travelled to Glasgow in the train for your education. Well, being a Lyle ... What about her?' Her glance was steady.

'We took her daughter, Beryl, to Craigton after ... Lionel died. She wrote to me, you see...' It was better to talk about him than to think about him all the time, obsessively, worse since this breast ... 'It was you talking about Donald Baxter that reminded me. Beryl met this Bruce Semple at Craigton, and now she's engaged to him. His family farm at Dumfries, so he's stayed put. Lucky for Beryl.'

'She'll have the wiles of her mother, maybe.' Margaret pursed her lips.

'Grace has met someone else. Beryl told Lisa. Some time ago now. She might well be married.' She despised herself for this gossiping. But it was as if to speak about him, or around him, helped. She knew when Lisa had suggested her coming here that it

82

would bring him alive.

That hut where he'd painted, down by the river ... Not controlled paintings like Mackintosh, his mentor, but undisciplined. She remembered one which he'd called 'Scenes from my Hut', the misty green of the fields, the trees, the river, different tones of green, you had to look a long time before you saw it. 'Only connect,' he used to say. Lisa would have got it right away. She had an eye like Grandfather Lyle, acute, perceptive.

'Like mother, like daughter,' Margaret was saying. 'But then Lisa's the spitting image of you, that fair skin and dark hair, determined...'

'Obsessional.'

'I don't know what that means. A'm just a country lass!' She laughed heartily. Margaret, who took everything in her stride, her childless state, her Alec coming home from the first war with a leg missing, accepting the job of caretaker here without a fuss because she had worked for the Lyles as a maid and felt in a way it was her home too. No grovelling with Margaret. She and Alec were the salt of the earth.

When she had gone with the tray Jean sat on. This place always stirred up memories, one reason why she tended to avoid it, although she'd had a good enough excuse with a family and a business to look after.

83

But everyone had to have a starting point, and this was hers.

Of course, her own mother hadn't thought much of the Craigs – a feckless family, she had called them, always short of money, and Lionel with his painting, refusing to take up a proper job.

She had envied him. She'd had to work hard to become a teacher, then he did the same exams off the top of his head, when it became necessary.

But, oh, those long talks and walks! 'We twa hae paidled in the burn' – he had loved Burns, had quoted him endlessly. They had kissed a lot, and fumbled a bit in the way of the times, but she always remembered she was a Lyle and might have to run the firm when her father died. She was an only child. And there had been her career waiting in Glasgow...

Grace McBurnie, daughter of the village grocer and serving behind the counter (how one's mother popped up her snobbish head from the grave), but the toast of the village lads. Pretty, though, even friendly, but always critical of Jean because she travelled to Glasgow every day to Hutcheson's, stayed for weekends in friends' houses, moved away from her roots.

Besides, in Glasgow there was the attraction of going to Lyle's after school, being made much of by the staff and helping her father to choose paintings for display. He told her about the background of painters, never attempted to teach her. 'The Glasgow Colourists,' he would say, 'some folk think they're merely copyists, borrowing from the Impressionists, but you have to make up your own mind, develop your own taste by looking, looking, looking...' She had done the same with Lisa.

And later, when she was studying for her teaching diploma, travelling back daily to Kilmacolm in the train with him, her eyes taking in the slope and dip of the fields, the contours of the hills, she would find pleasure in reading the landscape, in absorbing the light of her birthplace into her bones.

She remembered Margaret in those days, fresh-faced, smiling, serving at table, that big mahogany table meticulously set, and saying one day as she handed the tureen of soup, 'You'll never guess! Lionel Craig and Grace McBurnie are getting married.' Mother had always deplored Margaret's familiarity. 'You've forgotten the ladle, Margaret.' Her nose in the air.

The room had swung around Jean, blurred like one of Lionel's paintings. Her father had said, 'Maybe that'll settle him. Plenty of talent in that lad if he'd stop playing around.'

She could feel the pain even now. She had

run away from Kilmacolm virtually, sharing a flat with a fellow-student in Renfrew Street, ostensibly to be handy for the Art School but really to keep her away from her home here. The only pleasure had been working on Saturdays in Lyle's, gradually taking more responsibility as her father grew frailer, and giving up teaching altogether when he died.

That wasn't the only reason, she reminded herself. It had been because Lionel had turned up one day where she taught. 'Got a wife and child to support,' he had said. His eyes had changed. They had lost their vision. She couldn't bear to see that. It had twisted her heart so badly that she'd left...

She took what was the wrong decision and regretted it. James Cowan did the books for the firm, and when he proposed to her she accepted. It couldn't go on, this obsession. Somehow she had to get rid of it. And James was easy to live with. Where Lionel had great dollops of temperament, James had none. Only kindness, blandness. And then...

No more, she thought, no more. She got up and 'took a wander round the garden', as Margaret would say, but it didn't help. I want to go back to Glasgow, she thought, this place is too full of memories. I want to get back to Lyle's, to welcome clients, to go to see other dealers' purchases, visit galleries, smell the familiar smells in the back rooms – paint and glue, wood – choose a special picture for the easel in the window, drape it with black velvet. With the help of Bill Crawford. Or Lisa. Those were permanent things...

It was 1925. She knew it was that year because she had been looking at a poster which had come in that day, and which she would ask one of the staff to put up in the reception room tomorrow. She had been working late. EXPOSITION DES ARTS DECORATIFS. Art deco. Cubism domesticated, she thought now.

She was intrigued. Could she possibly ask Agnes, the maid at Holland Street, to stay over the weekend to look after Lisa? She must see it. James wouldn't go with her to Paris, she knew, but that would be better. He could keep an eye on things. She felt thrilled at the thought of seeing the exhibition, the paintings, wallpapers, furniture, Raoul Dufy, René Lalique ... She had always wanted her father to buy a few pieces of Lalique for display, but he had been too cautious, said they wouldn't sell ... The lock of the door clicked and she looked up.

'Lionel!' she said, and she heard the excited but fearful surprise in her voice, wanted to put her hand to her heart to steady it. 'Lionel! I was just looking ... What on earth are you doing here? We're closed.'

'But not to me.' He had a large square parcel under his arm. 'I've brought you some of my paintings. The best of them.' He came to the counter, propped the parcel against it and glanced at the poster which she had spread out. 'Art deco, eh? Well, that puts my stuff out of joint, eh?'

It was as if she had seen him yesterday now, the ease, the familiarity, and yet she had to steady her voice, lean on the counter. 'Oh, I don't know. I haven't seen it for years. But the whole thing's a roundabout nowadays.'

'Why did you run away?' he said.

'You know why. I was needed here. And I got married ... like you.'

'Before that. You left me and ran to the city, and when I followed you to where you were teaching, you ran again. Cruel, cruel.' His eyes were the same as she remembered when he had turned up there, almost haunted, the lack of brightness, of vision, of love of life. Had it been Grace who had told him to give up painting and go and earn his living?

'You were cruel too.' She couldn't bring herself to mention Grace's name. He looked at her for a long time, as if there were no words, or not the right ones, then looked down.

'These paintings. I'd like you to keep them

88

here. They're yours. I don't think I'll do any more.'

'I don't believe it.' She took a deep breath, felt calm now, could say her name. 'How's Grace?'

'Well, thank you. And there's little Beryl too, remember? Like her mother. Just as there's your little...? What's her name?'

'Lisa. Like her mother.' Their eyes met again and this time his were focused, there was life in them. Her heart suddenly flooded with love, overwhelming love, as it had never flooded for James; for him there was only a steady affection, such as one would have for the auditor of your firm, which he was, which was how she had met him. Steady, reliable, kind James, all those unimportant things compared with love. 'It's wonderful to see you, Lionel,' she said, 'let's have a look at your paintings.'

'No.' He shook his head. 'Not now. There's a letter inside the parcel. For you. Read it when I'm gone. For good.' He laughed, quoting, '"But now your brow is beld, John, Your locks are like the snaw..."'

'What are you talking about? You were always melodramatic.'

'That's me. That's how I paint. Very un-art deco. Well, I'd better be going. Not many trains to Kilmacolm, "where the tansies grow..."'

'Don't go. I mean ... We haven't spoken for

ages. I could make you a cup of tea, or would you like whisky? I keep it for signing deals.'

'Great! I'd like a whisky. Are you tempting me?'

'Yes, I'm tempting you.' She laughed with this new-old happiness, the feeling she'd always had when they'd larked about in the hut, such light-heartedness, unknown to her now. Why had she been so prim, leaving that school because he had turned up? She had forgotten how easy it had been with him, how ... joyous, the only person in the world who could make her feel alive.

'Lead on,' he said. He lifted his parcel and followed her.

It was a snug little room at the back of the premises; there was even an old green velour sofa which her father had put in for the female staff, if needed. It stemmed from the time when Jenny, one of the shop assistants, had felt faint because of her period. He wasn't stupid, he'd known.

'Snug,' Lionel said. 'So this is ben the hoose?'

'It's my hide-away when things get too much for me.'

'You look the same, Jean, not a day older than those times in the hut, but prim, yes, prim...'

'Maybe I was, but here I am, a sober married woman.'

'I'm not a sober married man. Should I be?'

'It's up to you.' She had found the whisky, and poured two tots. 'There you are, and I'm going to break rules and have one too.' He was sitting on the sofa and she sat down beside him.

'Thanks.' He sipped. 'Warms the cockles, eh?'

'Yes.' She sipped too. It took away the primness.

'I've made a lot of mistakes, but that was the biggest one, getting married to Grace.'

She shrugged. 'Our generation. Getting married because there was no other way of sleeping with each other.' She didn't think it applied in her case. 'I bet in years to come people won't make that mistake.'

'No gold bands or dog collars.'

'Free love.' It must be the whisky that was making her speak so oddly. She was thinking she would like to throw her arms round him... 'If you've finished your whisky you'd better go. I have to lock up.'

'I was going to have a cigarette. How about you?'

'All right, but then you must go.' Such decadence. Whisky and then a cigarette. She bent forward to the match he held and she felt faint, like Jenny, only it wasn't her period. She sat back, listening to him coughing. 'You always smoked too much,' she said.

'Yes, I've been told to cut it down, but what can I do when it's my only pleasure?'

'I don't believe that.'

'It's true, now that I've stopped painting.' He stubbed out his cigarette in a small opaque ashtray in front of him. 'I hope it's not Lalique.'

'No, it isn't Lalique.' She stubbed hers out too. She was shaking. 'I'll have to put you out,' she said, 'I'll have...'

She thought she kissed him first, and knew with the kiss that the die was cast. Fool, fool, fool, she was saying as he pushed her back on the sofa so that he lay on top of her. 'Stupid, stupid, stupid,' she whispered, 'when we had all the freedom of the world in the hut.'

Because they were both married, it seemed to dispose of the preliminaries. They knew the drill. Neither was a virgin. Only one thing mattered to her, that she possessed him or was possessed by him. She thought her heart would burst. She wept for the wasted years, wept and loved, wept and loved. There was all this love that had mounted up in those wasted years.

He used no endearments. He said, 'Why did you go away and leave me, you bitch? Why, when I needed you so much, for everything?' She wept and kissed his hands as if she was looking for absolution.

When he went away, she discovered the paintings where he had left them, propped against the foot of the sofa. She lifted the parcel – it was heavy – and carried it to the old press in the corner. She put the parcel inside, leaning it against the back wall, then turned the key. She put it in her handbag, put on her coat and left.

When she got home, Lisa was fractious and Agnes was cross because it was her night off, but James welcomed her and said, 'Have you had a busy day, dear?'

'Very tiring.' Later she put the key of the cupboard in the jewel case that James had given her. Yes, she was very tired.

Eight

'Did you find your way all right?' Betty asked, letting James Cowan into her front-door flat.

She looked very trim, he thought, in her black cardigan and skirt, in mourning for her mother, probably, but there was a glimpse of something white and gauzy underneath the cardigan.

'Good-evening, Betty,' he said, stepping into the hall. 'Yes, quite easily.'

'Let me take your raincoat.' She hung it up on one of the row of hooks behind the door.

'I know this district well.' He followed her into a sitting-room which faced the front. The curtains were drawn and there was a bright fire burning in the grate. He hoped she hadn't used up her ration of coal on his account.

'Sit down, James, and take a load off your feet.'

'Is this the new sofa? Very nice.'

'Yes, I made the chintz cover myself. I'm

94

not sure I like where the men placed it. You know Byres Road, then?' She sat down beside him.

'Yes. When I was a boy at Glasgow High I had a chum who lived in Hillhead, and we used to walk up here and on to Great Western Road to the Botanic Gardens. We must have done it for the walk, because neither of us was interested in flowers. Maybe it was the hothouses that appealed to us.'

'It's nice there. I sometimes go on Sunday afternoons. I don't go out at nights in the blackout. I wish the War was over. You get fed up with it.'

'Don't worry. Pearl Harbor will bring the Americans in. It took something like that to convince them. Trust the Americans to see which side their bread is buttered on.'

'They've got money, though. That's what Churchill is angling for.'

'You're right. My goodness, this room is cosy.' He leant back. 'Do you feel lonely, Betty, since your mother died?'

'Yes, I miss her, but then again there's something to be said for being on your own. You can please yourself. I've no regrets that I gave up the best years of my life to her.'

'But you're just a chicken yet!' he said, head back, thinking how much at ease he was.

'Thirty-eight is scarcely a chicken.'

'Well, you don't look it.' It was true. He could see her hands clasped on her lap, the dimpled knuckles, and wouldn't have minded stroking them. And those bright cheeks and her hair, alive, not like Jean's wig – that terrible wig. Once he'd gone into her room and caught her with it off. She hadn't heard him knocking. She had turned round and looked at him, as if to say, 'Here it is. I'm not going to hide it.' He could never look at her afterwards without remembering that shiny scalp...

Betty turned towards him. 'You look sad tonight, James. Is it your wife? How is she?'

'Bad.' He had been told by the doctor it was liver cancer now. 'She's got no energy, stays in her bed in a wee box room most of the time. She managed to get herself to Lyle's one day. Determined. Lisa helped her.'

'She seems a good girl, your Lisa. You couldn't have managed without her.'

'No, I admit that. We don't talk a lot, but, yes, she's good with her mother. And looks after us. Me and Tommy. He's a bit of a problem. Well, I think I've told you before, Betty, I don't know what's wrong, but we've never been a talkative family. It's funny, when I meet you at Cranston's we talk away like nobody's business.'

'It's probably become a habit that you can't break. But then, as I've said, I'm a chatterbox.' Her eyes left his and looked towards the floor. 'My goodness, you brought in your haversack and your tin hat! Why didn't you give them to me in the lobby?'

'I was stunned by your beauty.' He laughed.

'Flattery will get you anywhere. So this is your LDV night, or is it the Home Guard now?'

'Whatever you like. No, it's my night off, but I always carry them. You never know. I've got to be ready for any emergency. See, there's my armband.' He pointed to the sleeve of his jacket and she bent forward to look at it. He could smell her perfume. Carnation, he thought, or Californian poppy.

'Well, you're sitting on an emergency!' She giggled, the dimple on her left cheek twinkling in and out. 'I thought if you could help me to push the sofa at right angles to the fire instead of in front of it. I get chilblains on my legs in winter if there's a fire.'

'Delighted, I'm sure. And what's my reward?' He looked playfully at her.

She put a dimpled hand against her chin. 'Well, I've baked a cake, egg powder, flour and liquid paraffin – as good as butter – and saccharin, and a bit of icing sugar I'd hoarded. Although I say it myself it's quite good, and the liquid paraffin isn't supposed to have any effect...' She giggled. 'And some Irish coffee to go with it. I've got a wee bottle of brandy.'

'Sounds good. And I'll risk the cake.' He jumped to his feet and held out his hands to her to help her up. A wave of perfume filled his nostrils. 'Well, suppose we get going, since that's the purpose of my visit, helping a lady in distress. I'll take this jacket off.'

'Throw it on my bed – that's the door there,' she pointed to a corner of the room, 'and you might as well take your haversack and tin hat as well in case we bump into them when we start our furniture moving.'

'Right you are.' He lifted them from the floor, put his jacket over his arm and went into the bedroom. There was a rose-pink-shaded lamp on, just enough to illuminate it, and he laid his tin hat and haversack carefully down on the pink quilt. There was a doll lying there with its head on the pillow, a white, satin-skirted doll with long legs clad in white stockings. It had huge black eyes which seemed to stare at him. Very feminine, he thought, just like Betty. He couldn't imagine Jean with a doll like that, any doll.

When he came back to the room he saw that she had taken off her black cardigan, and the blouse underneath it he now saw was one of the voile Tyrolean kind, with a

98

drawstring neck and cross-stitch embroidery. Lisa had one.

'Ready for action,' she said. 'I was hot, too. You take one end and I'll take the other and guide you. Don't push too hard. I don't want you to strain anything.' Her laugh gurgled in her throat. 'Excuse me,' she said, her eyes dancing.

'Are you sure, Betty?' He tried to look solemn. 'You're just a wee thing. I could manage by myself.'

'I'm stronger than you think. I had to lift Mother on to the commode in her last weeks. Now, slowly does it.'

He noticed as he bent forward that her breasts seemed to push the voile taut, outlining their roundness, and he thought of Jean again. He had seen her bare scalp, but he hadn't seen where her breast had been. She didn't know that he had wept for her in his lonely bed a few times. She had always been so proud of her appearance. He had tried to make himself go into that little room, get in beside her, put his arms round her and say how sorry he was, but he hadn't been able to do it. If she had only asked...

Betty had no trouble in asking. 'I need help with my sofa.' Men liked to be asked, if they felt shy or awkward. And she had said once in Cranston's how she suffered for him. 'I know how it must affect you, James.'

'We're nearly there,' he said, 'a bit at a

time and it's easy ... Do you want it right against the wall?'

'Yes, but very gently, please. That's it. Inch by inch...' He felt his cheeks go hot. 'We're getting there, James.'

'Right-oh. The main thing is to get it to fit snugly.'

'Yes, I want it to fit snugly, James,' she said, looking up, smiling, one side of her mouth higher than the other.

He wiped his cheeks with his hand and took a deep breath. 'That's it. Right in.' She collapsed on the sofa and he did the same. She was laughing and he joined in, heartily. That's the way, James, he told himself. Relax. Take it easy. They nearly killed themselves laughing...

'When I've had a wee rest I'll make that coffee I promised you,' she said, 'and cut two slices of my cake.' She wiped her eyes with her handkerchief.

'There's no hurry.'

Both their heads were resting on the back of the sofa. 'It was a favourite of Mother's,' she said, 'Irish coffee. Bucked her up, she used to say.'

He had turned towards her, and he couldn't take his eyes off her breasts, her veiled breasts. They were heaving slightly, pushing against the material, in and out, in and out. 'You're out of breath,' he said. He touched one of her breasts and it pushed gently against his hand. He could feel the nipple.

'You shouldn't,' she said.

'Shouldn't what?'

'Do what you're doing.'

'What am I doing?' The word-play reminded him of long ago when he used to take girls out, see how far they would let him go. Some liked it, some slapped his face. He was always prepared for either. But these were girls. Betty was thirty-eight. Had there been anyone else in her life? 'You're an attractive girl, Betty. I bet there've been others...'

'With a mother keeping a check on me every night?' Her voice had changed, become harsh. '"Where have you been, Betty? You're ten minutes late. I want my tea ... I've been left alone in this place all day and then you come in when you like. I know what you've been up to..."' She leant against him and he put his arm along her shoulders and his hand under her armpit, resting on her breast. It was hardly noticeable.

'I thought she was good to you.'

'That's what I liked people to think. She ruined my life, James. Her constant girnin'.' She turned her face towards him and he saw that her bright cheeks were streaked with tears.

'You poor wee soul,' he said, and kissed

her. 'You need someone to look after you.'

'I've only told *you*.' She held up her mouth pitifully and when he kissed her this time he made a proper job of it, the kind you used when you were young, probing, searching. She pressed against him and he could feel her breasts, hard now. The thrill went all the way down. He hadn't felt that for ages...

Somehow they were in the bedroom, in the bed, both undressed, and she had put his tin hat on his head 'to see the effect'. She was as playful as a kitten, her cheeks pink, her pink mouth open, her Irish blue eyes screwed up with laughing, no tears now.

'We'll try it further down, just for a laugh!' She couldn't stop laughing, it was that funny, she said. 'Now you see me,' she chanted, whipping it off, then on. 'Now you don't.'

'You're a wee devil!' He took the hat away and pulled her on top of him so that her breasts were between them again.

The rest was easy. If she had never known a man before, it was still dead easy.

And it was just as easy afterwards, having his piece of cake and washing it down with Irish coffee, Betty in a Chinese kimono which parted at the front when she sat down. The fire was reflected on her flesh, turning it a rosy pink.

'When does your meeting stop?' she said with innocent eyes. 'Nine thirty?'

102

'Yes, nine thirty.'

'We couldn't have timed it better.'

He had absolutely no guilt. He saw that her head had drooped, her hair had parted, showing her white neck. 'What is it, Betty?'

'Your wife ... especially when ... she's the way she is.'

'I got carried away. It's all my fault. You don't regret it?'

'No. I'm lonely, James. And we're not causing any trouble to anyone.'

'No, we're not, and you looked so lovely.'

'You make me feel lovely.' She rested her head on his shoulder like a little girl. If only Jean had been like that sometimes, soft...

'I'll have to get off,' he said. She took her head away and he stood up. 'If you want any more furniture moved, let me know.' He felt like that man – d'Artagnan, wasn't it? – cocky, swashbuckling.

She went to the bedroom and brought his things and put the tin hat on his head. 'Suits you,' she said.

'Suits me anywhere,' he said, and felt her giggling against him.

When he got home the house was silent. He saw Jean's light was on, but he couldn't make himself go in. He told himself it might disturb her.

Nine

March 1942

You would have thought that, with her mother's illness, Lisa would have no room in her mind for Neil, but it wasn't so. She read the papers avidly in the tramcar going to and from the hospital, the *Picture Post* if she could prise it from Tommy, searching for any news about air raids, successes and casualties (there were plenty of both), and she picked his brains about Enigma and the effect decoding had on the RAF's successes. She kept to herself the shuddering fear which had swept over her when she had a short note from Neil saying he was now flying the Avro Lancaster bombers.

She thought it possible that her father saw her as a capable, cheerful daughter who had stepped in and run the house as well as his wife's business, kept an eye on Tommy and arranged for the rota of visits to the hospital. She saw him as an imperturbable man who never complained but never enthused – she hesitated at the word 'dull'. She could never imagine confiding in him, yet wished he could confide in her. Was he suffering deeply because of his wife's illness, or was his stoicism such that he accepted without complaint whatever fate dished out to him?

She said to him one evening at supper, 'Did you ever hear anything more from Mr McLean – you remember, the man you met at Craigton?'

'No, never,' he said, 'although golf's the last thing any of us have on our minds these days.' She looked at him, the mild, still-youthful face, except for the lines round his mouth. Why had Mother married him? 'Maybe they're growing cabbages at Hagg's Castle now,' he said with a sly glance at Tommy. Tommy shrugged, unresponsive. The cabbage joke was wearing a bit thin: 'How many cabbages today?'

Tommy's usual deadpan reaction sometimes reminded her of her mother's slightly weary but not-enough-to-be-impolite attitude to her husband. Had it been all along, or for many years, a dead marriage? But why had she married him in the first place?

Lisa worried about Tommy. He was in and out of school as it opened and closed according to the demands for its premises. He mooched about the town too much, presumably with his schoolfriends. Father should step in, have manly talks with him, cultivate mutual interests, but the truth of the matter was that there was little rapport between them.

Tommy, she knew, was deeply distressed about his mother; he always came back from the hospital with a white face and disappeared into his room. He was too old to comfort. Sometimes she felt the responsibility was too heavy, but never for long. It wasn't as exciting as the WAAF, but she was being useful, and it had one advantage, at least during the day: it kept her from worrying about Neil.

'Mrs Docherty has planted the plot at the back with tulips,' she told them. She had noticed their nodding heads this morning, the rich colours against the soft grass of spring.

'She gave me a bunch to take to Mother tonight,' Tommy said. 'I put them in a jug in the kitchen.'

'That was kind of her.'

Mrs Docherty had become an unlikely friend as well as neighbour, cemented by fairly frequent meetings in the Anderson shelter, especially last year when Clydebank had been bombed. She had kept the other tenants in fits of laughter with stories about her stage career, and sometimes one of her 'followers' would oblige with a song recital. They brought a distinctly theatrical aura into the motley bunch of neighbours sitting half buried in the ground under the corrugated roof piled with earth and sandbags, and helped them to forget that their feet were usually wet from the puddles on the earthen floor. Mrs Docherty, with her dyed hair and rouged cheeks was ... joyous, she would think, remembering the word Neil had used about her.

She knew she had the capacity for joyousness, like her mother, like Tommy, however deeply suppressed – but not, alas, like her father. Still, he didn't drink nor beat them. You couldn't have everything.

'We have to decide about Mother,' she said to 'the boys'. She thought of them like that to make her smile. 'Is it safe for her to stay in the hospital after those raids? The Western's pretty near.'

'And there's bound to be more,' Tommy said. 'They always said they couldn't fuel the bombers to fly as far as this, but they did.' They ate without speaking for a minute or two, their minds on the hundreds of homeless people who had come streaming away from Clydebank that terrible morning.

'I saw a barrow with furniture and a canary in its cage on the top,' Tommy said. 'I remember because the wee thing was singing away.'

Their father nodded, knife and fork poised. 'Did you, Tommy? Well, that's the spirit that will win this war.' He wiped his mouth with his napkin. He should be on a poster, KEEP THE FLAG FLYING, Lisa thought disparagingly. She was tired and worried.

'Margaret Currie has three families at the Glebe just now,' she said. 'The men are shipyard workers, and they travel back to the dockyards every morning.'

'Did she ask if she could?' Her father looked stern.

'Oh, yes. It's our war effort, Dad. It's better than having them here, if you like to look at it that way.'

'There's that,' he nodded, 'and in a way nobody would want to come here to the city, the eye of the storm, so to speak.'

'That's quite a good way of looking at it,' Tommy said, brightening at the thought of a discussion. There was a pause.

'So that means Mother can't go to Kilmacolm.' Lisa felt as if she was calling a meeting to order.

'And Craigton's impossible now,' Tommy said. 'The whole place has changed since Liverpool was bombed. All the shipping had to be diverted to the Clyde. There's a steel net across the Firth. Imagine! Bristling with boats, the shore-line chewed up with War Office buildings.'

Regret filled Lisa for a moment. This bloody war, she thought. It's even taken my dream place away from me: no quiet shore road now with the small waves stirring the pebbles, no Middle Wood where she and Neil had sat, no Neil, perhaps. There was no room in his heart for her. Flying filled it.

'You two get off,' she said. 'If Mother looks weary don't trouble her with suggestions. If you've finished, Tommy, go and get the flowers. Right, boys,' she said like a matron, 'on you go. She'll be waiting for you.'

She was glad to be alone for an hour or two as she washed up. It gave her the chance to be really miserable, to shed a few tears, to think of the uncertain prospect ahead for most people. She thought of the ups and downs of her mother's life nowadays, the remissions and the inevitable slipping back, the nurses with their cheerful faces, and her tears dried. Her mother's capacity for recovery always amazed her. And she had somehow become more beautiful, the blue-grey eyes at times startling in her emaciated face.

Once, when she had said, 'You must get fed up, Mother, not getting around,' she had shaken her head.

'For the first time in my life I've had a chance to think. Don't let yourself get too busy.'

And yesterday, when Lisa had visited her, she was sitting up and smiling. 'The doctor says I can go home soon. I'll tell the boys tomorrow when it will be. The specialist does his rounds tomorrow morning.' Her eyes had been lively, animated.

She would go and put fresh sheets on the spare-room bed, and get some flowers tomorrow. Mother didn't want to share a room with Dad any more, she'd said. 'Even though it isn't contagious.' Her father had made no comment. The small room was at the back of the flat, but there was a view of the spring grass and Mrs Docherty's tulips. They nodded cheerfully at Lisa as she made up the bed. 'Consider the lilies,' she remembered, 'they toil not, neither do they spin.' That was the advantage of a reliable education.

They took a taxi home at her mother's wish: 'I'm fed up with ambulances.' She tut-tutted at the doubtful red sandstone edifice of the Art Gallery as they passed it. 'Well, it's there now...' And Charing Cross charmed her, as always. 'There's the Grand Hotel. Many a wedding I've been to there. They lay on a good buffet.' She welcomed her little room – 'my nest', she called it – and declared her intention of visiting Lyle's in the afternoon.

'No, no, Mother, you've done enough for today,' Lisa said.

'No, I've to strike while the iron's hot. I want to see the place, and Bill, and have a wee chat with him on the sly and ask him how you're doing, and ... I want to go there.'

'All right. We'll have an early lunch and after you have a rest we'll go. I have some papers to sign anyhow. I've got a girl, Lilian, just left Skerry's, for the typing. She's good.'

'And pictures? Anything new?'

'I've got one I'd like you to see. It's got a lot going for it. A man brought it in.' She wouldn't say any more.

But, as Lisa had thought, Jean wasn't able to go that afternoon. 'No use, Lisa,' she said when she went into the box room to help her. She was sitting on the edge of the bed and her pallor was alarming – 'grave-like'; the word came unbidden.

Lisa sat down beside her mother and put her arm round her shoulders. 'There's plenty of time. I'm going to make us tea and we'll have a chat and then if you feel well enough I'll help you get ready for the boys coming home.' Her heart ached, an aching fear, at the thinness of her mother's body as she tucked the bedclothes round her.

'My scalp's itching like mad,' she said; 'this wig. Would it offend you if I took it off?'

'Why should it offend me? I'll give it a good brushing. It's quite smart really, with those wee curls.' She whirled it admiringly on one hand. She thought it was awful. 'How about a chiffon scarf?'

That word 'grave-like' came back again as

she looked at the bare scalp, the large eyes in their sunken hollows, the sunken but still-fine mouth. Good bones. Cancer couldn't hide that. She wrapped the azure-coloured scarf round her mother's head, tying it in a bow at the front.

'Mammy!' she sang, arms extended like Al Jolson. 'You're ready for the King's!'

Her mother's smile was to please her.

In the kitchen she brought out two china cups and saucers, and lacy napkins, put shortbread fingers on a flowered plate and made the tea in a fine rage against fate, against the too-slow advance of medicine, against God.

She had a bright false smile on her face when she pushed open the door of her mother's room. She was asleep. Her head, with the chiffon bow, lay askew on the pillow; her face was bone-white.

Ten

'Do you think you should, Jean?' James looked anxious. Lisa thought she detected a new tenderness between her parents, although her mother still occupied the box room, saying she was such a bad sleeper that she would only disturb him.

This morning she was at the breakfast table, saying she was ready to go with Lisa.

'Why not take it easy this morning and I'll take you in the afternoon?' Lisa suggested.

She looked wistful, but very fragile. 'All right, maybe I should.' She brightened. 'And we'll have tea in the snug at the back of the shop. That's what my father called it.'

'Maybe he kept it for his lady-friends?' Tommy, at sixteen, liked to shock.

'Now, now, Tommy,' his father said mildly.

'It had its uses.' Jean spoke quietly, looking away.

She seemed surprisingly fit, Lisa thought, as they set off in the taxi that afternoon, seeing her own likeness except for the lack of flesh on the bones. She recognised the set of the grey-blue eyes, and their size, but not the hair. No wig could reproduce that 'growing' quality.

Jean walked confidently into the show-room, smiling, her stick giving her presence as well as support, and was greeted by Bill Crawford.

'Mrs Cowan,' he said, taking her hand in both of his. His eyes were watery with a mixture of sympathy and affection.

'What's happened to "Jean"?' she said. 'I'm the same person.'

'I've never seen you look better.'

'Enough of your flattery, Bill. Are you going to take me to see the gallery? Not much in it, I hear from Lisa.'

'Aye, now, come along then. Now take your time. Mind they two steps. Lisa's right. There's no' much to show you, because there's no' that many folks interested in pictures these days.'

She stood in the middle of the room, resting on her stick, her eyes travelling round the walls. 'It's scanty-looking, I must say. These are all old ones.'

'Aye, but Lisa made a purchase the other day. She's got your keen eye. A beauty, it did me good to look at it.'

'Where is it?' She turned to Lisa.

'I'll show it to you when we get to the snug, Mother.' It was a pity about the rouge she had insisted on wearing. Against the pale cheeks it made her look like Mrs Docherty. 'Did you want to see the books? Bill could bring them there.'

'No, that'll keep for another day.' She was leaning more heavily on her stick now. 'But a cup of tea would be very acceptable, Bill. You're welcome to join us.'

'Thanks, but I have to keep an eye on these lads in the work-room. I've to mind Lyle's reputation. Lilian will bring in a tray. Lisa got her from Skerry's. Aye, you have a good deputy there.' He smiled at Lisa. 'We'll soon pull up the sales when this nonsense with Hitler is over. What do you think of the cheek of that man Hess, landing in the Duke of Hamilton's estate just ahint Cathkin Brae?'

'Maybe he just wanted a cup of tea as well,' Jean said pointedly. 'Come on, Lisa.' She walked smartly enough to the back of the premises but when she got to the small room she sank down on the sofa, looking exhausted. Not yet fifty, Lisa thought. Her heart sank.

'The showroom looked quite nice. Quite up to standard. That wrought-iron stand with the flowers was new. Where did it come from?'

'I picked it up in a junk shop in Woodlands Road, and I get Campbell's to send up fresh flowers every week. It's worth the expense.

115

Keeps the flag flying.'

Her mother nodded. 'You were going to show me that picture you bought.'

'Oh, yes.'

Lisa was shaking with trepidation as she turned and went towards the wall it was leaning against, lifted it, and placed it on an easel where her mother could see it. 'I couldn't resist it,' she said, steadying her breathing. 'You'll know...'

Her mother's eyes were fixed on the picture. The room seemed suddenly deathly quiet. It had been a mistake. The shock was too great. She looked casually out of the window, a back yard and a dreich day, then back to the small room, the round table with two chairs, back to the old sofa where her mother was sitting.

'How did you come by it?' The voice seemed to come from far down her throat.

'A Mr Anderson. He said his wife had sold all the others, off and on, and he wanted to check the prices she'd got. He hadn't told her about selling this one.' There was no reply. 'What's keeping Lilian?' Lisa said to break the silence.

'He hadn't told her?'

'No. That's what he said.'

'Don't tell me he doesn't trust his wife. Grace McBurnie. You said she had married again.' Her eyes had never left the picture, eating it up, drinking it in. Lisa had to say it.

116

'You know it's Lionel Craig's?'

It was some kind of derisive sound, not a recognisable word. 'I saw this one being painted. Of course I know. Sat and watched. I knew it was good; didn't say, though. He was always too bumptious, craved praise...' Her eyes had never left the picture. 'Well, Grace McBurnie has missed the best. In spite of her greed. Grace Anderson, I should say. He called it his water painting. It's the Gryfe.'

'I thought it was water by the tones. Flowing water. Limpid. You could nearly wring it out.'

'You're right. Water. The most difficult thing to paint. But he got it.' Her voice was low, hardly audible. 'I was there, at his side...' There was another silence. Her eyes hadn't moved from the picture. 'How much did you pay?'

'A hundred and fifty. He wanted two hundred.'

'You're a skinflint. You'll get two thousand for it when the War's over...'

'I know.' She looked at her mother and saw the exhaustion in her face, her clown's face. She wished she could take her handkerchief and rub off that colour ... That poor head with the doll wig, the row of stitching down the middle to simulate a parting, drooping as if she could no longer hold it upright, her outstretched hand like a claw gently stroking the green velour of the old sofa, back and forward, back and forward. My mother. Lionel Craig could have painted her like that. 'I'll go and hurry up Lilian,' she said. 'They evidently didn't teach her to make tea at Skerry's.'

There was no answer.

She found Bill Crawford in the workshop, strips of framing in his hand. 'Bill, what's that girl doing? Mother's looking like—' she stopped herself in time.

'Has she not brought it in yet? I told her...'

'She's in the lavvy, Mr Crawford.' One of the lads at the work-bench looked up, laughing. Bill frowned.

'Could she no' have waited?'

'Needs must, Bill.' It was a relief to smile at his scarcely concealed embarrassment. Bill Crawford was a betting man, a man who liked his whisky, but of the old school who didn't like any mention of bodily functions. Bella, his wife, was very prissy, of course.

'Once she has a drink of tea I'll get her home. Would you order a taxi to come in half an hour?'

'She's worse than I thought, Lisa.' He looked miserable.

'She's up and down.'

He nodded, biting his lower lip, his eyes full.

Lilian appeared in the doorway. 'I'm sorry,

Mr Crawford. I couldn't find the biscuits...'

'Tea in five minutes, Lilian!' Lisa said. She sounded like her mother.

Jean looked up when she came back to the room. Her smile was like that of her own ghost.

'Tea's coming,' Lisa said brightly. 'I'll just put this away.' She went towards the easel.

'No, leave it!' Her mother's voice was raised, and then died to a whisper as if she had worn it out with the three words. 'I've still to look at it. I haven't got it all, yet. It's ... subtle.'

Lilian bustled in, looked from one to the other and decided to address Jean. 'I'm sorry to be so long, Mrs Cowan. I got ... held up. I hope everything's all right.'

'Perfectly, Lilian.' She was gracious. 'Just put it on the table. Lisa tells me you're doing well here. Now you've been lucky to obtain employment in a fine business like this. I hope you appreciate it. If you take my advice and stick in, you'll not regret it.' Very much the *grande dame*. If Lilian had been told off by Bill she had by now brushed it aside.

'Not for me, thanks all the same, Mrs Cowan. I'm just waiting to get into the ATS.' She smiled round, confident. 'Well, I'd better get back.' She bounced out.

Lisa laughed at her mother's expression. 'She wouldn't have done anyway. I'll have

119

that tea now.' She leant back on the sofa while Lisa poured the tea and put her cup and saucer on a small table beside her.

'To be fair to her, Mother, she was quite honest. She told me when I took her on that she wanted to join up.'

Her mother's interest had gone. She sipped her tea. 'You can put the picture away now. I've got it in my head.'

'All right.' She lifted it from the easel, stood it against the wall. 'The taxi will be here soon.' She came back and sat opposite her mother. The sadness in the room made her throat close.

'What happened to Neil?' Jean's voice was stronger. 'You don't talk about him.'

'I've nothing much to say. As far as I know he's fighting the War single-handed.'

'What does that mean?'

'He doesn't write much. He's dedicated. He's flying Lancaster bombers now. It's his whole life. Nothing else interests him, not even me.'

'Don't get bitter. It doesn't mean he doesn't think of you.'

'I know that.' So much sadness in this room. She wouldn't add to it. She watched her mother's hand stroking the green velour, and met her eyes.

She was looking shyly up at her, the eyes nearly falling out of her face. 'Lionel Craig and I were lovers.' The eyes clung.

Lisa didn't reply at first, and yet she wasn't shocked, although she might well have been considering she had reached nearly twenty-one and hadn't had a steady boyfriend, far less a lover. Beryl Craig had been wallowing in connubial bliss for six months now, as had her mother. 'Well, it's more than I've had,' she said at last, and then they were both laughing, her mother as if it hurt. She held her side.

'I thought as much by the look of you. You can tell. Is it that you've got too much on your plate just now?'

'No.' She couldn't add to this woman's burden. She said lightly, 'I'll have more time when Tommy joins me. He sees himself already as Grandfather Lyle's successor, swanning over to Paris every month to live the life of Riley.'

Her mother's eyes were on her. 'You're strong-willed, Lisa. I see myself ... Well, tell me about Tommy.'

'He's talented, inclined to mooch about, but he gets a lot of time on his hands with the school's erratic timetable. I thought it would be good for him later to have a year at a lycée in Paris. After the War. If there is an after...' She saw clearly Neil's brooding eyes, the lean beauty of his face, felt the sharp pain in her heart. 'If there is an after...'

'He's Lionel's son.'

121

Now she *was* shocked. She watched the hand stroking the green velour, gently, softly, and repeated the words to herself, *'He's Lionel's son,'* over and over again, hoping that they made sense. But they had to. Her mother wouldn't say that as a joke.

'Did he know?'

'No, I never told him. Then he died. Everybody supposed he was James's. But I ask you, does he look as if he were James's son?'

'No.' She shook her head slowly. 'They're quite different. Does Father know?'

'I never told him, but he might have worked it out. I broke his heart, Lisa.' Her eyes were beseeching.

'Oh...' Pity for her father at first overwhelmed her, and then she wondered if her mother *had* broken his heart, or was it that he was incapable of great excesses of feeling in any case? A temperate man. 'Why didn't you marry Lionel Craig in the first place?' Her voice was stern.

'I ran from him. I thought he should have a proper job. It was the way I was brought up, not realising that men with proper jobs were as dull as their jobs. And Grace McBurnie stepped in. I expect he needed somebody in his bed. Most men do. I've made a mess of things, Lisa. All those times in the hospital I've thought of it ... At least it took my mind off the pain...'

There was nothing to say when her heart was full of pity and love. She said at last, 'The biggest mistake I've made so far is that I haven't made any.'

'You'll never know until it's too late. Where's that taxi?'

She got a grand send-off from the staff clustered round the door as Bill Crawford opened it for her. 'Come back soon, Jean,' he said, taking her hands again. He wanted to kiss her but couldn't.

'Oh, you'll not get rid of me,' she said, and to Lilian, 'Enjoy the ATS.' To the young gawping apprentices, 'Stick in, lads.'

'A grand send-off,' she said to Lisa in the taxi.

She died in her little room the same month. She was heavily sedated because of the pain, but even then she was racked by it. Her flesh, what remained of it, fell away from her bones, and she shrank to the size of a mannikin.

In between the bouts she had long talks with James and Tommy, and Lisa didn't ask them what she'd said. Tommy spent a lot of time in his room, and James went to the LDV meetings, keeping the War going.

Lisa stopped going to Lyle's, except weekly to pay the wages, which meant first a trip to the bank, but she saw Sauchiehall Street as through a veil, and answered with an expressionless face the manager's enquiries about her mother. 'A true Lyle,' he said once, 'a very special lady. Give her the bank's kindest regards.'

Bill Crawford supported her more than her father, whether the latter felt it was essential to keep a cheerful front for her sake she didn't know, but she found it impossible to confide in him her occasional bouts of terror at what lay ahead.

'Sometimes I feel so alone,' she said to Bill when she was sharing a quick cup of coffee with him. 'My father has never taken an interest in Lyle's and it's almost as if—' She stopped herself at the enormity of the thought which lay at the back of her mind, that he was applying the same lack of interest to the imminent death of his wife.

'Well, it cuts both ways, Lisa,' he said. 'This was very much your mother's domain. I don't think she ever said he couldn't come, but he might have thought it.'

'Her territory?'

'Aye. And then there's another thing. He's the head of the family. Maybe he thinks he has to keep cheerful for your sake and Tommy's. Some men go to pieces, others don't. I don't know what I'd be like if it were Bella. She's always supported me.'

'Maybe you're right, Bill. It's difficult for everybody, and we've never been a demonstrative family. And I'm possibly giving the same impression to Tommy.' *He's Lionel's son.* It seemed as if the words were burned into her mind, other times that she had dreamt it. 'I'm holding myself in, for her sake...' She looked round the snug so that he wouldn't see how her eyes had filled up. 'What's in that cupboard, Bill?'

'I don't know. It's locked, and I haven't the key. Maybe you could ask Jean, if you find the right time.'

He had a large bunch of hothouse roses for her. 'Bella bought them. And there's a card inside. We're not sick-room visitors, and a know a'd just disgrace myself. I've written to her telling her what I couldn't say. And that I want to remember her as she was in her glory here...'

'Yes, she got it. She said you were quite right. She didn't want to see you crying in front of her and she knew you would. "Bill's a sentimental old codger," she said.'

A few weeks later she said to Lisa in a quiet spell – there weren't many now – 'I think I've straightened things out. As far as I could.' That day Mr Cuthbertson, her lawyer, had come. 'My father always said, "Commit it to paper."' She tried to laugh. 'A businesswoman to the last.'

'Have a drink.' Lisa held the cup to her lips, giving her time. 'I'm going to do some cooking before the boys come in.' She got up, leaving the door open.

The next evening, after Mr Cuthbertson had called, she looked contented, had even smiled and said, 'That's everything tied up.'

'Lisa...' She heard the faint voice and she went swiftly. She had been expecting it, had kept listening as she peeled potatoes, sliced carrots, perfectly calm because she didn't believe it and yet knew it was going to happen.

Her mother indicated with her head that Lisa should sit beside her. She did, and bending forward kissed her forehead, then stroked her cheek, gently. There was a blue tinge under the eyes, and at the side of the nostrils. She felt a great calmness.

There was a long silence while her mother lay with her eyes closed and Lisa watched her, telling herself to be ready. They were in a strange country beyond speech. It was merciful, she thought, that in spite of all the pain it was leaving her alone now.

In the quietness of the house the wag-at-the-wall struck rustily, an old clock, and she saw the eyelids flicker, then felt her mother's hand on hers, caressing it, shakily, slowly, gently, backwards and forwards, as it had done on the green velour of the old sofa.

After a time the hand fell away.

It was very strange to be alone in a house with a dead woman, her mother. Someone who didn't look like her mother now, just a shell. No one would have liked to take her like that to bed, not even Lionel Craig. All kinds of strange thoughts went through her head until she stirred herself and went to leave a message at the doctor's.

After that she walked for a long time about the city, gazing into shop windows and not seeing anything, reading the placards on the sandwich-men's boards – WAR, WAR, WAR, they said in various disguises – thinking she must buy a black hat for the funeral then turning away as it was shut, somehow putting in the time until Tommy and her father would be home. It was raining; she had no umbrella and the rain and the tears which were like rain made a mess of her hair and face. No one noticed. They don't in cities, not even in Glasgow.

Eleven

It took Lisa a few days before she felt she
was operating as a human being. She went
about her duties in the house and at Lyle's
in a kind of half-world, being as supportive
as she could to Tommy and her father, and
polite to customers and staff at Lyle's; putting on a brave face at home was the more
difficult.

She said at supper one evening, 'I took all
Mother's things to a charity shop where
anybody who's been bombed out can go. It's
what she would have wanted. She had some
lovely coats and suits, but it's nice to think
of someone else getting pleasure out of
them.' She saw Tommy's down-bent head.
'You think it will be a good idea, Tommy?'

'They'll be a gift to somebody.' He snort-
ed, something between a sob and a laugh.

She smiled at him. 'We've just to remember her as she was, when she could wear
them.' Lisa thought of a mauve suit her
mother had, lovely material, the frilled voile

blouse, the high-heeled black patent court shoes, her 'all-together' look, not a hair out of place.

'There was no one like her for smartness, that's for sure,' her father said. 'But we must look to the future. You two have a life ahead of you and I'm ... not in my dotage yet.' His smile was cheerful, and she saw Tommy look at him as if this was somebody he didn't know.

He further surprised her by taking in hand all the arrangements for the funeral, which was to be at Kilmacolm, leaving only the letter-writing to Lisa. If she hadn't known it was impossible, she might have thought that there was someone at his elbow telling him what to do.

Tommy, fortunately, was back at school. The governors had obtained smaller premises that were not likely to be commandeered by the government. The discipline came at the right time.

'You know,' she said to him, 'Mother always thought you'd go to Paris to finish your education. So if I were you, Tommy, I would work hard. This war can't go on for ever, and at least it's something to look forward to.'

'I know,' he said, 'she talked about it to me once, the Seine, and the bridges. I quite fancy mooching about the Left Bank – the *Rive Gauche* – it's called, looking in those stalls for books, and pictures. She bought a Sisley there once.' His sad face had lightened, and she thought their father had been right: the only saving grace for the three of them was to look forward.

Tommy had stayed close to her at the funeral as if she were a surrogate mother, grim-faced and dry-eyed. Margaret Currie, who had no difficulty in expressing her feelings, gave them all a hug as they came back from the interment at the family plot, even her father. Lisa saw his face soften.

'Now that you aren't so tied at Holland Street,' Margaret had said, 'you should try and come here at weekends. The Clydebank folks have been given accommodation nearer their work.'

'Yes, we could try,' Lisa had promised.

'You could make some new friends here, Tommy, go to Baxter's farm with Alec. Some of the young lads about the place would take you fishing and that. Set you up, now that spring's here.'

'It's a good idea, Father, isn't it?' Lisa had appealed to him.

'Well, I'll have my Home Guard duties, but you two should certainly think of it. Lisa here looks as if she could do with some fresh air.' His smile was kindly.

She had written to Beryl Semple, and she and Bruce had turned up at the funeral. Beryl looked too happy for such an occasion. 'We felt we had to come for old times' sake,' she said, 'didn't we, Bruce?' She and Bruce were the picture of wedded bliss, plump and oozing sexual satisfaction with their married state. 'I worried about leaving wee John, but Bruce's mother was dying to look after him, wasn't she, Bruce?'

'That's right, Beryl.' Lisa thought he looked slightly sheepish when she caught his eye.

'How is your mother, Beryl?' she asked.

'Oh, she's living in style in Helensburgh, a lovely bungalow. Mr Anderson seems in quite a good way of doing.'

'I'm sure he is.' Mr Delmino, their London dealer, had given £750 for the picture. Mother would have been pleased.

But when they were back home and had taken up their duties, Tommy turning out each morning for school, the impact of her mother's death hit her. The tit-for-tat bombing at home and abroad seemed pointless, although in Glasgow they had been free since the Clydebank raids.

Where was Neil in all this? She got the occasional short note, but leave was impossible, he said. She shuddered every time she heard of another historic city being ruined, places she had hoped to visit with him in happier times. 'I love you deeply,' he wrote, but there was no commitment, no planning for the future. Because he didn't believe there would be any future for them? She fought depression by throwing herself into managing Lyle's.

Bill Crawford was her mainstay. 'You're run-down, Lisa. Everything looks black. I can guess what it's like without Jean. There's no easy way. And there's your young man in constant danger. If I were you I'd take up the suggestion you told me about and go to Kilmacolm every weekend. It would do you a power of good.'

'I'm back to thinking I should join up,' she confided in him. 'I'd feel part of it.'

She wanted to say, 'Nearer Neil.'

He dismissed that. 'Have you seen yourself in a mirror? They wouldn't pass you looking like that. Get some colour in your cheeks before you even think of it.'

She took his advice and every weekend she and Tommy set off for Kilmacolm. Their father said again he was too busy with the Home Guard to join them, but he could manage fine. Tommy joined Alec Currie at Baxter's farm as soon as he arrived, and Lisa let Margaret spoil her by 'feeding her up'. And having a few good cracks over their morning coffee.

She wanted to build a picture of her mother when she was young and living here with her parents. The photographs Margaret had kept of a bright, laughing girl were a far cry from the dying woman she had looked after, but they helped to dispel the image. 'It was the loss of her spirit,' she said, 'all that brightness gone. That was the sad part...'

'You're right, it was a kind of inner brightness. She wasn't a noisy child, nor young girl, and I think she sometimes wished she could be more like Grace McBurnie, surrounded by boys. She was too fussy, maybe because she was an only child, a bit hoity-toity, a bit old-fashioned. Yet underneath there was this radiance.'

'Did Granny and Grandpa keep her down?'

'Mrs Lyle did. She liked to hobnob with the toffs, hoped Jean would get in with the county set. *He* wasn't like that; he was quirky, wrapped up in his business.'

'Did my mother fall in with Granny's ideas?'

'Not at all. The only one she ever fancied was Lionel Craig, the direct opposite of her, a bit lazy, a law unto himself. You could see she was taken by him, but she never said. And he wasn't one of your lily-livered kind, down on his knees begging for her favours, oh, dear no...' Margaret looked away, shaking her head, then went on:

'She haunted that hut of his down by the Gryfe where he painted. Folks told me. Mrs Lyle got a hint of it and she was furious. Truth to tell, the Craigs weren't much, lived

133

in a tenement near the Village Cross, didn't even have a job into the bargain. He was bright, though, it was looking out of his eyes. Tommy reminds me of him, that same look of promise.'

'Yes, Tommy's bright. He'll make his mark.' She avoided Margaret's eyes.

'To tell you the truth, Lisa, I worried about her hanging about that hut, her being so fond of him and him being well ... himself. I held my breath often in case...'

'...She got pregnant?'

'Aye. It wouldn't have been the first time around here. It's the smart ones who know how to avoid it, and she was as innocent in that department as a new-born lamb.'

'I doubt it, Margaret.' She smiled.

'Well...' Margaret tossed her head. 'He was a devil, but you couldn't help liking him. He had the nerve to come here for her, though he wasn't made welcome, I'll tell you, but he says to me, with that devil-may-care attitude of his, "Where's my bonny Jean? Is she at home?"'

'I wonder they didn't get married, in spite of Granny and Grandpa.'

'It was the Lyle bit in her. She wanted it both ways. She wanted him to fit in with their conventional outlook, and she wanted him as he was. Anyhow it seemed to peter out when she started travelling to Glasgow to that fine school, and then she was studying for a teacher and stayed up there. The next thing I heard was that he and Grace McBurnie were getting married. I've often wondered how she managed it, if she tricked him...'

These talks did more than help her to cope with her own anxiety. She gained an element of peace at Kilmacolm because it belonged to her mother's life. The poignancy she felt about Craigton and Neil was her own.

In the Sunday quietness of a sunny afternoon she wrote a letter to him. She knew as she wrote that he had never truly been out of her mind, only pushed to the back of it because she had been caring for her mother. It seemed that now he was the sole occupant of the space which Jean's death had left. It was like talking to him.

Dear Neil,
I'm spending this weekend and others in our house at Kilmacolm. It's been lovely. I've watched spring arriving in the white flourish on the trees, in the fresh springtime grass under my feet, the spring flowers pushing through it. You forget what it's really like when you live in the city, all that stirring...
I have a view over the farmland to Pacemuir Mill and the Gryfe, the view my mother loved so much, and where

she liked to walk.

She died in March, and I'm slowly coming to terms with the fact that the person I loved most is no longer here. I had scarcely time to think of you, but often in bed I would picture those lovely times we had at Craigton, and think how circumstances have changed for us.

I remember my first sight of you, perched on that umpire seat, all arms and legs, and your clear voice coming to me, 'Game to...' Sometimes I imagine it's my name you're calling, but that is only when I'm tired. And it isn't a game now, is it?

Each day I feel I should start a new life, help in the War as you are doing, but then I'm swallowed up in my day-to-day existence. Remember I said that I was going to join the WAAF and be posted beside you?

I still talk about it, but I know I won't. Bill Crawford, the manager at Lyle's, says they also serve who only stand and wait, but it's something to do with knowing where my duty lies ... so like my mother.

Since she died, I realise you've always been in my mind and in my heart. Sometimes I didn't know it, but you were there, a presence, a sweetness. I don't mind confessing that. I know you, far more than me, can't look ahead. Every time I read of a raid by the RAF I think of you. I'll never get used to that fear for your safety, but then I remember it's what you wanted, to be up there. The escape, you called it.

Do you remember how we walked in the blackout and how cold it was? But I was happy because I was near you, complete, happier than I have ever been, before or since. I pray that you'll come back safely – I don't look beyond that.

My love to you, Lisa.

Twelve

1942

Mr Cuthbertson, their lawyer, had request-
ed their presence at his office, and on a
breezy May morning they set off. He had
asked that the whole family should attend.
Tommy was looking more settled, she
thought, sitting opposite her in the tramcar.
The discipline of regular schooling suited
him, and he was working steadily towards
his Highers. He had a new teacher with
whom he had struck up a rapport, a young
man called McIlroy who had been invalided
out of the Army after Dunkirk.

Her father had grumbled when the letter
came. 'It's not very convenient to take a
morning off, and I have a lunch appointment at twelve thirty...'

He, too, looked well, and she hoped that
she herself had got rid of the woebegone
appearance which had looked at her from
the mirror a few months ago. Personal

sorrows couldn't be allowed to dominate your life when there was so much tragedy all around.

There was no doubt about it, they had all got used to a greater or lesser extent to Jean's death; routines supported them. Lisa was probably reminded more of her mother because she took upon herself the job of clearing out drawers and wardrobes. She noticed that her mother's jewel case was missing, but when she mentioned it to her father he wasn't perturbed.

'Mr Cuthbertson saw her before she died, if you remember, and he took possession of it. I'm sure he left a receipt with me. I'll have a look for it.'

Normally he would have fussed about the loss, but there was a new forbearance in his attitude. Lisa mourned that everything passes, even grief, or at least intense grief, and recognised that she herself had a new hopeful outlook, thanks to Margaret's cooking and her walks about the peaceful countryside around Kilmacolm.

It had such an air of permanence, she thought, the old houses, the old names. She remembered her mother telling her that the Earl of Glencairn had taken communion from John Knox. The present house still looked stately on the banks of the Clyde, the river peaceful there compared with its other persona at Clydebank as home to the great shipyards bustling with activity. And there was the old Duchal House, several times rebuilt, with the ruins of the even older church of the same name.

By contrast nowadays there were the forward-looking designs of Charles Rennie Mackintosh. Perhaps I'm seeing for the last time the Kilmacolm I knew, she thought. After the trauma of war people would seek out a place like this for a quieter life.

On one of her walks along the banks of the Gryfe she had come across the remains of what looked like a wooden hut, only a few timbers, a few beams of a fallen-in roof, and she had wondered if it might be the place where her mother and Lionel Craig had met, a young girl tied by conventional pride and a free-spirited unconventional young man. All in the past, she thought, both dead, and now this appointment with their lawyer was in a way a final shutting of the door...

The three of them got off the tram at St Vincent Street and were walking towards St Vincent Place. The lift was rickety at the lawyer's address, and her father cracked a rare joke: 'I hope we're not all rushing to our doom in this rattletrap!' But when they reached the floor where Mr Cuthbertson's office was, he reminded them that they weren't going to spend all day with him.

'I don't mind a morning off,' Tommy said.

'Neither do I,' Lisa agreed. 'You and I will

have our lunch in town after we've finished. We're quite near Argyle Street here.' Their father had gone ahead and was already opening the door.

Mr Cuthbertson welcomed them with a solemn shaking of hands and expressions of condolence. He seated them in a semicircle in front of his desk, then sat down behind it.

'I must apologise for taking so long to get in touch with you, but there's such a thing as probate, as you know.'

'Yes, we understand,' her father said. 'And it gave me time to find the receipt for my wife's jewel case. We were all too disturbed at the time.' He took a slip of paper from his pocket and placed it on the desk.

'Good. Well, this won't take long. Perhaps if you're ready, I'll go ahead right away and read out the will. Your wife dictated it to me, Mr Cowan. She had evidently given it a lot of thought. Such a sterling character – like her father. A sad loss to you all.'

'We're coping,' he said, 'and Lisa looks after us well, as she did throughout her mother's illness.' He smiled at her, and she felt her eyes fill. It was the first time he had ever made any reference to her part in their domestic arrangements, far less publicly.

'I'll spare you all the fiddle-faddle at the beginning,' the lawyer said. 'It seems, Mr Cowan, that you gave your wife a generous housekeeping allowance. She didn't use it

141

all, and you'll be surprised to know that it accumulated to the tune of seven thousand pounds. She leaves this sum to you.'

'But that's ridiculous!' he said. He looked upset. 'She could hardly have used any.'

'She was a good housekeeper, and the maid, Agnes, whom she employed when the children were young, was paid out of her own pocket.'

'I didn't realise that.' He looked genuinely abashed. 'I must admit I hadn't been made office manager then, and things were a bit tight. She was the major earner ... but she shouldn't have paid Agnes.' He turned to Lisa and his regret was obvious. 'I've just realised you've managed without a maid and you've been running your mother's business as well.'

'I didn't have children to look after...' she smiled at him, 'unless you like to count yourself and Tommy.' Mr Cuthbertson chuckled.

'There's a clause in her will saying that you mustn't stint on help, but that's to be paid by you, Mr Cowan, until the War's over and Alexander Lyle and Son is earning enough.'

'We can settle that between ourselves,' Lisa said.

'I'll leave it to you, then. I'll read you the rest of the will now before you make any decisions.' He lifted the document again.

'"I leave to my daughter, Lisa, the firm of Alexander Lyle and Son, on the under-standing that when my son, Thomas, is twenty-one, she offers him an equal part-nership. Should he refuse, it remains in her hands, but he will be entitled to an equal share of the profits. Should Lisa marry she retains her share, and Thomas, if he has become a partner of the firm, takes Lisa's place as managing director. I want him to be partly educated in Paris, so that he will be *au fait* with the opportunities which exist there for enlarging our business."'

The lawyer looked around the three of them. 'Is everything clear? Please ask me any questions if not.'

'Yes,' James said. 'I think that's fair. I never took any interest in the firm, but I have benefited from it in many ways when I wasn't so well-placed as I am now.'

'Thomas?'

Tommy looked at his father and Lisa, then at Mr Cuthbertson. He was very pale. 'It's too much. I...'

'It's what your mother wished. Think of it as a token of her love. You accept, then, Thomas?'

Tommy nodded. 'Yes, thank you.'

'Lisa?'

'It's generous, but like Mother, and I can think of nothing better than following in her footsteps.'

There was a pause. Mr Cuthbertson looked round the three of them and cleared his throat.

'Er, a delicate matter ... Mrs Cowan asked me to say that it was her earnest wish that you should remain as a united and devoted family although you're aware that Tommy's father was Lionel Craig.'

So she told him, Lisa thought. And Father ... 'Tommy will always be my dear brother,' she said. She smiled at him. His eyes met hers gratefully.

'And my dear son.' Her father, like Tommy, looked close to tears. They smiled tentatively at each other.

'Well, that's all right, then,' Mr Cuthbertson said briskly, as if he was afraid they'd make a scene. 'Now, to the jewel case.' He took the green leather-covered box from his desk and opened it. 'There's an inventory of the jewellery inside which has been willed to Lisa, naturally, but she can distribute some of it at her discretion in the event of either Thomas marrying or Mr Cowan remarrying.'

'I'll keep it safely,' Lisa said. Tommy looked uninterested; her father's gaze had shifted to the window.

'That seems to be the substance of the will,' Mr Cutherbertson said, leaning back. 'You will each receive a copy.' He looked at Lisa. 'Are you aware of a locked cupboard in a small room in the premises of the firm – I might say, "your firm"?' He smiled.

'Yes, there is. In a room we call the snug.' The blood seemed to race through her veins. She felt her cheeks flush. 'I meant to ask Mother what was in it, but then she was so ill, and I didn't want to bother her.'

'Quite. There are four paintings in it by Lionel Craig. They are yours, because the firm is yours. You have to dispose of them or keep them, as you wish. Any decision you take is your responsibility.' He looked intently at her over his spectacles. 'If you will take advice from an old codger like me, take your time.'

He stood up. 'I think that is all the business for today, but no doubt you will keep in touch. I shall be happy to go on serving the firm of Alexander Lyle and Son as long as I am able.'

They went down in the lift in silence. They were all too full of thought to speak. At the main entrance their father turned to them. 'We can talk tonight. I'll take time off the Home Guard. Now, I must get on.' He left them, striding swiftly towards Buchanan Street. He looked remarkably ... virile. Yes, that was the word, Lisa thought.

'I'm glad Mother told you about your father, Tommy,' she said.

'Yes, when she was dying.' His voice was low. 'I'm glad Mr Cuthbertson sort of ...

broke the ice for me.'

'Typically Mother. "A sterling character", he calls her. Everything ship-shape. Come on, then, we'll have lunch at Miss Cranston's, anything you like, then we'll go to Lumley's and buy you some shirts. You're growing so quickly. Have you any tennis ones?'

'No. Why should I want that?'

'Well, Margaret was reminding me of the club at Kilmacolm. I used to play there. I thought if you got fed up mucking out byres with Alec at the weekends you might like a game there with me. I used to be quite good.'

'You played at Craigton a lot.'

'Yes, I did.'

He glanced at her. 'It must be worrying for you, Lisa.' He looked awkward. 'I mean Neil McLean, flying ... You never say ... We're both bad at saying...' He smiled uncertainly. She couldn't speak for sudden tears clogging her throat. He looked at her then went on in a casual voice, 'I like fishing better, actually. I miss Craigton at times. It's as if it was in a ... time capsule.'

'That's a good name for it.' She swallowed, repeating the words. 'A time capsule...'

They had reached the restaurant and Tommy was soon tucking into his meal with boyish gusto, the full luncheon menu, soup, steak pie and chips, ice-cream. He didn't want coffee: he would take the chance to go to the model shop in the Argyll Arcade and look at the new ones. He was interested in the Avro bombers. 'Thanks for the lunch, Lisa,' and he was off. Still just a boy, she thought fondly.

On the way to the cash desk, Lisa glanced for some reason at the corner tables on her left. At one of them she saw her father with a woman. He was leaning towards her, and the angle of his body conveyed an eagerness ... something she had never before seen in him. Tommy was ahead of her, intent on his mission. She wouldn't mention what she had seen to him.

Thirteen

For once they had plenty to talk about at supper. Lisa, looking at her father, saw him with new eyes. The trite phrase rang in her ears: 'How long has this been going on?' She hadn't had time to notice the woman sitting opposite him at the table in Miss Cranston's. What remained in her mind was the eagerness, the animation of his attitude as he leant across the table towards her. These were words she never could have applied to him before.

'I was bowled over by Mother's generosity,' he said. 'I feel badly accepting it.'

'It's your money,' Lisa said. 'And I'll repeat what I said in Mr Cuthbertson's office. I don't need a maid. Mother had small children. I can remember that maid, Agnes.' She said to Tommy, 'Can you? She came just after you were born. "Wooden", Mother called her years later when she was talking about her to me.'

'I remember her smell,' Tommy said, wrinkling his nose, 'kind of fishy. Pass the potatoes, Dad.'

'She was always desperate to get away. Maybe she had a boyfriend...' She glanced at her father. He was busy eating.

'Not with a smell like that,' Tommy said.

'I think we've had enough of Agnes.' Their father looked up. 'As far as I remember, she did adequately what she was paid for. And that your mother made her sign a paper to the effect that she mustn't lift a hand to you. Maybe that made her a bit doleful.'

Have I known a different man all my life? Lisa thought, listening to him.

'There are the paintings,' she said. 'I think the best thing is for Bill and me to have a look at them and then we might get them valued. I expect we would all like to know their worth.'

'They were done by Beryl's father?' He was casual.

'Yes.'

'Lionel Craig.' His eyes were empty. 'I don't expect they're up to much.'

'We'll see.' She had been going to tell him about the one she'd bought from Mr Anderson, Grace Craig's new husband, but decided against it.

The next morning a letter arrived from Neil in reply to hers, much sooner than she had dared to hope. She went into her bedroom to read it. It was dated 14 May 1942.

Dear Lisa,

I wept for your loss when I read your letter. I know how you loved your mother. You must feel bereft. Here, death becomes an everyday affair, and announcements no longer continue to shock, although we grieve for a particular friend. You tell yourself that the only name you won't hear is your own, which is at least a comfort.

As a matter of fact I haven't been flying for a week. My legs suddenly wouldn't hold me. At first I thought I'd had a stroke, but the doctor diagnosed it as nervous exhaustion, and had me put into hospital and sedated. I lay in bed, didn't read, didn't even think, didn't want food, a zombie. In a strange way I've never been happier.

This doctor, Squadron Leader Cramond, had to see me before I reported back to duty. He's a Highlander, big, solid, jokey – you couldn't find anyone more different from me. He gave me as much time as he could – I suspect it was his off-time – and he'd soon diagnosed what was really wrong with me, as if I didn't know. But I told him the lot, and how much I loved you. He didn't hesitate.

'Go and see her,' he said; 'don't write

long-winded letters torturing yourself. Tell her face to face. I've passed you fit for your next mission, but if I were you I should nip up to Glasgow immediately after.'

I feel a different person. I'm looking forward to flying again, but I'll want to live now, not die. Let's make it the 31st. It'll be over by then. We'll meet at the Shell, but then we'll take another train to your Kilmacolm and walk in your fields, and by your river, and I'll talk and talk ... 'She sounds the right type of girl to understand,' Charlie said. He asked me to call him that, to treat him as a friend.

I'll get the early train and should be in Glasgow by midday. Please be there, my darling. It's so very important to me. I can hardly wait, I feel so ... joyous. And relieved. And truly happy. My dearest love...

She sat for a few minutes on her bed, her heart full. She wouldn't let her mind dwell on what he was going to tell her – all along she had shut it against suspicion, against fear, against doubt, telling herself that eventually he would tell her. This doctor who had persuaded him ... she felt very grateful.

It was good Neil had suggested Kilmacolm. It felt right. It had been her mother's

151

home, and perhaps they would find there the same peace that she had felt as a young girl.

She breathed deeply and got up. Everything was going to be all right. Meantime, she had better get off to Lyle's. She would find plenty there to fill in the time until they met.

She met Bill Crawford in the gallery.

'You look good, Lisa,' he said.

'I've had good news.' She felt the smile spilling over her face. 'We can do with good news. Anything new, Bill?'

'No, fairly quiet. Do you want me for anything special?'

'Yes. I heard from our lawyer that there are some paintings locked in the cupboard in the snug. They were given to my mother by the man who painted them, Lionel Craig.'

'Lionel Craig?' His surprise was genuine. 'If that's the case, you have a treasure trove in your possession.'

'Why did you say "my possession"?' Her smile was ready because of her happiness.

'Because, knowing Jean, she'll have left the business to you. Am I right?'

'Yes, you are. But Tommy will be joining us when he's twenty-one, if not before. If he wants to, that is.'

'He'll want to. Blood is thicker than water. And you're both like old Alexander. I see him in the two of you: something that can't be taught, that has to be passed on. But she didn't forget me, your mother. I had a letter from your legal man this mornin'.'

'I knew she wouldn't.' She patted his shoulder. You wouldn't dare kiss Bill. 'Nor will we.'

'How about they paintin's then?' He didn't want to be accused of being 'saft'.

There were four. The same basic palette had been used on all of them, giving Lisa the impression that they had been done as a set. Bill propped them up on a counter side by side, and they both stood back. Neither of them spoke for a few minutes. It took that time, it took longer, to let them sink in, to get inside them.

'He's got it,' Bill said at last. 'By God, he's bloody got it, pardon ma French. What did you sell that last one for?'

'I got seven hundred and fifty from Mr Delmino in Old Bond Street.'

'He got a bargain. These are four-figure jobs.'

'You're a mercenary old devil,' she said, laughing.

'Put them away till the fightin's over then bring them out one by one, and your fortune's made.'

'They're the family's, not mine.'

'They're yours if they're on the premises, and they're your premises.'

'That's what the lawyer said, but stop

talking about money, Bill. Just look...'

'I see rows of noughts.' He laughed. 'Only teasin'. Now you give me the artistic viewpoint.'

'First of all they're Scottish. They couldn't have been painted in any other place. Not like the Glasgow Colourists, who painted French, Provençal colours. They didn't convey the subtlety of *our* light, nor were they meant to. But when Lionel Craig wanted his to sing, by God he knew how to do it, pardon *my* French!'

'Granted.'

'D'you see that river one, and that dab of blue-green iridescence? A kingfisher? I've never seen a kingfisher on the Gryfe. That misty autumnal one, with that patch up in the corner there, maple red? It shouts at you!' She was suddenly excited. 'I get it! It's the four seasons, spring, summer, autumn, winter! He didn't need titles. It's as if he'd settled everything before he lifted a brush. So different, and yet so much the same. How sad that winter one is!'

Had her mother seen them? Had she unlocked the cupboard, untied the parcel when the staff had gone away and seen her lover in them? The parcel had been loosely tied, as if it had been opened again and again.

She would do the same. There would be no hurry. It would be her own treasure trove

154

before she shared it with the family, with the world. There was no rush. Her mother hadn't been in a hurry. When she had looked at them she had looked at her lover, had felt that winter sadness, and then been gladdened by the spring, felt the happiness of summer and the poignancy of autumn. The four paintings contained the essence of him, and somewhere she was there too. She had known where to look.

Fourteen

'Poor boy,' Betty said, 'you've had a bad time.' They were in bed at the Byres Road flat, because, as Betty said, they were resting at the same time. 'But it's a blessed relief when there was no betterment for the poor soul.'

'Yes.' He nodded, his chin touching Betty's curly head and resting there like a bird in its nest. 'She was brave, though, Jean. She was never a whinger. Right up to the end. The day before she died she sent for the lawyer and made her will. That was typical of her.'

'A brave woman.' The curls nodded. 'May she rest in peace.'

She broke the small silence. 'I don't suppose she left you the business all the same?'

'No, but I didn't expect that. I wouldn't know how to run it. That goes to Lisa, and Tommy when he's twenty-one. But there was a surprise. I had been giving her a housekeeping allowance, naturally, never asking how she was doing. My firm had given up Lyle's account for some reason. Interested only in big companies. That's by the way. Well, she'd banked the allowance, never spent it.'

'There would be a tidy sum tied up in it over all those years?'

'Yes. Seven thousand. She left it to me.'

'Well, well, that was generous. But she could afford to.'

'Before the War, perhaps, but not since. Lisa told me she'd been digging into capital in order to keep the flag flying. She's doing very little business. And by the time the staff's paid, and the rental – Sauchiehall Street rents are enormous – she's just avoiding running into debt. By God, she's got a good head on her shoulders, Lisa, and her only twenty-two. I don't know how Tommy and I could have got on without her looking after us.'

The curls moved fractiously. 'Maybe you'd rather have Lisa than me. Just go on in the flat being looked after by her?'

He put his hand under her chin, lifted her face to his, bent down and kissed her. 'Lisa could never give me what you do, my lovely, a new life.' Her arms raised, went slowly round his neck. He felt the swell of her breasts between them, 'Oh, Betty...'

Some time later she said, flushed and tumbled, 'Where were we?' Giggling against him.

'You're a wee rascal. Oh, my!' His sigh was one of satisfaction at himself and satisfaction in her. 'All the same, I've got to get up and go home, much as I'd like to stay here. But I'm still in the Home Guard, remember?'

She looked at him, pouting. 'I hate it when you go.'

'Needs must.' He scrambled out of bed with that wonderful feeling of well-being she always gave him.

He knew she was watching him as he put on his clothes. It was strange. He had never liked to dress or undress before Jean – she had been the same with him – but here with Betty it seemed natural. He pulled on his long drawers, and when he met her eyes he gave a lewd wriggle with his hips to make her laugh. Now his semmit, well tucked in, doing up the front two buttons, sticking out his chest as he did so, manly-like. It was as good as making love. Nearly.

Now his shirt, and with the tie and the Home Guard blouson he felt serious, a servant of his King and country, and saluted. 'All present and correct, madam.'

She giggled, slightly, as if the joke had worn thin.

'You think Lisa won't mind if you tell her about us?'

'Oh,' he shook his head, 'I couldn't right away, Betty. It wouldn't be ... seemly. But in due course...'

'Yes, I know. Only sometimes ... Maybe in the near future I could be introduced to her, maybe be asked to come for tea, and that ... get to know her. Then there's your son, Tommy...'

He sat down on the bed beside her. 'Tommy is not my son,' he said. He hadn't thought it could be so easy. Maybe it was the love-making, feeling like a man, but there, it was out. 'Tommy is not my son.'

'What are you saying, James?' She had sat up against the pillows, one strap of her nightdress slipping over her shoulder. 'Tommy is not...?'

'He's Lionel Craig's. Jean told me when she was dying.'

Betty's lady-like qualities seemed to have temporarily deserted her. She grabbed his arm.

'Who the hell is Lionel Craig?'

'A painter.' He saw her shocked face. 'An artist. Her childhood friend. The man who should have married her instead of me. She was a Lyle, through and through, dedicated: she couldn't stand his feckless ways, which he didn't try to change for her. As for me, a humble accountant for their firm, I couldn't believe my luck when she said she'd marry me. I knew then she didn't love me. It was Craig all the time, though she told me she only saw him once or twice afterwards.'

'My God!' She lay back on the pillows, her eyes wide. He saw that she'd be better left alone to get used to the idea.

'I'll have to go, Betty. But I had to tell you.' He stroked her arm. 'I want there to be no secrets between us, unlike Jean and me. It was a marriage of pretence from start to finish, on both sides. I was glad to marry into a good family; she was running away from Craig.'

'Well,' she sighed, and her breasts heaved – one was on show, but he hadn't time – 'I must say you've given me plenty to think about.'

'A clean start. That's what I want for both of us.'

'I've nothing to tell!' She shrugged. 'One or two half-baked affairs with one or two half-baked men, who scampered when they thought they were taking on my mother as well...' She held out her arms. 'Give me a kiss, James.'

He bent down. He said, between several kisses, 'It's going to be different this time, a clean start, and as soon as I can make it.'

On the way home he took out the *Evening Citizen* from his pocket and opened it at the headlines. They hit him between the eyes. RAF SENDS 1,000 BOMBERS TO COLOGNE. His eyes travelled down the page. 'The moonlit sky was filled with bombers last night, 1,047 aircraft rushing to shatter the German city of Cologne...'

Thank goodness Tommy was too young to be embroiled in that kind of thing. He was interested in the progress of the War, but as an onlooker; James had never heard him express a burning desire to be in the thick of it. Lisa had talked about the women's services, but thought her place was at home ... a fine girl.

It's surprising, he thought, that I worry about Tommy when he's not mine. But I've seen him grow up, which Craig never did, and although we never talked much together, I've always admired him and his cleverness. I provided for him – I didn't know Jean was going to give me back the money – I provided for him in good faith, a husband and a father...

When he got home Tommy was in the sitting-room. Lisa had gone to bed, he said.

'Have you heard the news, Tommy?' Strange: since he'd known he wasn't his son he could talk to him like a friend.

'Bomber Harris on the rampage. Do you know, the crews had to drop their bombs and clear out in ninety minutes! They say it was like Piccadilly Circus!'

'If it hurries on the end of the War we'll all be happy.'

'This is the Beginning of the End,' Tommy said in a fairly good imitation of Churchill. Yes, he was a true Lyle, the fine skin, those intelligent eyes, wide-set, taking in every-thing; even on his youthful features there was that look of competence Old Man Lyle had. 'There's a lot more to come.'

'Don't tell me you want to be there?'

'No, I want to live. The casualties will be enormous.'

'Was Lisa all right?'

'I think so. She had to meet someone at the station but they didn't turn up. She said she would just go to bed.'

'I think I'll do the same. I've had a busy night.' He was half tempted to say, 'You know what I mean, eh?' and tap the side of his nose ... as if he would. But the relaxed feeling he now had with Tommy made it almost possible.

Lisa was very different. She was his daughter. If he had to choose between them it would always be Lisa. He hoped she would like Betty. It seemed more important than Betty liking her.

She had waited for an hour, but she had known all along that he wouldn't be there. Ever since she'd heard that announcement on the wireless, 'More than a thousand bombers...'

'I'll want to live now, not die,' he'd said in his letter.

It had been going to be a special meeting. He had wanted it so much. It was to be a meeting that would explain everything, and maybe then they'd be able to plan, or at least hope that they could begin to plan. Start again.

Central Station was busy. You couldn't see the Shell for the hordes of couples in uniform, meeting, parting, kissing, laughing, weeping. 'More than a thousand bombers...' Statistics were crowding into her mind: 1,047 aircraft, 65,000 men ... How could there possibly be anyone left?

'After the next mission,' he had said in his letter, but he had miscalculated, its timing and its importance. Missions were dependent on logistics, weather, not if someone had decided to meet someone else at Central Station in Glasgow on the same day. It would be better to go home. She had kept secret her arrangement with Neil from Tommy and her father. She was glad about that.

The fear when she got into bed, a black beast of fear, tore at her with cruel claws. She heard the rumble of voices, Tommy and her father, discussing the Cologne raid, Father just in from his Home Guard duties. She heard their goodnights to each other, their bedroom doors shutting. The black beast of fear was back with her, tearing, tearing. She had to stifle the moans.

It was another Lisa who ran Alexander Lyle and Son for the next few days, outwardly calm. She shopped at lunchtime for the boys, she made nourishing soups with a scrag end of mutton, she didn't look at newspapers.

When Tommy tried to enthuse about the Cologne raid, she silenced him with a look. Her father was kindly: 'Lisa doesn't want to talk about it.' And to her: 'Wasn't that lad Neil McLean in the RAF? I never heard from his father about that game of—' His face changed when she turned and looked at him. 'We'd better keep off the subject, Tommy,' he said, cowed.

Betty was different. 'Oh, James, don't tell me those awful things!' she would say, snuggling into him. He could cope with that very well, thank you; being made to feel that he'd been turned into a pillar of salt was a different matter.

She was almost glad when it came at last. This terror would kill her. She knew when she went into the sitting-room that she had been right. He wasn't going to meet her at the Shell. Ever. She knew when her eyes fell on the orange envelope lying on the table, knew by Tommy's face. Father would be at the Home Guard.

'I opened it, Lisa. You have to do that in case there's a reply.' The tears were running down his face, a big boy of seventeen, ready to sit his Highers and everything. Her heart melted for him. The fear went. Sick certainty took its place.

'We regret to inform you that Flight-Lieutenant Neil McLean met his death on 31 May 1942 when he was shot down over Cologne. He died for his country.'

Now there was only the blackness of despair, which was worse. She sat down opposite Tommy at the table and pressed one bunched-up fist against her mouth, her eyes on him, pleading.

'You remember him at Craigton, don't you?'

'Yes.' His face crumpled. 'Oh, I wish Mother was here. She'd know what to say.'

'It's all right, Tommy. All the saying in the world won't make any difference now. He's dead.' Her eyes wouldn't leave his face, they clung as if to a lifeline. 'What did he look like, Tommy?'

'Look like?' The question seemed to alarm him. 'Look like? Tall, lanky, long legs and arms. He could be ... very funny at times?' His eyes said, 'Will that do?' then he went on quickly. 'Only sometimes. Other times he sort of ... left you. Bruce Semple didn't like him.'

'Didn't he? Didn't he?' Her eyes still pleaded, Tell me more...

'He was really keen on you, Lisa ... dead keen.'

She put her head down on the table between her arms, but she couldn't weep.

Her eyes were like hot coals.

She was like that when James came back from the Home Guard. She knew he stopped in the doorway then came over to the table. He smelled of perfume. He put his arm round her and guided her to her room.

'I know, Lisa. It's hard. Lie down and rest. Tommy's making you a cup of tea.' She met his look of infinite sorrow and shook her head. Nobody knew. He stood at the door for a second and then she heard it quietly shutting.

She was lying on her back, motionless, her hand pressed to her mouth, when she heard the rattle of a cup in its saucer on her side-table, and Tommy's voice, gruff.

'Your tea, Lisa.'

She could only nod.

Fifteen

If she had been able to think coherently, she would have recognised that it was a good idea to take Tommy off school to go with her to Kilmacolm. She was useless at Lyle's. She had gone in the day after she got the telegram, but sat in her office staring at the wall. She had prepared the evening meal and then gone to bed, exhausted by grief.

On the third day Bill Crawford had come in. 'Your father thinks it would be a good idea to go to Kilmacolm with Tommy till you feel better. He's told Tommy to ask his teacher.'

'You're all busy on my behalf,' she said, her face expressionless, dry-eyed.

'Because we love you.' She saw a deep flush spread over his face, even showing through the grizzled beard which covered his chin. Her eyes filled.

'It's terrible, Bill,' she said. 'I don't think I can stand it. You see, he was going to ... going to...' She bit her lip.

167

'You stood Jean's death. You'll stand this all right. Now, just you tell me if there's anything urgent to be attended to and then Lilian will take you home.'

'I don't need Lilian.'

'She'll be useful crossing the road.' Lisa thought of the lorry she had almost stepped in front of the day before. 'Just let yourself be treated as a parcel, to be safely delivered to the Glebe...'

'COD.' Her smile was half a grimace. 'All right.' She flicked the letters lying on her desk. 'These came in today. You deal with them. And Friday's pay day. Go to the bank and lift the money for the wages. They know what to give you.'

Lilian knocked at the door, fresh-faced, not showing too much pity.

'You're my wardress, then, Lilian?'

'Aye. It's Mr Crawford's idea. I'll help you with everything, packing and that. We'll wait for Mr Tommy to get back.' She was *au fait* with all the arrangements.

'We'll walk back to the flat, then. I could do with some air.'

The girl's detachment was better than pity.

'Suits me. Anything to get away from this dragon.' She grinned at Bill, confident in the face of authority. Lisa admired her for that. She had always respected it too much.

Lilian chattered all the way back about the

ATS uniform. 'It's quite smart, the cap's great, but I wish you could see the knickers! They'll itch like mad.' Lisa had a sudden desire to say, 'As long as you keep them on,' and wondered if she had taken leave of her senses.

'What a lovely flat!' Lilian said when Lisa opened the door and ushered her into the hall. 'I always wanted to see where you lived. And isn't it roomy? All these doors. Ours is a room and kitchen in Uddingston with four of us squeezed into it. No wonder I want to get into the ATS.'

She chose Lisa's wardrobe and packed it while Lisa sat on the bed, not caring. Grief was odd. One minute she was almost making a rude remark, the next she was so overwhelmed at the thought of Neil, no longer alive, that she wanted to scream at this girl who had taken over her life, or throw herself on the bed, face down, and pray for her own death – anything to escape the pain.

'That's done now,' Lilian said, snapping the locks of the case. 'Now, show me your kitchen and we'll have a cup of tea. Your brother will be here soon.'

They were drinking their tea and Lisa was pretending to eat the sandwich Lilian had made when she heard Tommy's key in the lock. He came into the kitchen followed by a young man in a raincoat and wearing horn-rimmed glasses. That was all she registered.

'Lisa, this is my teacher, Mr McIlroy. He has the afternoon off for prep and he's offered to run us to Kilmacolm.'

'That's kind.' She looked. A long nose in a long face, a wide smile. 'There's no need.' Then, aware that Lilian was sitting at the table with her: 'This is Lilian ... I've forgotten your other name, Lilian...' She was ashamed.

'Fletcher. I'm the typist at Miss Cowan's, and I came back with her. Mr Crawford thought she wasn't fit to cross the road. Have you got a motor, then?' Her eyes were fixed enquiringly on Mr McIlroy.

'Yes, a rattletrap. I get a petrol allowance because I do a bit of voluntary driving in my spare time.' Hadn't Tommy said he had been invalided out after Dunkirk? People carried on after all kinds of disasters.

'It's very kind of you, Mr McIlroy, to give up your free time for us.'

'I'm glad to. And I know the way. I've driven to the Quarriers' Homes at Bridge of Weir with a patient.'

'I'll get away, then,' Lilian said. She looked disappointed that the conversation had turned away from her.

'All right, Lilian. And thanks.' But the whole situation had drifted away from Lisa as well. It was like a play in which she had been pushed into the leading part when she should be back in her business, getting on with running it. 'Have you packed, Tommy?'

'Yes. I'll get my case.' He was cheerful, but then he had only known Neil briefly. *He was really keen on you, Lisa ... dead keen.*

She sat in the front with Iain McIlroy, and he seemed willing to talk about anything except Neil, or Dunkirk.

'Tommy and I are armchair soldiers,' he said. 'At the moment we're interested in Rommel. He's trying to get to Tobruk.'

'Yes? We'll have to stop him in his tracks.' *Tall, lanky ... He could be ... very funny ... at times...*

'We've done that for the time being, but he's not called the Desert Fox for nothing.'

'Don't forget the American Grant tanks the Eighth Army have.' Tommy, in the back. *Don't forget the diver ... Tommy Handley.*

'God bless the Americans,' Iain McIlroy said, saluting, but keeping his eye on the road, which was fortunate as he was driving along busy Sauchiehall Street. Lisa saw amongst the crowds on the pavement two stalwart American soldiers – were they all tall and stalwart, with that indefinable air of being better fed than ours? If her mind hadn't been fixed on Neil all the time she might have got to know one. There had been that officer who had come in one morning and asked if he could look at the gallery. 'I do a little painting back home.' What a gift for Glasgow girls those Americans were, with their insouciance – and their money: a pair of silk stockings for a kiss. Two pairs for ... Those kisses of Neil's. Strangely enough, it was the ones which had been sweetly chaste that she remembered.

'Milngavie,' Iain McIlroy said. Her mind must have been wandering for ages. 'Pronounced "Mulguy" just to confuse the English when they cross the border...'

'They do the same with us,' Tommy said. 'Did you know Cholmondley is pronounced "Chumley"?'

'Your Highers are in the bag, son,' Mr McIlroy said. 'He's hoping to get my job, you know.' He and Tommy were teasing each other.

She drifted away; green fields, farms tucked between them, the gleam of water ... Oh, Neil, if only you'd had the chance to tell me. I was so faithful, I believed in you, nothing would have made any difference ... nothing ... Pastoral ... Lionel and Jean ... lovers ... they had been lucky.

'That's our house, Mr McIlroy, the Glebe. You go through the double gates at the side. Stone pillars.'

'Right. Lovely house. Suits you both.' He pulled up at the door.

Margaret had a meal ready for them. 'I don't know what to call it. It's after two, but

172

I thought you'd all be hungry. And don't you worry, Mr McIlroy' – she had taken him in her stride when she was introduced – 'there's plenty for everybody. Tommy's always ready for food, a growing boy.'

'I'm always ready for a meal like this,' Iain McIlroy said. 'I'm in digs. A change of cooking is a lovesome thing, God wot...' Margaret gave him a 'they teachers' look. She had to go to the village to get some messages, but if Lisa liked to come...?

'No, thanks, Margaret. You go on. I'll see to...' She nearly said 'the boys'. She sat watching while they both tucked in, doing full justice to Margaret's steak pie. 'You don't have to rush away, Mr McIlroy,' she said when he pronounced himself replete.

'That's kind of you. Would you like me to take you for a walk?'

His eyes seemed full of kindness. She wanted to refuse. She wanted to go into her room, draw the curtains on the world and lie down. 'I had...' she began.

'You're lucky to have a house in the country. My digs are in Maryhill. You can imagine the difference...'

'I don't mind,' she said. This compliance. Ingrown. Did it come from generations of Lyles brought up to please the customer?

'I'll go off to the farm,' Tommy said. 'I'll see Alec and some of the Kilmacolmers there. I went to the primary school here, Mr

173

McIlroy. They all wanted to be farmers. I was one of the few who travelled to Glasgow every day. You have a walk, Lisa. It will do you good.' His eyes were full of kindness too for this bereaved sister who had two faces: one white, expressionless, the other an amiable hostess who liked to please her guest. 'Thanks for driving us, Mr McIlroy.'

'It was a pleasure. See you next Monday. And don't forget some revision, lad, to keep your hand in.'

'Sure.' It seemed an easy relationship, just what Tommy needed.

They set off. Iain McIlroy didn't talk much, and it enabled her to examine her grief, to say, I think it's not as bad as it was five minutes ago, it must be the gentle landscape, this quiet man at my side. Besides, reason told her that eventually it would grow less, as her grief for her mother had grown less, and all that would be left would be a sense of loss ... She knew that it was just a question of working through the agony...

'Is Tommy clever?'

'He's bright. Much better. Not a swot, but he's got an intuitive intelligence. Just right for art. He's not a mathematician. He'd be no good as an accountant.'

'That's what my father is.'

'Well, they're needed.' He didn't apologise.

Her steps led her on farm paths to the Gryfe, towards Pacemuir Bridge. Mother. Lionel Craig. Now Neil. Still, three against the thousands who had been lost fighting wasn't much. And there was this Iain McIlroy minus something or other, along with thousands of dismembered arms and legs and what remained of Neil McLean...

'I'm a city man and yet the countryside is for me. Some day ... a cottage, a garden, time to study, to think, a simple life...'

'A dream that will have to wait...' And most dreams didn't materialise. Neil ... having him as her own ... strangely enough she had never thought of marriage and children; her dream hadn't been domestic. She would have kept on working, like her mother, whether or not she married, because it was in her bones and in her flesh; of course, she would have taken time off to be with him ... But he was dead. There was no future now.

Iain McIlroy knew about architecture. He recognised the different influences in the big houses of the parish, he could name names, Burnett, Tait, Honeyman. The great one, Charles Rennie Mackintosh.

'Domestic architecture,' he said. 'It's fascinating. You see the Scottish castle influence in so much of it, derived from the French château ... you'll have books in your father's study, I expect...' Lisa remembered he had looked impressed when they had passed its

175

Stockton Public Libraries Borough

open door. 'I advised Tommy to make use of it while he's here.'

'Now you sound like a teacher,' she said.

'That's another passion of mine, to bring out the best in an enquiring mind. Sounds pretentious but it's not meant that way. He's keen to go to Paris later. You should encourage him.'

'Later, yes. Unless I write to Hitler and ask him to stop the War.' She was amazed that she could talk so normally with this man, as if only one pathway in her brain was being used while the others were stultified with grief. She said seriously, 'I worry he'll be called up before it's over.'

'There's that,' Iain McIlroy said, 'there's that.' His voice was bitter, and then he was saying, mildly, 'it was a good idea of your father's, you coming here. He must be a sensitive man.'

'Even if he *is* an accountant.' She could actually make a joke, forget the grief, even for an instant. She almost added, 'Maybe his woman-friend is teaching him a thing or two.'

He left after he'd drunk a cup of tea which Margaret made. They'd met her bustling up the garden path as they were going into the house.

'A kind man,' Margaret said, as they watched him driving off in his rattletrap.

'Yes, but with definite opinions. I wonder

if he passes them on to Tommy.' She didn't quite understand what she meant.

She was there when Tommy came back with Alec, but she didn't join them for their evening meal. 'I've done nothing but eat all day, and I haven't been heaving hay like you two.'

'Haystacks,' Tommy said. 'When we lifted one there was a nest of baby mice under it, little pink things. Embryonic.' The word sounded like one of Iain McIlroy's, and looking at Tommy she saw a vulnerability in his face, as if the sight had touched him more than he'd thought.

Before she went to bed she went into her father's study and found a book of Robert Burns's poetry. She found the poem easily enough: 'Oh, what a panic's in tha breastie...' It hadn't been panic, nothing like that, more a vulnerability, strange for a strapping young man of seventeen. But she forgot it in her grief, which seemed to be waiting to engulf her.

A day or two later she discussed with Margaret whether she should call on Neil's parents, but remembered she hadn't their address. Perhaps her father knew it? But she dismissed the idea. His mother had been unfriendly, odd, and she would think it more odd should Lisa call or write. She had no proof of her involvement with Neil. No ring. And she felt sure he wouldn't have discussed her with his parents.

She gardened, she walked, she helped in the kitchen, and she was there hulling strawberries on the day before she and Tommy were due to leave when she heard the doorbell ring. Margaret was at the foot of the garden fruit-picking, and Lisa went, only stopping to rinse her hands. She noticed the tips of her fingers were still pink when she opened the door.

A man in Air Force uniform was standing there, tall, broad; there was a glint of gold in his brown moustache.

'Are you Miss Cowan?' he said, taking off his cap. His hair was brown with the same glint of gold at the hairline where it was brushed back.

'Yes, I am.' Her voice was shaking. Had there been a mistake? Was this an official come to tell her that Neil hadn't died after all? The sun had brought out the spicy smell of the pinks bordering the path, stronger than usual.

'I was Neil's doctor when he was in hospital ... May I come in?'

'Yes.' She held the door open for him, said, 'Follow me, please,' and led him into the sunny drawing-room. In the new villas they were building now they liked to call it 'the lounge'. 'Please sit down.' It was the amiable hostess speaking.

'Thank you. I'm Squadron Leader Charles Cramond. Did he ever mention me?'

'Yes, he did, in a letter.' She folded her hands, saw the pink tips of her fingers.

'I had a few days' leave. I thought I would come and tell you about him. That it might help. I know he was going to see you.' No, he was dead after all.

'Yes. He didn't ... turn up. Then I got a telegram.'

'Yes.' He nodded. His eyes were on her, grey-blue like his uniform. They were searching, medical eyes, but kind. He seemed to have brought in with him the spicy smell of the pinks. As a child she had buried her face in them.

Sixteen

'How long had you known Neil?' Charles Cramond said.

'Since September 1939. He was already in the Air Force. It had always been his ambition, I think.'

'Yes, of course, he was in the Voluntary Reserve. I once said to him that his natural element was the air.'

'He loved it. Did he ever speak to you of St Exupéry, the French airman?'

'No, I don't think so.' He looked puzzled, and Lisa thought, Why am I talking to this stranger so freely? and immediately felt embarrassed. The amiable hostess disappeared. As if on cue Margaret knocked and came in, then drew back in confusion.

'Oh, I'm that sorry!' Her hand flew to her mouth. 'I thought you were on your own, Lisa.'

'No.' It was her turn now. 'This is a friend of ... my friend ... Remember?' She couldn't bring herself to say 'Neil'. 'Squadron Leader...' She had forgotten his name.

'Cramond. Charlie Cramond.' He got up and held out his hand.

'Mrs Currie. He knew him, Margaret. Neil ... The same squadron.'

'How do you do, Mrs Currie.' He smiled. 'I'm the interloper, I think. But I decided to call and see Miss Cowan since I'd been a friend of Neil's.'

'Oh, aye.' She nodded. 'Bursting in like that! Would you like a cup of tea, Mr...' His title defeated her.

'I'd really like that.' He turned to Lisa, eyebrows raised, and it was her turn to nod.

'That would be fine, Margaret, thanks.'

'She's been with us for ages,' she said when Margaret had shut the door behind her. 'She and Alec, her husband, act as caretakers when we're in Glasgow.'

'Worth their weight in gold, I should imagine. You wouldn't like to show me your garden while we're waiting? I had a glimpse of it coming in.'

'All right.' It would be easier outside.

The garden was as her grandfather had left it. His wife's requirements hadn't gone beyond it being 'tidy', and it hadn't been changed since the house had been built: a rockery bordering the lawn with its circular bed of roses in the centre, then the vegetable patch and fruit bushes running down to the fields, a typical country garden.

'Full of lovely smells,' Charlie Cramond

said. 'What a treat after hospitals!' He sniffed. 'I can pick out honeysuckle.'

'That's from the arbour.' She led him to a three-sided wooden structure weighted down with the honeysuckle and clematis garlanding it. 'I'm not much of a gardener, but Alec keeps it in apple-pie order. The vegetables and fruit are his pride and joy. The arbour was my own little house when I was a girl. There's a lovely view from it. On quiet summer afternoons you could hear the burn down there.'

'Yes, I hear it now.' They were walking towards the foot, and the sound grew louder. 'We get that sound all the time up north.' Now she noticed his voice, the Highland lilt.

'Isn't it more a rushing sound, a bigger sound?'

'If it's a river, yes, but our burns ripple, or "purl".' He gave the word the Highland inflection.

'I love the vegetable garden. Alec plants in such straight rows. And look at that clump of rhubarb. The size of the leaves! In spring he puts a pail over a plant or two to make the stalks tender for Margaret's rhubarb tarts.'

They had reached the burn. 'I paddled here when I was wee,' she said, 'and fished for baggies. Do you know what baggies are?' She heard herself being almost frivolous.

'Minnows? Sure do. I go after the larger variety now. Trout.'

'Ah, well, trout. You'll get trout up there. This is just a wee burn...' 'We twa hae paidled in the burn...' Don't say it. He might not be a Burns fan.

'So peaceful,' he said. They were standing at the stone wall, overlooking the fields. 'Even the cows are placid. It's the scene men dream of in the forces. I don't think they dream of cities, even if they've lived in them, do you?'

'That I wouldn't know. Except that it's nature, and nature's ... natural. That must sound silly.'

'I think you've got it. Nothing man-made.'

She turned and saw Margaret at the back door, gesticulating and pointing into the house. 'That's Margaret trying to tell us tea's ready,' she said. Again, she had talked too much when all she wanted was to know about Neil and then let this man go away.

'Where did you first meet Neil?' he asked when they were back in the drawing-room and he had been served with tea in the best china and offered a strawberry tartlet as a sample of Margaret's prowess. He'd smiled at her, eyes widened.

'Craigton, on the Clyde coast. I believe it's cluttered up now with submarines and destroyers, but it's still the same to me, quiet, gentle ... We met playing tennis...' *Game to*

Miss Cowan! She heard his voice clearly in her ears, saw him on the umpire's seat, long legs twisted round its legs. 'We had just three or four days to get to know each other and then he had to report for duty. The beginning of the War. Tell me,' she couldn't bring herself to say either 'Squadron Leader' or 'Charlie' to this stranger, 'do you know what Neil wanted to say to me?' His eyes were on her, as if to encourage her, but he didn't answer. 'I've had all kinds of thoughts in my head. I knew he had a secret worry, but I tried not to think of it because at the same time I knew he loved me...' His eyes were still on her, assessing. 'Do you know what it was?' She heard the strangled sound of her own voice.

'Yes,' he said, putting down his cup with a swift movement. 'Neil was a homosexual.'

I tried not to think of it ... She remembered Bill Crawford's blush as her face flooded. It couldn't have been worse than this. She felt the sweat in her armpits. 'Homosexual' wasn't a difficult word to understand if you took it to bits, even if it wasn't entirely unknown to her. 'Homo', man, 'sexual'. He, Neil, only liked men.

'Were you ... sure?' Her voice shook.

'Oh, yes, I'm sure. So was Neil, although he tried hard not to believe it, at first. We had long talks. Trying to make him accept it.

He truly loved you, but...' he looked straight at her, 'he could never have made love to you as you would have wanted it. I think most of the crew guessed. He wouldn't be the only one.'

She remembered that Bruce Semple hadn't liked him.

'How did he come to tell you, when he couldn't tell me?' Now she felt bitter, tricked.

'He was ill when I saw him, exhausted mentally, physically, emotionally, delirious when he was brought in. He let enough out so that I could ... start from there. I think he was dying to tell me. We had become friends in a fairly casual way in the bar. He told me he had to screw up his courage to tell his father when he left, and asked him to tell his mother. She couldn't take it, couldn't take it at all. She had adored him too much...'

She was still feeling bitter, cheated. 'So he didn't really love me after all, or he would have confided in me?'

'You're wrong there. Put yourself in his place. You were what might have been, you represented normality to him. There was still a chance ... *he* thought. If it had been possible for him to love women, I mean in the sexual sense, it would have been you. Am I being too crude for you?'

'No, oh, no!' Her voice quivered. 'Factual. Confirmation in a way. I knew there was

185

something, but I wouldn't let my mind dwell on it. Our time was so short...'

'I understand.'

'You see, it's so hard to take! I loved him, needed him.'

'Don't feel sorry you loved him. He needed love, that boy. He had been treated as a freak by his own mother.' He leant forward and touched her hand, and when she looked at him she saw his smile, a humorous, it's-not-the-end-of-the-world smile. 'You have to grow up sometime. What age are you?'

'Twenty-two.' She resented that about growing up, tried to justify herself. She wanted to say, 'Don't patronise me.' 'I know there are different kinds of love,' she said. 'It was just bad luck...'

'You're not regretting the love, I hope?' His voice was stern. 'He wanted to see you because of that love, and to tell you...' he gave her a judgemental look, 'how much he regretted that he couldn't give you what he knew you wanted. For goodness' sake' – he smiled at her – 'a lovely girl of only twenty-two, there's all the love in the world waiting for you, *swilling* around. And if Neil had lived he might have found the kind *he* wanted.'

She sat silent for a time and he respected her silence.

'How,' he said, at last interrupting that

silence, 'does that affect your grieving?'

'It's different.' She looked at him and liked his eyes. 'I'm grieving now for ... the best of friends. Grieving that I didn't help him when he needed it.' And, she didn't say, grieving for that wonderful, exquisite tremulousness I felt close to him, a once-in-a-lifetime tremulousness.

'Good. If it's any consolation, I imagine he died happy, although it was probably the first time he'd flown wanting to live.'

'Poor Neil.'

'Don't pity him. Remember him with love.'

'I'll do that.' But she'd remember always that incredible sweetness when she *hadn't* known...

She saw him off shortly afterwards. He was going home to Speyside, which would use up all his leave, but next time, maybe ... She wasn't interested. She had enough to think about, and the thinking would have to be done on her own. What was the point of telling anyone? Certainly not her father, with his conventional views ... Maybe Tommy, but not right away.

'A nice man, that,' Margaret said when she was clearing up.

'He liked your strawberry tarts.'

Margaret looked gratified but pretended she wasn't.

'But fancy me bursting in like that!'

'You weren't to know he was there. It was a surprise to me too.'

'Aye, that's right. Was he able to give you any comfort about your friend, Neil?'

'In a way.'

'True, you can't bring the dead back. But you're only twenty-two, Lisa. There's all the world afore you.'

'That's what he said.'

Tommy came in later with Alec, sunburnt, hair dusty with hayseed. 'It's a great life,' he said to Lisa when they were alone, 'but it's not for me.'

'It's a healthy enough life.'

'Yes, but somehow I've grown away from the lads. We look at things with different eyes. Apart from girls, they've only one thing on their minds, rushing bald-headed into the War as soon as they're old enough.'

'It's natural. I thought you felt the same.'

His eyes didn't meet hers.

'I had a visit from the doctor who attended Neil McLean before ... his last flight.'

'Goodness!' His eyes were now full of interest. 'Had he anything to tell you?'

'Just how brave he was.' And not only in the air, she thought.

'Pity he didn't get home to see you.'

'Yes...' She stood up quickly, smiling unsteadily. 'Still...' If she broke down she would tell Tommy everything and maybe she should wait until she could say it calmly. It was too soon. 'Just remembered something...' She went quickly out.

Seventeen

He hadn't told them at supper the whole story of the baby mice, or any of it, come to that.

At first the lads had been innocently amused at the nest and the squirming pink bodies, then one of them, Ken Johnson, tow-haired, red-faced, had said, 'C'mon, lads, this'll gie us some fun!' Tommy remembered him at school, always taking the mickey, even trying it on with poor old Miss Chisholm.

So they had set the dogs on these baby mice lying there in their nest, a pink, squirming mass with seven pointed heads, a small forest of long whiskers. If Alec had been there he'd have given them all 'a clout roon the earhole' – Alec's way of talking; he never used it at the Glebe, frightened of Margaret.

That was when it had become nasty. There were three dogs, two of them collies, the other an evil-looking mongrel, and it was soon running about with a hairless pink body dangling from its mouth, the other two in full cry after it, slavering, barking. Tommy saw Alec look up from where he was working at the foot of the field, but he wouldn't be able to make out what they were up to. He had a pair of steel-framed spectacles he wore nowadays to read the paper.

It wasn't only the dogs. The lads seemed to have gone berserk, trying to pull the dead mouse from the jaws of the mongrel, then Ken Johnson, laughing and egging them on, went to where the nest was and threw it, full of squirming bodies, into the air for the baying dogs.

The words occurred to Tommy. Blood lust. The lads were killing themselves laughing, shouting, tearing around, trying to grab the morsels of mangled pink corpse from the jaws of the dogs and, when they succeeded, throwing the pieces of flesh and tiny bones into the air so that the dogs would jump up and catch them.

He went mad too, but in a different way, a sickening kind of rage boiling up inside him. 'Stop it, you bloody fools!' he screamed. 'You stupid bastards! Alec's looking. He'll have the hide off you if you don't stop it!' In a frenzy of anger he took up a hay fork and brandished it amongst them. 'Stop it or I'll use this! Stop it!' He saw Ken Johnson's bursting red face, the jaw hanging open in surprise, and then he heard one of the others, Willie Ray it was, saying, 'Aye, we'd better stop, lads. Alec'll dock oor pay!'

'Ach, he's just a cissy!' Ken Johnson was standing his ground, his chin up now, a mixture of fear and bravado. 'He'll never use it! Not Tommy Cowan! Fancy being worried aboot a litter o' mice anyhow. Vermin, that's aw they are, bliddy vermin!'

Tommy saw Alec striding across the field and rested the fork against the haystack.

'Whit's aw the commotion?' Alec had reached them, panting slightly. 'You lot are supposed to be workin'!'

'The dugs went mad aboot some wee mice, Alec. We wis tryin' to stoap them!' Johnson looked at Tommy boldly, daring him to speak.

'It's that mongrel, Alec,' Willie Ray said, Johnson's henchman. 'Starts the ithers aff.'

'So you say.' Alec looked at Tommy, then at the rest. He hadn't seen him brandishing the fork, Tommy felt sure. 'You lot go doon to the foot o' the field and work there till six. Tommy and me have to get back to the Glebe.'

'Wull yer tea be ready, Alec?' Ken Johnson scoffed. 'Aye, ye canny afford to be late for yer teas!' There was a half-hearted titter from the other lads.

He had walked home in silence with Alec

except for a casual remark or two. After a bit Alec kept quiet too. It was uphill, and it took all his time not to slacken his step. Tommy slowed down to suit him at the steepest part, surprised at the still-rapid beating of his own heart.

He had meant to tell Lisa, but she'd had a visit from Neil McLean's squadron leader, she said. Lisa never made a fuss, but he knew when she was affected. She went pale and looked like their mother. The pain showed in her eyes.

Of course, she had been obsessed by Neil McLean. She'd gone about in a dream at Craigton when he was there. He wondered if the squadron leader had told her that he was queer. Tommy had guessed, but never in a hundred years would he have said anything. Bruce Semple knew, but he played the innocent with him. He didn't want dirty talk.

But he would have liked to talk to Lisa, to tell her about the incident at the farm. 'It was blood lust,' he would have said to her, 'sheer blood lust. And I wasn't much better, but in a different way. I would have run that Ken Johnson through with the hay fork if it had gone on much longer. I was seeing red, brandishing it above my head like a wild thing.' 'That's not the way we're supposed to behave,' he would have liked to say to her, 'how we behave in wartime, like savages, ruining the world...' But how could he have said anything like that when Neil McLean had been killed flying a Lancaster bomber?

'What's the point,' he could have said, 'us flying above a city dropping bombs and killing and maiming and destroying and then them doing the same to us?' *'Coup de théâtre,'* Harris had called it, so he'd read, 'to demonstrate the power of our bombers'. And his own power.

Well, he had done that all right. Thousands of innocent people killed, injured, rendered homeless. How many young men died with Neil McLean, fell with their planes into that inferno? No, he couldn't have said anything like that to Lisa, going around white-faced and hollow-eyed in her grief.

The strange thing was the change in *him* since that madness at the farm. At the time of the Cologne bombing in May he hadn't felt like this. Was it because of Iain McIlroy?

There was no point in blaming McIlroy. Tommy knew his own nature: he was suggestible, almost too much so. They had got into the habit of having chats when he had been kept in after school to do his homework and Mr McIlroy had sat at his desk to keep an eye on him.

'This hurts me more than it hurts you, Tommy. You're arrogant. You think you can get by without doing any prep.'

Once when he had finished and handed his work to McIlroy he had said to him, 'You never talk about Dunkirk. Were you glad to be out of it all?' He had never said what his injury was.

'Since you ask,' the teacher had said, 'yes. I got off lightly.'

'You saw plenty who were worse?'

'What is this?' he'd said. 'Do you want a blow-by-blow account? Parading my damaged kidney like a medal? Yes, I saw worse things, but the worst was the mental effect on some of them. It was the demeaning quality, men stripped of their dignity, feeling desperately for missing limbs, bleeding to death, calling for their mothers ... I said "men". Boys. That's what stays with you. Boys not much older than you. Read de Vigny on the military condition. It's not all glory.'

Tommy wouldn't leave it alone. 'And those rumours of German camps, Belsen, Buchenwald, where they were tortured, starved? Men who did nothing, really. I read that some from the Channel Islands were sent there for illicit use of radios.' He had added sententiously, 'It's an insult to humanity.'

One side of McIlroy's mouth had lifted. '*War* is an insult to humanity. Get that into your thick skull. Go right back and you'll find there's always someone fighting someone else. Ask yourself why.'

'Territory?'

'Right. Greed. War, war, and rumours of war ... But don't be too high-minded. Don't forget that a lot of men are fighting for their own bit of territory – even, God help us, for their King and country. You're too young to see it through their eyes.'

'It's more than that. It's...' The incident with the mice hadn't happened then.

'Ah, well, everybody's entitled to their ideals at your age. I had them too. Now I can think what I like, and I'm doing what I like best. There are still the eternal verities, thank God. How did we get into this?' He had laughed. 'It's time I was back in my salubrious residence, and you too.'

His eighteenth birthday came and went. On Iain McIlroy's advice he applied and was accepted at Gilmorehill to study English. 'A good grounding first. Helps you to express yourself. After that Paris for art when the War's over.'

For the first few months at the university he was absorbed in settling down, joining societies, meeting girls; but then the doubts were back again. The more he found out how much his own city was contributing to the progress of the War, the more ashamed he felt that he did not rush to enlist like so many of his fellow-students.

He heard about the changes at Craigton. Six deep-water berths had been built by five thousand men on a new harbour with a waterfront of one and a half miles. Barges carried equipment form the ships berthed there to railroads. Most of the American Army and equipment were landed there. Mulberry harbours were being built for transfer ... the invasion at last?

He didn't sleep at night. Would he be branded a coward? Would he be laughed to scorn if he said what had finally made up his mind, a trivial incident in a sunny field at Kilmacolm? He knew the answer to that...

But in March 1943 one of Greek Thomson's most admired churches was bombed, and, although it was irrelevant in the scale of things, it was responsible for him finally coming to a decision.

His mother had taught him to admire the city's architecture. She had said to him once, sitting in the St Vincent Street church with its Palladian columns, 'My religion is in the stones...'

He finally admitted to himself that he loathed the whole concept of war. He didn't want to kill, to be responsible for deaths and desecration. Always the initial purpose of wars got muddied in their execution. He knew he was quoting Iain McIlroy, in substance if not in fact. He would register as a conscientious objector.

He was aware that if he refused to take part in civil defence or work in factories he could be sentenced to three months in jail. He was summoned to attend a tribunal. The die had been cast.

He told the family one evening when they were gathered round the table at Holland Street, Lisa, Father and his lady-friend, Miss Smith, who was now there quite often. Lisa had told him that their father had been frank with her. He and Miss Smith had been friends for a long time. She hadn't been surprised, she said to him.

Strangely enough it was not Lisa who had most influence on his father, who was grim-faced and disapproving, but Miss Smith – (she had asked them to call her Betty).

'Come on now, James,' she'd said, 'don't be an old fuddy-duddy. The boy's entitled to his own opinion, or should I say "young man"?' She had given him a distinctly sexy glance. He'd thought, although he hadn't said so to Lisa, that his father might want them to clear out of Holland Street so that Betty could move in. Anyone with half an eye could see that they were sleeping together.

Lisa had tried hard to understand how he felt. She said she saw his point of view, that of course all war was evil, but ... He could see that Neil McLean was the stumbling block.

She hadn't got over it. If she wanted someone who was fighting for King and country, she would be far better off with that squadron leader who had called at the Glebe to tell her about Neil's death ... Well, fighting in his own way. He was lucky that being a doctor he was non-combatant, and therefore his conscience would be clear.

Tommy knew he would be no good at that kind of thing, field ambulances and so on. Anyone who worried about a nest of bald baby mice wouldn't be much good at helping the wounded. He longed for his mother, her sharp, clear mind, the rapport they'd had. She'd have seen underneath.

The day of the tribunal arrived. They didn't shout him down as he had expected. They listened to his reasons for feeling unable to engage in warfare. 'Principles' was a word they had heard often, they said, but they respected his willingness to work on the land. He told them of the school allotments, and they then went into a huddle over his termly report from his tutor. The fact that he would eventually be the 'son' in Alexander Lyle and Son made the chairman look up at him as if he might be worth preserving. He was asked to wait outside and then was informed that he could go now and await their decision.

Someone in the school or university must have given him good references. Maybe Iain McIlroy. Maybe they were sympathetic that day and thought that a young man of eighteen attending the university could be allowed to slip through the net since things were looking up on the war front. The British bulldog was stirring at last. They would soon have Hitler on the run. 'Run, rabbit, run...'

In a few weeks their decision came: he could grow for victory.

Eighteen

Lisa didn't think Tommy realised the rift he had caused in the family by his announcement. She wished their mother had been there to help. She and Tommy had always been very close.

It took a week before Father would even talk to him, and it was Betty Smith who was responsible eventually for his reluctant acceptance. Lisa found her as different as night from day from their mother, and there rested the attraction, she supposed, for her father – girlish femininity as compared with calm pragmatism – and yet it didn't take her long to see that Betty could use her head. And that her father had a comfortable and long-standing relationship with her. And that she was the boss.

'Call me Betty,' she had said when they were first introduced. 'I know that you and I are going to get on like a house on fire.' And later, when she was helping Lisa with clearing up after supper, 'Your father thinks the world of you. That's good enough for me. I want you to know that I would never come between you.'

'I'm sure you wouldn't.' And then, being diplomatic, 'I suppose he was lonely after Mother died.'

'He's a softie, James. He needs a woman. We're happy together.'

Lisa took the plunge. 'Are you thinking of getting married?'

'Oh, yes. In due course. We thought I might move in here when *you* got married.'

She laughed. 'Come night come ninepence. Have you heard that old saying? Don't wait for *that*. I'll move out whenever you like. There's our house at Kilmacolm.'

'Yes, I know about that. James prefers the flat. And I know about Tommy's real father.' Was there anything this woman didn't know about them? 'But it won't take long for a girl looking like you to get married. You've got class. It's just that you haven't been applying your mind to it because of that friend of yours, the airman, who got killed.' She was certainly direct.

'It was in that big raid over Cologne.' It was a relief to talk about it.

'I know. A terrible shock. There would be other grieving hearts as well as yours. But you have to look ahead. There's that doctor you've met, a squadron leader, no less, James tells me.'

Lisa hid her embarrassment, yet was amused by Betty. She pictured her father and Betty lying cosily in bed, gossiping, his arm round her. It was what he had needed all the time.

'What did you think of Tommy's announcement?' She was curious.

'You could have knocked me down with a feather ... a white one!' Betty giggled at her own wit. 'What a bombshell! But I think I made James see sense. That's how the boy feels. As I said, he's had the courage to act on it. I wish I'd been as brave. I allowed myself to be tied to my mother till I was well into my thirties. I was destined to be a crotchety old maid if James and I hadn't fallen in love.' Her face softened.

She's changing our lifestyle, this Betty, Lisa thought. As a family they were not ready communicators, but that night they had chattered amicably because Betty had set the tone. Now that she came to think of it, it was her presence that had encouraged Tommy to drop his bombshell.

A few days later she said to him, 'What made you change your mind about being called up? You were so interested in the progress of the War at one time. You could hardly wait to grow up. I remember you saying you could be an officer because of being in the OTC at school.'

He looked at her, thin, tall, his eyebrows

drawn together as if he was disappointed at what he was hearing. 'I wouldn't expect you to understand until you get over Neil McLean.'

She felt snubbed. She hadn't realised that he had changed with growing up, that he was able to make his own decisions and, if necessary, change them.

'I'm sorry, Tommy,' she said. 'Of course you know your own mind.' She wouldn't mention it again.

Betty Smith would have been pleased to know that Charlie Cramond had written to her after his visit, and Lisa had replied. He was a better correspondent than Neil had been. His latest letter was from the Middle East.

'It's a romantic terrain, this,' she read, 'when you get time to notice it.'

Life is very hectic in a field hospital, as you can imagine. Sometimes I go to the tent mouth to get a whiff of fresh air, and at night the moon is immense in a sky of navy blue, with thousands of stars. Do you remember those Bible stick-on pictures we used to be given for good attendance at Sunday school? That's what the vivid colours here remind me of. In the daytime the sky is a fierce, hurting blue against the yellow sand, so fierce the contrasts and colours that you find yourself longing for the soft grey skies of the Highlands. Some day I hope to take you up there to see that sky, preferably with an eagle soaring against it and the mountains as a backdrop...

She began to warm to him, to look forward to his letters...

'El Alamein. The calm before the storm,' Charlie wrote on a scrap of paper, and then had to stop as he heard his name called. They were checking for the nth time the equipment in the field hospital behind the enemy lines. Monty was an organiser *par excellence*. Nothing must be forgotten.

Lisa had been on his mind all the time he'd been here: the first battle last month, now early in November the second one. He'd never properly explained to himself, far less to her, why when they had asked for volunteer doctors for the front he had been one of the first to offer. Perhaps it had been the same with that young brother of hers who had decided to become a conscientious objector – simply a gut feeling.

There was last night, when the men had been bracing themselves for the greatest battle yet. Some had played cards in the moonlight, the junior officers joining in. He had come across one sitting alone with his head bowed. He had looked sheepish when Charlie had said, 'OK?' He had thought the face raised to him looked like that of a boy of nineteen. Perhaps he had been praying.

He should be doing the same thing, but thinking of Lisa was as good. He was wishing her well, hoping that some day, when all this was over, he could break her reserve. He had no doubt about his own feelings, but she was a closed book.

He had known the first time he saw her at that pleasant little village in Renfrewshire, Kilmacolm. She had opened the door to him and that was it. This is the girl I've been waiting for, he'd thought. It was as definite as that.

She didn't know herself yet; twenty-two, and with that untouched look in her eyes. Neil McLean had been her prince, but, to put it crudely, he didn't have what it took to waken her, a young woman made for a mature, strong, sexual love. Bright, intelligent, running a business in Glasgow, looking after her father and brother, no doubt expertly, like Monty, a good organiser. But emotionally a child, a Sleeping Beauty. If only she could come to love him as he had loved her from that first time, he knew in his bones she would be a wonderful wife and lover.

She would give herself unreservedly because that was part of her character, she was whole-hearted in everything she did. Although she didn't as yet realise it, what she had felt for Neil McLean had been a girlish awakening to love, romantic, destined to be always unfulfilled. The poignancy she felt, the nostalgic tenderness, even the romantic grief for a lost dream, was no part of a mature love. There had to be more.

He was looking at his watch when the desert seemed to be split open by the crash of a thousand guns. Nine forty. He got up, stuffing the half-written letter in his pocket. He was ready. The casualties would be coming in thick and fast. As he took up his post in the tented hospital he heard the faint skirl of bagpipes and was ashamed of the tears that flooded his eyes for an instant.

Another terrific crash seemed to split his eardrums. No victory without death. He heard a high-pitched shriek from a man being carried in on a stretcher, and all thoughts of Lisa left him. He hurried down the ward, speaking harshly to the young officer who had been praying: 'Get some nurses here pronto for God's sake! This one will have to be held down.'

Nineteen

1942–3

Towards the end of 1942 her father went with a contingent of the Home Guard to parade triumphantly before the King and Queen at St Paul's Cathedral, and Betty went too, 'to see the fun', as she said. She came back excited by her first visit to the capital.

'You have to go to London, Lisa! It takes your breath away. Ask your squadron leader if he's due any leave soon. Take my advice. You're only young once...'

'He's not *my* squadron leader, Betty,' she protested, but she was infected by her excitement. 'I *should* go, all the same. I want to see an art dealer about some pictures my mother left.'

'There you are then! Kill two birds with one stone.'

She wrote to Charlie, telling him of her proposed visit, but surprisingly there was no reply.

Christmas came and went, but still she hadn't heard from him. Had she been into quotations like Betty she would have said that 'the best laid schemes of man gang aft agley'. But being Lisa she kept quiet.

She was unexpectedly busy at Lyle's for the first part of 1943, and it was March before she thought again of her London trip. There was still no word from Charlie, and when she wrote to Mr Delmino he had a sad tale to tell.

I don't know when I shall be in London, unfortunately. A *protégé* of mine, a close friend's son, was killed recently, crushed to death while sheltering in the Bethnal Green Underground from one of those terrible daylight raids. One hundred and seventy-eight casualties. His father was in such a bad way that I took him down to my cottage to recuperate.

We grew up in the East End together, both Italian immigrants, and although I moved away we had remained close friends; as I had never married, Nathan, his son, was learning the business with a view to taking over from me when I retired. He was like a son to me as well.

The whole tragedy has made me nervous of living in London while those raids go on, but I shall certainly get in touch with you whenever I return.

She wrote and commiserated with him, saying she quite understood his anxiety. She herself had been awaiting news from a friend for some time.

Had Charlie been injured, she now began to wonder, or even killed? If he had, there was no reason why she should be informed. There had been nothing official between them. She was so worried that she confided in Betty, and she, always practical, got her the address of an association to which she could write for information. 'That'll start the ball rolling,' she assured her. 'You should have made enquiries long ago. Why didn't you get in touch with his parents?'

'We weren't at that stage,' she said. 'I'd only met him once,' and was embarrassed when Betty asked her why then she was worried. There was no reply to that.

She had to resign herself to staying put in Glasgow and getting on with running the business, but, with Tommy away from home and in digs near the allotments where he worked, she began to feel that she should clear out of the flat so that Betty could move in.

As usual, she turned to Lyle's to make life purposeful: she was her mother's daughter. Fortunately, a new development came from Tommy. In the little time he had to himself he had been dabbling in photography, and one evening when he came to the flat he showed her some of his work. She was impressed.

'How long have you been doing this?' she asked.

'Quite a few months. I found an old Kodak when I was rummaging in the cupboard of my bedroom here, and I took it away. I saved up and bought some film and, well, these are some of the results. What d'you think of them? You've got a good eye, Lisa.'

So have you, she thought, looking at them closely. Pictures of the allotments, mainly, the straight rows of beans, the square beds of planted annuals, sturdy marigolds, sweet williams and pansies bordered by curly cabbages, in the background a round water-butt and the figure of a man at the door of a garden shed. Each photograph was a composition, as a painter would have done it. After all, he was Lionel Craig's son. 'It's you who have an eye, Tommy,' she told him. 'They're good.'

He grinned, pleased. 'I look at the plot every morning when I start work, and I think, That's a subject, the light's different today. Each day it's different. I have to put it down. Painting would be better, but there's an art in photography too ... I never would have thought that. Composing.'

'Did you know your grandfather was a dab

211

hand at photography?'

'Vaguely.'

'Have you ever heard of collodion?' She remembered leafing through his old note-books in the snug at Lyle's.

'Pyroxylin. Ether and alcohol. It's used for making photographic plates.'

'Right. I've been thinking for some time of resuscitating the Photographic Department. Not just for photographs of soldiers on leave, wedding photographs and that...'

'Did you ever hear from that squadron leader who came to see you?'

'What made you think of him?'

'Soldiers on leave. Airmen too.'

'We did correspond occasionally, and then he stopped writing.'

'Do you think something's happened to him?'

'I'm not brooding about it, but it's ... funny.'

He had eyes like their mother, probing.

'You'll hear. Medics don't get killed so often. They'll have shifted him somewhere else. Mail gets lost.' She felt immediately cheered.

'About the Photographic Department. We lost two good men but you could help me to set it up again. And we might get one or two from school as apprentices...'

'It would have to be at night when I'd finished work.'

'Are you keen?'

'Dead keen.' His eyes were shining. 'I could take photographs of our paintings in the gallery...'

'Better than that. You could take photographs of your father's paintings, and we could make prints.'

'And there could be original stuff. Thomson churches, those fine houses at Kilmacolm, some of them Mackintosh's. And special portraits, not run-of-the-mill ... I've got a lot to learn, and the allotments come first ... I haven't forgotten I'm a CO.' He looked at her. 'When I was agonising, knowing that I would be hopeless in an ambulance unit – quite a lot of COs do that ... It's the pain and suffering, the blood, the terrible wounds that appal me. I'm not proud of that. But at least I thought I could be honest about how I feel about the taking of life, and the uselessness of any war ... But I never thought of war photography.'

'They wouldn't have given you just the nice photographs to take, so that's out. There would have been blood and guts.'

She thought he paled.

'Something happened to me...'

'What?'

He shook his head. 'I can't explain. It's complicated. Leave it, Lisa.' He was definitely pale.

'Right. You made your decision. You opted

out. Stick to your principles.'

'By God, you're like Mother.' For a second his voice was a man's.

'I could do with some of her courage.' She was thinking of Lionel Craig as she spoke, and her giving him up. She'd suffered for that. 'Don't worry too much, Tommy. You're going to be all right. You won't be growing cabbages for ever, and now you've got a ready-made career waiting for you. Count your blessings.'

She gave him back his photographs. She would have liked to give him a hug as well, but didn't.

Twenty

Tommy was right. A letter came from Charlie the following day, from Tripoli.

'I hear the mail is pretty bad these days, especially as we're being shifted about. I hope you haven't been worrying – but in some ways I hope you have – just a little! I have to warn you I'm going into Italy soon, so there may be more hold-ups...' It was a short letter, with a promise that he would write again soon. Because of her relief she replied almost immediately.

'I admit I was worried about you. Betty persuaded me to write to SSAFA, and I felt guilty about that. It wasn't as if we were married...' She tore that up and started again.

She had to admit to herself that he was becoming her anchor, because of his letters, which were coming fairly regularly now. She told him of her worries about the business, because, she said, she had to keep a poker face in front of everyone else, and it was such a relief to let her hair down with him.

In return he told her of his patients, and how he worried about them and admired them, 'especially those lads who look as if they'd just left school', and sometimes his opinion of the political scene as he saw it.

Rommel has been ordered home on sick leave. That to me, in my amateurish way, means they're getting cold feet. When there's a conflict between personalities, when Rommel begins questioning the two dictators, which I'm sure he does, I bet there will be a break-up. He's smart. He'll accuse them of false optimism. Roll on the end. I can't wait to see you. Do you know what I'd like to do? Whisk you off to a register office, however much you protest. We couldn't be more suited.

That shook her. Was he being facetious? She decided to ignore the remark meantime, and then wondered if she had offended him, because there was nothing of that nature in his next letter. Was that her fault?

She was in a state of confusion, not helped by feeling that 1943 was the most tedious and yet the most significant part of the War so far. There was a feeling of progress at last, but at the same time there seemed to be an increase in its size and fierceness. It had become a global war.

All thoughts of going to London had been put to one side for now. Mr Delmino was still in Sussex and advised her not to venture into the capital for the time being because of the persistent daylight raids.

In one of his letters Charlie said, 'By the way, are your father and his lady-love married yet? I hope so...'

She immediately felt guilty. In her unsettled state of mind she had forgotten about them. Betty came every week as usual, and her father was still in the Home Guard and coming in late ... I wasn't born yesterday, she thought.

The next time Betty came she broached the subject.

'I've been thinking, you two, that it's high time I cleared out of here and let you have the run of the place. Why don't you get married?' She saw Betty's face light up.

'I thought you'd never say it! I've said to your father to, sort of, bring it up, but he wouldn't. Men are so pussy-footed!'

'Betty,' James said mildly.

Lisa shook her head. 'No, I've been at fault. Anyhow I've rented a flat in Woodlands Road which is nice and near for Lyle's, and I'll always have Kilmacolm at the weekends. The travelling might be a bit difficult in winter. So will you two get busy and get the banns called or whatever they do?'

'Will we no'?' Betty said, getting up and throwing her arms round Lisa, then going to James and to his obvious embarrassment sitting on his knee and giving him a resounding kiss. 'I'll let you up if you promise to go to that press of yours and bring us all a wee drink to celebrate!'

'She's the limit, isn't she?' James looked sheepishly at Lisa.

'You do what she says, Father. I want to drink to the two of you. And maybe you'd like to have a honeymoon at Kilmacolm after the ceremony. Betty looks tired.'

'I'm no' that tired that a good trail round the shops to buy my wedding outfit won't cure,' Betty said. 'My, my! What a surprise for the office!' And, when they were drinking their whisky, 'Here's hoping you and the squadron leader will be next!'

'I'm not in a marrying mood.'

'Don't let your thoughts dwell on someone who's dead. Look to the future.'

'Supposing you concentrate on planning your *own* wedding,' Lisa said, laughing to hide the sharpness of her remark. She met her father's apologetic glance, and felt prim and old-maidish.

James asked Tommy to be his best man, which Lisa thought was a generous gesture, and she advised Tommy to accept. 'She's going to be your mother-in-law, Tommy. They'd both be really disappointed if you refused. She's always been your champion.'

It was a simple wedding in a Bath Street Church – Betty had insisted on a religious ceremony – and afterwards they had a meal in the Grand Hotel where the bridal pair were staying the night.

'You won't mind if I do a wee bit of refurbishing in the flat, Lisa?' Betty said. 'I'd like our bedroom to be a bit more frilly. You know, feminine.'

'Of course I won't. It's yours now.' Betty wanted to remove any traces of the woman she was replacing. She could understand that.

Tommy said he'd have to get back to his digs as he had an early start; because she was feeling sentimental after the wedding, Lisa gave him a hug. 'You did well, Tommy.' He looked pleased.

The flat in Woodlands Road felt strange and unwelcoming when she let herself into it, and she sat for some time at the window watching the trams sailing past. She was so seldom alone. Had Charlie Cramond meant what he said about wanting to marry her, 'whisk her to a register office'? It was hardly a proposal, and in any case was Neil McLean still lingering in her mind, as Betty had implied, his sweetness, the effect he'd had on her, the poignancy? 'Don't let your thoughts dwell on somebody who's dead,' Betty had said. But he was the first person who had occupied her thoughts so exclusively, who had left such an indelible memory. She could scarcely visualise Charlie's face, but she could see Neil's quite clearly, the dark eyes, the sweep of dark hair on his brow ... She got up quickly and put on her coat, thinking there was no good feeling sorry for herself, and went running downstairs into the dark street. It was only half past seven but it looked deserted.

Tears blurred her vision as she walked. The last time I did this was when Mother died, she thought. So much has happened since then. She felt very lonely.

But you'd like Betty, Mother, she said to herself, stopping to look into Elders at the utility furniture – a come-down for them – but really to dry her eyes. And she'll make Father happy. You knew what that meant, if only for a short time, with Lionel Craig.

Before she went to bed she wrote a letter to Charlie.

You'll be interested to know that I'm living alone in a flat in Woodlands Road. You asked about my father and his 'lady-love'. Well, today they got married and you never saw a happier couple. I'm sure my mother would wish them well. Tommy was best man and I walked behind carrying a bouquet of carnations my father gave me. He also gave one to Tommy for his buttonhole, white with maidenhair fern, and Betty could hardly be seen behind her red roses. A true marriage of love, and it united what has tended to be a rather disunited family. I think we're lucky to have her.

I hope you're well. I had plans that we might meet if you came to London, but that seems unlikely just now. I should have liked to see you again. We only met once, and I can barely recall your features, only a general impression of 'hail-fellow-well-met-ness'. That's because I can't think of a better word – oh, I've just got one: '*bonhomie*'.

Neil didn't give me that; he was rather melancholic, in fact. Is that why I see him so clearly, because of the poignancy? But Betty says you can't dwell on someone who's dead, and that's true enough.

I wish I could see you. I wish this war would stop. I'm feeling the weight of it. I'm looking at the carnage through Tommy's eyes for a moment, and then thinking of how you're doing your utmost to patch people up. But why damage them, kill them, in the first place? I feel you would say that that is part and parcel of all wars, if the cause is just.

Good luck. Betty calls you 'my squadron leader', which makes me blush, so you see I'm not always the self-contained girl you say I am.

Lisa.

Twenty-One

1943–4

Turkeys were scarce that Christmas, but Betty must have used her charms on their butcher because she put a fat eight-pounder on the table, roasted to a turn, to the admiration of the family gathered round at the Holland Street flat. The four of them wore funny hats from the crackers that Lisa had run to earth, but, glancing around, she had the feeling that only her father and Betty looked happy and carefree.

Betty was a homemaker, without a doubt. Their mother had always been too engrossed in the business to spend much time in the flat, but Betty had made it a cosy nest with a sparkling fire, shining doggy ornaments – she had a penchant for white and brown collies – soft cushions, footstools, everything designed for comfort.

When Lisa had laid her coat on the bed in their bedroom, the lights had been rose-shaded, and a white satin doll lolled on the pillows. Her own bedroom had been made into a study for James, with his books and pipe-rack.

It was evident that he had never been happier. He had changed, grown portlier, was urbane instead of bland. He was a good and generous host, and their presents reflected that generosity: a fitted attaché case for Lisa and a pair of furlined boots for Tommy, both from R.W. Forsyth's. He had remembered that Tommy had once said his feet were on fire from chilblains.

'And how's your squadron leader?' Betty asked when they were sitting round the fire with their coffee and small glasses of 'likoors', as she called them, not to mention a bon-bon dish of chocolates from the Belgian shop in Sauchiehall Street – a favourite haunt of hers.

Lisa laughed. 'He seems all right, from his letters.'

'We've got them on the run at last,' her father said. 'The Big Day won't be long now.'

'The planning's going ahead,' Tommy ventured. 'A combined effort. We've got American soldiers at the allotments, Nissan huts and the lot. They've given them part of the golf course for training. They're a great bunch. Very friendly.' Not like some of our own, Lisa thought. He had never spoken of the open hostility he suffered from, but she knew it existed.

They left together. 'Are you fed up digging for victory?' she asked him.

He shook his head. 'There's the photography now. It satisfies a need. I'm lucky, thanks to you.'

'Rubbish. It's your place as well as mine.'

'Are you worried about Charlie Cramond? You don't talk about him much.' They were walking in Sauchiehall Street. It was packed with young men and women, mostly in uniform. The American accent seemed to predominate.

'You'd think we'd become one of the States.' She avoided his question.

'They're not here for fun. It's coming, the Big Day, as Father calls it.' She noted the 'Father'. When he was older would they come to some agreement? Perhaps he would call him 'James'. 'You'll know when they clear out and go south. They're scattered all over the country just now, for training.' She thought what a contrast his interest was in the progress of the War and the fact that he had refused to fight in it, whereas Charlie Cramond wanted only to 'see it out'.

'You didn't answer my question,' he said after a pause.

'Yes, I'm worried. I didn't want to talk about him. His letters are few and far between now, and sometimes I think, Why isn't he offered a home posting? and then again that, of course, he always wanted to be in the thick of it.' She didn't look at Tommy. He should be used to taking brickbats. 'And I sometimes wonder if he's been injured ... or worse.'

'It couldn't happen twice.' She knew he was thinking of Neil. 'Don't you know his parents? They're bound to get official letters if something happens.'

'No, I know of them, but that's all. I mean, I'm not ...I mean they might not have heard of me. Don't let's talk about it, Tommy.' She turned to him. 'Why don't you come home with me and stay overnight? It's a long way out to the South Side at this time of night.'

'No, thanks. I'd better not. My landlady's not too keen on me these days. She might throw me out.'

'Has she a pretty daughter?'

He laughed. 'She's got a daughter. I've got to watch my step there.'

'Has she set her cap at you?'

'I couldn't care less. But I've got to keep my digs. Not everyone will take me in.'

'You'd better take the tram then. I'll wait with you at the stop and see you on.'

'OK. But don't let any of these Americans pick you up.'

'Not a chance.'

She waved him off on the last tram, watching his lithe figure swing on to the platform, watched him clatter upstairs. Tomorrow he would have his fur-lined boots to keep out the cold. And they'd made arrangements to meet at Lyle's and do some work in the Photography Department. The panacea of work was ingrained in both of them.

A week or two later Lisa got a letter at Lyle's, signed 'Elspeth Cramond'. She had looked at the strange signature and then read the contents with trepidation.
'Dear Miss Cowan,' it began.

I'm writing to you without Charlie's knowledge, but, knowing what a stoic he is, I thought I should put you in the picture. He told me of meeting you at your home, but I had to ferret out your address, which wasn't difficult. He had mentioned the name of your family's business, along with other things, all complimentary.

He's had an injured foot since he went to Italy which seems to be giving him a lot of trouble. I don't know how he got it – some accident, I expect – but knowing my son he has given all the care to his men but not himself. We've just had a letter from the doctor in charge of the hospital to say that the infection has spread and he's being sent home for further investigation.

We've been to see him at the hospital in Bucking hamshire where he now is, and were appalled at his condition. The news is not good and there is the possibility that the leg may have to be amputated...

Lisa put down the letter because of the sharp pain which shot through her chest, making it difficult to breathe. *Amputated!* This was war at close quarters. Charlie Cramond, once full of *bonhomie*. What was he like now?

'He's very ill,' she read, 'but he managed to say, "Tell Lisa. Tell her I'm sorry"...' Sorry! The word sent the pain through her again like a sword. Stupid, was more like it! Why should he *not* tell her?

'The nurses say it's your name which is constantly on his lips. If you don't know how much he loves you it's time you did. I've written the address of the hospital at the foot of this letter and how to get there.'

She wept in a confusion of concern and indignation. 'Sorry', indeed! Did he feel she'd had enough to bear with Neil's death? That she had no feelings left to spare for him? In the ordeal that stretched ahead for him she must tell him that she wanted to be involved, to do anything she could to alleviate his pain. Amputation! That dread word. In his lucid moments he too, as a doctor, must realise the possibility.

Her mind worked swiftly. She'd go right away to the Central Station and book a ticket to London for tomorrow morning, and then tell Bill. The panic she'd felt was subsiding. There was relief in action, and the desire not to waste time.

There was no problem with Bill Crawford. He heard her out and said immediately, 'You do that, Lisa, go and see him, the sooner the better. Friends come first.' She had the same response when she went to Holland Street that evening.

'She's doing the right thing,' Betty said, 'isn't she, James? What a sensible woman his mother sounds. But aren't men the limit? Afraid to upset you. The very idea! That's what we're here for, to be upset!'

'Would you like me to see you to the station tomorrow morning?' James asked.

'No, I'll get a taxi,' she said, and was surprised that her eyes filled with tears. 'I'll get off, then. I have to write to Charlie's mother.' If she didn't go she would find herself weeping on Betty's shoulder.

She wrote a short note when she got home, thanking Elspeth Cramond for letting her know about Charlie, saying how concerned she was and that she would be setting off for London tomorrow morning. She stopped herself saying more.

She went out and posted the letter at the corner of the street, feeling the loneliness that sometimes comes to one in the middle of a great city, and remembering other similar times – when her mother had died, when she'd moved into her flat. Is it by choice, she wondered? Am I a solitary by nature, or am I on the brink of a different kind of life, of involvement with one person?

She walked back quickly through the darkness, meeting no one, and feeling the familiar smirr of rain caressing her cheek, real Glasgow rain, not enough for an umbrella. Good for the complexion, everyone said. A cat slid past her, intent on some nightly pursuit.

I like having time to think, she told herself. Had she accepted Betty's invitation to stay the night she would have had to chatter with her, amicably, but perhaps saying too much before she could analyse her own feelings. 'If you don't know how much he loves you it's time you did.'

She packed a suitcase when she got into the flat, tidied up and went to bed. The word was there again with all its connotations, and with it again the sharp pain in her chest.

She was up early the following morning to catch the train and arrived at Euston Station at lunchtime without incident. She took the Tube straight away to Marylebone Station, where she had only half an hour to wait for a train to Aylesbury.

When she got there she walked up the street leading from the station into the square, where she thought there might be some hotels. She was lucky in finding a room at the King's Arms, and was also given a bus timetable by the receptionist. The travelling had only increased her anxiety, and after freshening up she set off for the bus station.

There was snow lying in the gutters as the Green Line bus trundled through the Buckinghamshire countryside, and also lying thickly in the vast grounds of the hospital as she walked up the drive. She was surprised to find her knees trembling, but whether it was anxiety or tiredness she wasn't sure.

She remembered the same sensation when she had been going to meet Neil, but she saw that now as a tremulous kind of adolescent love, not the mature feeling of concern tinged with panic which she felt now. This was no time for magic.

She reached the entrance, an imposing façade to what looked more like a country mansion than a hospital, with its towers and turrets. There was no doubt when she pushed open the swing door, however. It was clinically white and spotlessly clean. She went to the reception desk.

The smart nurse behind it gave her a quick glance when she gave her name and that of the patient she'd come to see, and directed her to Ward Nine. Here she was met by another nurse who asked her to take a seat in the side room while she informed Sister. Lisa's anxiety increased.

In a short time an older woman arrived, seated herself behind the desk and introduced herself as Sister Chalmers. No friendliness, such as there had been when she was visiting her mother at the Western Infirmary: 'In you go. She's waitin' for you.' It must be a Scottish characteristic.

'You're a friend of Squadron Leader Cramond's?' She did smile, however.

'Yes, I am.'

'Miss Lisa Cowan?'

'Yes.'

'His parents told me about you. The situation is this, Miss Cowan. He came to us from Italy with a serious foot infection, and the doctor here is worried that there is no improvement. We have a specialist coming to see him tomorrow morning from London.' She paused, then went on. 'It's better to be frank with you. There is a possibility that amputation will be necessary.'

'Yes, his...' Lisa felt an unexpected wave of faintness. The word seemed to swim in front of her eyes.

'Are you all right?' The sister's tone was kindly.

'Quite all right. I'd been forewarned by his

mother. Is there still hope?'

'That it won't be necessary? There's always hope, and Mr Rosmer, the London surgeon, is particularly experienced in this field.'

'Could I just ... see him for a second?'

Sister Chalmer's eyes were still on her. 'Well, perhaps for a second. Are you staying locally?'

'Yes. At the King's Arms in Aylesbury.'

'Good. I suggest after you see Squadron Leader Cramond you have a good night's rest there and come back tomorrow afternoon. Did you come a long way?'

'From Glasgow. I left early this morning.'

Sister Chalmers nodded and got up. 'Just for a second, then. He's very weak.' Lisa got up also and followed her.

Charlie seemed to be sleeping, and he didn't look like the Charlie she knew. His face was gaunt; there was a dull flush on his cheekbones. But the glint of gold was still in his hair.

She stood looking down at him, the sister at her side, saw the outline of a cage under the counterpane and thought again, This bloody war. He opened his eyes and looked at her, but there was no sign of recognition in them.

She bent forward and said, 'Charlie, it's me, Lisa.' She put a hand on his cheek. His eyes closed as if he were too weary to keep them open. She imagined the side of his mouth lifted a fraction.

She kept looking at him, hoping against hope that he would open his eyes again. After a time she heard the sister's voice: 'He's tired. Not a good day. I think you should go now.' She put a hand on Lisa's arm in a signal of dismissal.

'Do you think he knew me?' Lisa asked when they reached the entrance to the ward.

'It's difficult to say.' She looked doubtful. 'But come back tomorrow around this time. We'll know more then.'

She didn't take the sister's advice about having a good rest. At least, not immediately. She had been so obsessed about reaching the hospital as quickly as possible that she felt restless and unable to relax.

Aylesbury under snow looked like a picture-book English small town, with its clock-tower and square surrounded by buildings of different shapes and sizes crowded together. There were one or two narrow streets running off the square, and she walked along one, unlit but still with a few people scurrying in and out of the small shops which seemed to be converted from the old houses lining them. She found one which had TEA SHOPPE painted on the window, and she went in, heralded by a dangling bell on the door.

She asked the refined lady in an unsuitable mob-cap who came to her table if she might have tea and a scone. The woman had to ask her twice to repeat her request.

'Oh, you mean a *scone*,' she said with prune lips, looking at Lisa as if she were a very strange creature indeed. You'd think I had antlers, Lisa said to herself.

She did a rare thing for her when she went back to the hotel. She went into the bar and asked for a single whisky, and there the man served her with a pleasant smile and no appearance of surprise. In Glasgow pubs a middle-class woman, which she supposed she was, asking for a tot would have been frowned upon. Pubs were not a place for ladies. At least that was something to be said for the English.

At dinner the waiter asked her if she would like wine, and she said yes, a glass of red would be acceptable and she would leave the choice to him. He was equally pleasant and she decided that she obviously fared better in hotels than tea shoppes.

She lay in bed with anxiety eating into her, but relieved in a peculiar way to feel herself a more vulnerable, more tender Lisa than the one who ran a business in Glasgow. At this moment it couldn't be further from her thoughts.

She fell into a troubled sleep with the picture of his wan face, the unseeing eyes, in

front of her. Just before unconsciousness
Elspeth Cramond's words curved her lips in
a smile. 'If you don't know how much he
loves you it's time you did...'

Twenty-Two

The early part of the following day seemed like a week to Lisa.

She explored the back streets of the town again, thinking that this part of it had remained untouched for a couple of centuries. She came across a large house set in its own grounds, like an oasis in the centre of the higgledy-piggledy of houses, some of which had been turned into solicitors' offices, doctors' surgeries and the like.

On the wrought-iron gates of the house there was a board announcing that it was a school, borne out by the sound of children's voices singing inside. So innocent, she thought, so unaware of the turmoil the world was in.

She went back to the centre and to fill in more time boarded one of the buses waiting there. It took her on a compulsory tour round some of the nearby villages, quiet snowbound havens, deserted except for a few people going about, generally elderly, occasionally a farmer on his cart; each one a facsimile of the one before with the self-same village church, village green and duck pond.

At last it was time to catch the afternoon bus to the hospital, once more to walk up the drive, still snowbound, and present herself at the reception desk. 'Sister Chalmers told me to come back this afternoon,' she said to the nurse who raised the window when she rang the bell.

'Just a moment, please.' Professional detachment while she looked up a ledger. And then, 'Will you go to Ward Nine, please?'

Sister Chalmers was waiting for her. Nothing could be read from her face. 'Good-afternoon, Miss Cowan. Will you come in here, please?'

'You said I had to come back today, Sister Chalmers?' She couldn't keep the questioning note out of her voice.

'Yes, but I'm afraid I have no definite news for you. I'm sorry.'

'You mean...?' She kept her back straight.

'The position is, Mr Rosmer doesn't wish to commit himself at this juncture, Miss Cowan. He appreciates how difficult it is for you, but Squadron Leader Cramond's case requires careful consideration. It's a question of avoiding more drastic measures ... if possible.'

'I see.'

'He would have seen you himself, but he had to get back to London immediately.'

'Is there a certain length of time ... after which...' she didn't know how to put it, 'a decision has to be reached?' She thought the sister's look was appreciative.

'That's exactly it.'

'Is he hopeful?'

'I think it's necessary to be hopeful. As a surgeon he would always want to avoid radical treatment unless it was absolutely necessary.'

Once again Lisa saw the world swimming before her, but this time she didn't feel faint. The possibility had lost its first dreadful implication. An old Scottish saying came into her mind: 'You can get used to anything but hanging.'

'Could I see Charlie?' She saw the sister's face soften.

'Unfortunately, no. He's been sedated and he hasn't to be disturbed.' She hesitated. 'If you will take my advice, Miss Cowan, you should go back home. His parents have been sent for, and they'll be here shortly. Quietness for their son is essential. You'll be notified ... if there are any further developments, or if a decision has been reached.'

Was he dying? Did the surgeon think it wasn't worth operating? Should she wait and see his parents? She was in misery, and then her good sense prevailed. She wasn't going to become one of those hysterical women who were a nuisance to hospital staff. 'I promise you.' The Sister's eyes were on her. 'You could get back here in a day, couldn't you?'

'Yes, I could. Easily.'

'Good.'

That was it, then. Lisa was silent, thinking. At least Mr Rosmer wasn't rushing at anything, and the fact that Charlie's parents would soon be here didn't necessarily mean there was a particular urgency. It could be kindness on their part, their staying away while she was here. She knew her own temperament: she would be better working than trying to fill in time here.

'I'll leave tomorrow morning, sister. But, remember, I could get back in a day. I wouldn't mind a bit, if you just let me know.'

'Don't worry, Miss Cowan. We'll let you know.' And when Lisa stood up she put a comforting hand on her shoulder. 'Everybody is doing their best. That you can be sure of.' She walked with Lisa to the entrance and there gave her another reassuring pat. 'Try not to worry,' she said. Lisa thanked her and said she would try.

She had plenty to keep her busy when she got back to Lyle's. Bill had carried on nobly in her absence, but he had bad news for her.

'I've been told I have angina, Lisa. The doctor doesnae stop me from workin' awthegether, but he says I have to slow doon.'

'I'm so sorry, Bill.' It took her mind away from Charlie. 'Did you suspect it?'

'Just a bit puffed. But I'm quite able...'

'No, you must do as the doctor says. Slow down. Come in later in the morning, go home when you like. With Tommy helping in the evening in the Photography Department, it's a pair of extra hands.'

'If you're sure, Lisa...'

'I'm sure.' Now she was the comforter.

She threw herself into reorganising the staff to make it easier for Bill, taking on another girl from Skerry's and another apprentice from the Art School. Tommy, when told, was only too willing to come in every evening he could; it was easier, he said, in the short winter days when there wasn't so much to be done in the allotments.

Every morning she searched her mail, but there was no word from the Buckinghamshire hospital...

Twenty-Three

Tommy was giving himself a real treat. Mrs Doyle was out; Jenny, her daughter, was working late at the munitions factory; Jock and Bert, with whom he shared this room, had gone to a holy rollers meeting (he only called it that to himself).

He had slipped down to the kitchen, filled a basin with hot water from the kettle on the hob, refilled the kettle and carefully carried the basin back to their bedroom. He took off his shoes and socks, having first found a bar of yellow soap and a flannel where he had hidden them in the shaky wardrobe, and slowly immersed his feet in the hot water. He sighed with happiness, feeling the warm water flow between his toes.

His feet gave him a lot of trouble. He'd had to go back to the cheap boots because the fur-lined ones his father had given him had proved unsuitable for his work. The fur lining got quickly soaked and matted, and he had to keep them for wearing indoors as superior house slippers.

Lisa had offered him money but he had refused it so often that she had given up. 'I get sufficient for my needs,' he'd said. Necessities, he thought now, not needs. His father had only asked him once if he were 'all right', but Betty invited him fairly often to supper at Holland Street, and he went willingly, liking her, but most of all for the excellent meal she gave him. He was ashamed about that.

He wriggled his toes in the water and thought how simple most of his pleasures were. It reminded him of paddling at Craigton when he was small, the same pleasure when the salt water ran between his toes, making little cuts smart, and that time when he had skiffed a pebble and it had accidentally struck Lisa on the leg.

He had thought of Craigton when he'd read that they were making Mulberry harbours there in preparation for the great invasion. Strange how he retained an interest in the progress of the War when he had elected to stay out of it. Jock and Bert didn't want to know, said it was a sin against Our Lord. It was easy for them, but sometimes they drove him up the wall with their prayers and their hymns and their clapping.

The water was lukewarm now, but he daren't go downstairs again for some more from the kettle. Mrs Doyle might come in.

He made a tent for his legs with his towel. Long ago, it seemed, when he was a schoolboy and came home with a cold, his mother would fill a basin with hot water, put in a few spoonfuls of Colman's mustard, and wrap the towel round his legs, saying, 'There, that'll sweat it out of you.'

He saw clearly her calm face with that magnolia skin, the beautiful eyes, the permanent look of unhappiness behind them even when she smiled. What a strong bond of love there must have been between her and Lionel Craig, his father.

She had stroked his hand when she'd told him before she died. 'Difficult for you, Tommy, but you're old enough to know. And you can be proud of him, a fine painter, a remarkable man ... I was so immature...' Her voice had trailed away on the words. He remembered her skin, paper-thin and white, the magnolia warmth gone.

Not that she had ever made Father – he must think of him now as his stepfather – suffer. There were never any rows in their household. Maybe it would have been better if there had been.

'Well, well, well,' Jenny Doyle said from the doorway, 'what sort of carry-on is this you're up to?' Tommy looked round. She was so like her mother, the same red full lips, and in Jenny's case the accented bow which permanently showed her white, rabbit-like teeth, and gave her a petulant but provocative expression. She wore cheap dangling earrings and a flowered dress, tightly belted at the waist.

'Hello, Jenny,' he said. 'I'm washing my tootsies. Getting the potato dirt out of them. Any objections?'

'Whit do ye do about washin' the rest o' ye?' she said, coming over and sitting on the bed beside him.

'Try getting into that bathroom of yours when you want to! And your mother hardly ever lights the gas under the geyser. The water's only lukewarm.'

'Aye, she's mean wi' it. A just gie masel a sponge-doon in ma room, stand on a towel. You should come in wi' that camera o' yours and take a picture o' me.' He ignored this, and the lewd look which went with it.

'You're lucky to have a room of your own. There's three of us in here.'

'Well, you're lucky to get a place at all. Maist folk won't take conchies. Ma faither would kill her if he knew. Lucky he's in Burma. And if he knew whit she gets up tae...' It wasn't prayer meetings, Tommy thought, with the amount of titivating her mother did in the scullery when they were having their tea; kiss curls, she called them, those snail-like wisps of hair she trained to lie flat on her forehead. 'Hurry up, youse yins,' she would call; 'a'm late fur ma

245

appointment.' She had a laugh like a banshee.

'Where's your mates?'

'Out.' He was busy drying his feet. He padded across the room to the drawer that had been allotted to him and found his other pair of socks, which he had washed and dried. The pleasure of pulling them on ... he lifted his fur-lined boots.

'Don't bother wi' them,' Jenny said, lying down on the bed, her arms behind her head, her legs parted. 'Come on an' hae a lie-doon beside me. You must be tired wi' aw that exercise.'

He hesitated. Jock and Bert had teased him often about Mrs Doyle throwing Jenny at him. Jenny didn't need any help, he thought. 'She's hopin' you'll get her in the family way and then you'll have to marry her,' they had said. He had laughed scornfully.

She was inviting, all the same. It was that mouth. It would be nice to close it with a kiss, get hold of that upper lip between his and bite it softly. He felt an ache in his groin. He flung himself down beside her and immediately she rolled on top of him.

'That's more like it!' She supported herself with her arms on either side as she looked down at him. 'We don't often get the chance, do we?'

'Someone will come in, Jenny.' The

beating pulse in his groin could nearly be heard. How easy it would be, he thought, hating himself, to loosen his clothes, to release himself into her. He had never had a woman. But he wasn't like Neil McLean. He was ready...

'Ride a cock horse,' Jenny sang, moving on top of him, 'to Banbury Cross. Dae ye like it, eh?' He heard the door bang, and the heavy steps of Jock and Bert on the stairs. He pushed her off him, got to his feet and lifted the basin of dirty water, meeting the men at the door.

'Whit's this?' Bert said. 'Are ye gawn to throw th' water ower us now? Baptise us?'

Jock, who had more of the devil in him, laughed.

'Wur ye washin' Jenny?' She was now sitting on the bed.

'No, my feet.'

'Then it was ma turn,' she said pertly. 'But youse yins interrupted us.'

'You shouldnae be up here. You're no' wanted. Stop runnin' after this young fella. He's no' your type.' Bert was unctuous.

'How dis an auld Jessie like you know whit's ma type?' She shrugged. 'Anyhow, who would want a conchie and be shouted at if a went oot wi' him? A'd rather hae a threepenny seat at the pictures wi' a sodger.' She got up, saying as she passed Tommy, 'Dae ye need them to fight your battles, saftie? Too scared to go into the Army in case you get hurt?' And, turning on the two other men, 'An' you two wi' your prayers and hymns and holy meetings ... you make me sick!' She banged the door behind her.

'You want to watch them,' Bert said, 'her and her mother. Alley cats, baith o' them. This is no place for a young toff like you.'

And who asked you? Tommy wanted to say, but only shrugged. He had to live with them.

'I can't afford the Central Station Hotel. Well, I'd better empty this basin.' He went out of the room and poured the water down the lavatory rather than go back to the kitchen.

The men were digging into a newspaper parcel of chips when he went back to the room.

'Want some?' Jock offered.

'Don't mind if I do. I feel great since I washed my feet.' He said companionably, munching, 'We'll soon be moving. It's nearly over now, thanks to Monty and Eisenhower.' Bert looked at him.

'A couldnae care less. But a've often wondered why a fine upstanding lad like you became a conchie anyhow. Your father workin' in an office an' that. Educated.'

'He's not my father. Stepfather. My real father was a painter.'

'Oh, aye? Well, you could start him on this

room right away,' Jock said. 'Look at they patches o' damp, and the paper's peelin' aff.'

'Not that kind of painter,' Tommy laughed, 'a painter of pictures.'

'Oh, like the art galleries an' that? Well, that accounts for you bein' a conchie. They're an odd lot, they painters, bare scuddy women and snakes crawlin' up them...'

'You're thinking of Adam and Eve. The Bible's getting to you, Jock.' He half wanted an argument. 'It's not factual, it's an allegory...' Bert jumped to the challenge.

'Aye, it's gettin' to us. We're gawn to be two o' the Elect at the end o' the world, when you'll be crawlin' aboot on your hands and knees, beggin' for mercy.'

'What has that got to do with me being a conscientious objector?'

'We were directed by Jehovah, that's whit! No sheddin' o' blood. You don't know why...'

'Come on, noo,' Jock said. 'Ur there will be sheddin' o' bluid here tae. The three o' us agreed a long time ago there wid be no argifying if we've to live together.'

'Aye, so we did,' Bert said. He held out his hand to Tommy. 'A offer you the hand o' friendship, brother.'

Tommy took it.

He watched them later, kneeling at their beds in prayer before they lay down, and

249

thought, They're happy, which is more than I can say.

He got into bed and put out the light. Had it been worth it, he thought, his stance? He had suffered no injuries, except once from an irate woman who had rushed at him in the Co-op and knocked him over. Well, he couldn't blame her if her husband was fighting. And here he was, nearly at the end and not sure if he had done the right thing. He envied Bert and Jock. They had their Jehovah to tell them what to do, their place in their own society, happy to be members of the Elect. They had been obedient. Their reward would come.

But what about him? He had no place. Lisa was in her own flat now, and there were fewer invitations to Holland Street from the newly married couple. He didn't fit in, either in one or the other. But what of the Jews? How could he ever complain when he thought of what they'd gone through, taken from their homes, persecuted, tortured and put to death? He'd seen some dreadful pictures.

That was one thing he would have liked to have done, been a war photographer. But could he have borne to take pictures of such sights? Hadn't Lisa pointed that out to him? A failure, he thought.

He tried to lighten his mood with mind pictures of Paris where he had always wanted to go, the Champs Elysées, of lights, music and laughter, but all he could see were those terrible images, and one particular one, a man, a living skeleton, holding out a beseeching hand, the terror-stricken eyes falling out of his head. A failure, he thought again, a 'saftie', as Jenny had called him.

And then another picture came, one of a much-lauded airman, hero of many trips to Germany, where thousands of people had been killed and maimed, those weary, tit-for-tat air strikes. The airman's eyes weren't terror-stricken. His smile was confident; he didn't hold out his hand...

Twenty-Four

London in the late spring of 1944 didn't look any different, except that the streets were seething with uniformed men and women, British, Canadian, American, Free French, Polish – Lisa was able to recognise most of them thanks to Tommy's interest.

There seemed to be an undercurrent of excitement, like a thrill running through everyone, making eyes grow brighter, shoulders straighten, and giving Lisa, walking amongst them, a fellow-feeling of pride and joyful anticipation. 'Soon!' seemed to shape the lips of everyone who passed her by. The great offensive they'd been promised for so long was at last going to happen.

Everyone was on the move, arriving, passing through, including Charlie. His letter was in her handbag and she was going to see him today. 'I'll call for you at your hotel at six o'clock. I told you I'd be there.' She had never doubted him.

In the hotel they kept her well supplied with newspapers. General Montgomery, she had read this morning, was visiting his troops, visiting factories; Omar Bradley, less formally, was photographed sitting on the grass chatting to his men. One paper commented on the relaxed attitude of General Eisenhower, another on Montgomery's swagger. All of them told that the Allies were advancing triumphantly on Rome.

Her room was a little zone of quietness in the middle of such frenzied activity. Even the quietly spoken staff relaxed, as if wishing to share in the excitement. The girl who brought her breakfast tray confided, 'I feel all of a dither! Oh, I hope my Bob's all right!'

She felt at one with the excitement as she set off for her first appointment, to see Mr Delmino in Old Bond Street. He was now back in residence in his London home, he had told her in his letter.

'Great, isn't it?' she said to the taxi driver as she craned her neck to see the crowds milling around Piccadilly Circus.

'Yeah, this is it!' She saw his grin in the mirror.

Mr Delmino's neatly trimmed goatee beard, his twinkling eyes, showed that he had recovered his spirits, and his black tail coat and grey satin tie with the diamond pin that business was flourishing despite

Hitler's efforts. He had coffee waiting for her in his private room.

'Miss Lisa, at last!' He got up to greet her. 'You chose the right time. Did you feel the excitement when you were coming here?'

'Yes, I did. My heart's fluttering!' She laughed and sat down on the chair he indicated. 'Did your friend come back with you?'

'No, he prefers to stay in Sussex and look after the cottage. He's never got over losing Nathan, I'm afraid. But London beckons me. This is where the action is!' He poured out two cups of coffee, handed one to her. 'Cream or sugar?'

She shook her head. 'My father thinks I'm quite adventurous coming here, but I wanted to see you, and I have another appointment also.' Her eyes must have given her away.

'I'm not surprised, a beautiful young woman like you. If I've guessed right, you'll want to say *au revoir* to someone and wish him good luck.'

She sipped her coffee, smiling.

'Loads of good luck. I had a friend who was shot down and killed in his Lancaster bomber – the Cologne raids. It's hard to take.' As she said that she searched for the usual ache when she thought of Neil but it had gone; just a memory remained of sweetness, and his youth, his underlying sadness. 'But that's life.'

'You sound like your mother,' Mr Delmino said.

'Do I? I still miss her. She influenced me a lot.'

'But only for good, I'm sure. Jean was a stalwart, but I always thought that underneath she was an unhappy woman.' He looked questioningly at her, and she thought, Why not?

'She married the wrong man, Mr Delmino.'

He nodded. 'Life is never straightforward, but sometimes unhappiness is the spur we need.' The cosy intimacy made it easy to confide.

'Lovely coffee.' She put down her cup. 'The man whom my mother loved was a painter, and he gave her four of his works. They're in my possession. Do you remember the one you sold for me a long time ago?'

'Ah, yes, a gem. It caused some interest in my gallery. Suffice to tell you, Lisa, that I made a killing.'

'You would.' She smiled.

'I'm a dealer first and foremost, but also a connoisseur. The buyer got a bargain. I'm also a human being. I didn't fleece him.' He smiled mischievously.

'It was done by the man I've told you about. Lionel Craig, my mother's lover.'

'So ... And you have another four of his?'

'Yes. I didn't bring them, but Tommy, my brother, has taken photographs of them.' She lifted her briefcase and brought them out, handed them to Mr Delmino.

He studied them intently, giving her time to decide if she would tell him any more.

'They give a faint flavour,' he said. 'Enough to let me see their worth. Fine photographs. Well executed.'

'They were taken by the painter's son, my stepbrother, Tommy.'

He looked at her, his eyes surprised, and then he nodded as if the information pleased him. 'Did it break up the marriage?'

'No. I think now it would have been better if it had. There wouldn't then have been three unhappy people.'

'The War has made a great difference to how people think. That's one good thing. Is Lionel Craig dead?'

'Yes. Of cancer. Then she got it. It was like a final ... affirmation of her love.'

'My dear,' his eyes were sympathetic, 'if you choose to think that ... why not?' He changed the subject. 'In view of what you've told me, do you want your stepbrother to have those paintings?'

'Yes, eventually. Meantime, what I wanted was your valuable advice. Should I put them into safe custody, or keep them at Lyle's for the time being? They're a set, four paintings of the seasons. They're exquisite.'

'If you say so. I trust your judgement. And they'll get better all the time. You could ask one of your excellent art galleries to care for them, but it could be bombed the following day. A cornered beast can be ugly, and when we invade ... there could be repercussions – well, you know what happened to Nathan.'

'Lyle's could be bombed too.'

'That's so. Nothing's sure any more. My advice is to keep them where they are, but insure them for at least fifty thousand. Their price will go up all the time. That I am sure of.' He smiled at her. 'It's a good nest-egg for your brother.' She decided not to say that Tommy was a conscientious objector. Mr Delmino was a Jew.

'Yes. And make him proud of his real father.'

'An added bonus.' He smiled at her. 'I tell you what, when the War's over – it won't be long now – I'll come to Glasgow and see them for myself, if I may.'

'I was hoping you would. I can put you up in our country house.'

'No, thank you. I never stay with friends. You lose them that way. I'll sample again your excellent Central Station Hotel.'

She said as she was leaving, 'My father has married again.'

'Good. He must have suffered too.'

It had been a highly satisfactory meeting,

and she made her way back to the hotel feeling ... joyous. That was Neil's word. She would have a leisurely bath and get ready to meet Charlie in her geranium dress. She had bought it on one of her shopping expeditions with Jean: 'Never wear blue. It makes girls with colouring like yours look insipid. You'll look striking in red.'

She didn't know about 'striking', but it made her hair look burnished, her eyes a deeper grey, her skin pale but glowing. Mother was always right.

She thought Charlie looked dapper as she went downstairs to the hotel lobby to meet him, Then again, no, he was too big to be dapper, too masculine. The sun was slanting through the long windows, a shimmering, river-tinged sun, and she saw the glint of gold in his hair as he took off his cap to greet her.

They got into a bit of a fankle at first. She was wearing her silver fox cape; he had a stick, and therefore only one useful arm; and the stick caught in the fur cape, which made him sway slightly off balance when they kissed, and they laughed and she said, 'We'd better sit down.'

'You look a dream in that outfit.'

'I feel a fool in this cape, but I had on a sober suit earlier, and the cape added, I thought, to the London businesswoman effect ... I'll take it off.' She did.

'I should take it with you. That dress looks ... well, flimsy. I don't mean it doesn't look wonderful.'

'I might be cold? OK. The main thing is, How do *you* feel?'

'Tremendous. Ready to go. I've to stay in base headquarters at first but when it hots up, as it will pretty quickly, I'll join in the fun, I hope.'

'With your stick?'

'Oh, that's just for show.' Their eyes met and he hesitated, looking shy for him. 'This is the greatest thing for me. It's sad it will also have to be goodbye for the present, but it will be over before we know it.'

'Especially with *you* there,' she teased him. 'But I must admit, there's a tremendous feeling of optimism.'

'You feel it? Right!' He smiled at her. 'Are you ready to go on the tiles?'

'Yes,' she said. 'I've been looking forward to it for ages.'

In the taxi he said, 'We could go to a stiff upper-crust sort of place after we eat, or a rowdy place full of fun. Which would you prefer?'

'Oh, rowdy, every time.'

'But to begin with I've booked a quiet place for dinner so that we can talk. We're just about there.' He peered, then knocked on the window behind the driver. 'Drop us here, please.'

'Right, sir.' The man drew up at the kerb, and they got out. She noticed Charlie was fairly able, but was glad of a helping hand. At the entrance they were met by a waiter and led to a corner of the room. It was as quiet here as her hotel.

'This is nice,' she said when they were seated.

'We'll see to the inner man first. I wanted it quiet so that we could talk, and I could look at you.' She was slightly shy, but not tremulous, as she had been with Neil.

It was as if he had read her thoughts.

'Have you got over Neil's death?' he said.

'Yes, I think so.' She had to be honest. 'I think it was part of my growing-up phase.'

'You look different, perhaps older; no, I shouldn't say that, more ... mature.'

'Like cheese?' she said, laughing.

'*Not* like cheese.' He grinned. 'Something far more romantic, and beautiful.'

'Now you're making me blush. *You* look older.' There were lines round his eyes, and she wondered if they had been caused by pain.

'Maybe I grew older in hospital. Lying still doing nothing doesn't suit me.' He lifted the menu. 'Now let's decide what we're going to eat.'

'You choose for me,' Lisa said. 'I'm sure anything here will be good.' She glanced around. The restaurant had a subdued elegance. Even the other diners seemed to speak in subdued tones.

'Right. I hope you're not averse to champagne?'

'Not me. Champagne sounds just right.'

They chatted about nothing while the maître d'hotel hovered, while his minion brought the silver bucket and was banished, while he poured the champagne.

When they were alone she said, 'You asked me about Neil. I wanted to say, maybe meeting him made me more mature. Anyhow, it was good for me. I'm left with his ... essence.'

'I get it.' His eyes were steady on her.

'I'm glad he had you as a friend, and that you were able to help him. I think that was what he lacked all his life. A real friend.'

'He would have had that if he'd lived. A new life, I hope.' He raised his glass. 'Let's drink to him.'

She sipped the champagne, and the sweetness and sadness of Neil were there, and the sadness of her mother also.

Their food came. She was aware of its quality rather than the name of the dishes, white frilled baby cutlets of lamb which melted in her mouth like no lamb she had ever known, and a pudding which had a sharp lemon tang. Perhaps a bowl of porridge would have served the same purpose while she talked and listened to Charlie. She was deeply interested in him, how he looked, how he talked. She found herself assessing him as she assessed a good picture, felt the same pleasure.

A delicate Sauterne had followed the champagne, then claret, a liqueur followed with black coffee, all of it, like the food, a pleasant accompaniment to what was becoming a unique occasion.

'Did I tell you that my father has married Betty, a cuddly, curly-haired woman?'

'Yes. You did. I can just see Betty,' he said. 'Does it affect you?'

'No, I like her. I've got a flat nearby. I'm a big girl now.' She laughed at him. 'Mature.'

'But *not* like cheese?'

'Right. Oh yes, I live alone now, I can come to London on the train all by myself, and dine with a squadron leader.' She enjoyed teasing him. 'Betty was very impressed by that ... and I'm going out on the tiles with him later.' His eyes were dancing.

'You know, I wondered at first if you were too serious for me, but I see now you had nothing to be not serious about. I'm glad I came along at the right time.'

'Don't flatter yourself!' She laughed, then said, 'I'm glad too, Charlie. I'm beginning to see that serious things shouldn't necessarily make you serious.' She stopped there.

She had wanted to say, 'I think you've been very brave,' but decided against it. That would have been too serious.

'What age is your brother now?' he asked.

'Nineteen. He might not have been called up right away – he was at the university – but in spite of that he registered as a CO.'

He didn't look surprised. 'I can never understand the powers that be; I mean, how their minds work. Why didn't they let him go on educating himself? Young men like him will be needed after the War.'

'Tommy insisted on being "directed". Anyhow, he's growing food for Britain on a former golf course. At least it's original.'

'We all have to eat, and golf isn't essential.' He smiled at her. 'Does it distress you, about Tommy?'

'It did at first. In my serious phase. But now I think, How can you expect to understand anybody else's mind, even a brother's – I mean a stepbrother's?'

'Oh. Were your father or mother married before?'

'No, my mother had a lover.' The wine made it easy. 'He was a painter. That's one of the reasons why I'm in London. He gave her some paintings of his, which she left to me when she died.' His eyes were encouraging her. 'He was the love of her life. At least there's Tommy to show for it. And the paintings, of course.'

'That's really interesting.' He nodded, assimilating, 'Really interesting. Have *you* found the love of your life yet?'

'She held up her hand. 'Hey! That's a leading question!'

'*Have* you?' He wasn't letting her off.

She met his eyes. 'I think so.'

'Good. That's two of us.' She thought he would become soulful but instead he said, 'Do you want some advice about Tommy?'

'I probably could do with it.'

'He's not your brother. He's got a different father, a man who had unique talents as a result of his unique personality. Possibly complicated. Tommy could have inherited those. Don't try to understand him. Some people would have wondered why you didn't see right away that Neil was homosexual. I bet Tommy did. But you didn't want to see it. You were in love with love.' She thought that was possibly true, but she didn't want to let him think he was right.

'Is that the end of the lecture?' she said.

'That's the last thing I'd do. Lecture you. Don't you know you're the queen of my heart?' His eyes held her until she turned away, blushing. 'Are you ready to go out on the tiles, then?' he said.

'Yes.' She stood up quickly and felt her head swim. Goodness, she thought, her eyes widening. 'I'm ready.' She hoped she hadn't

264

slurred the words.

'You've forgotten your cape.' He lifted it from the chair and put it round her shoulders. She felt the pressure of his hands through the fur.

Twenty-Five

The noise in the Piccadilly ballroom knocked Lisa sideways as they went in, or perhaps she was still a little unsteady on her feet. She was glad of Charlie's hand through her arm. Laughing voices, shouting voices, clinking glasses, almost but not quite drowned the band, twelve or more players in immaculate evening dress swinging in unison as they played their saxophones behind the crooner at the microphone, a great blast of sound.

She saw Charlie's lips move rather than heard what he was saying. He was pointing to the bar. She nodded, and he steered her to the long mahogany counter at the back of the dance floor. They found two vacant stools and sat down thankfully.

'I don't see an empty table,' he said, looking around. 'We'll have to sit here until we see someone leaving.'

'All right.' She was bemused by the atmosphere, the seething life of the place.

'Sir?' The barman was at Charlie's elbow.

'I don't really want anything,' Lisa said.

'Sure? I'll have a beer, then.'

'Try a shandy?' The barman spoke to Lisa and she nodded out of politeness.

She leant forward to Charlie. 'Do you get it? The excitement? Everybody's determined to have their last fling.'

'Can't blame them. Most of them will be on their final leave. Making hay while the sun shines.' She felt glad to be there.

After a time they danced, or rather moved slowly around, close together. Once or twice they were nearly knocked off their feet, except that there wasn't room even to fall. His arms felt strong, and when he bent his head and put his cheek against hers she was entirely happy. Except that the noise and the heat made her feel a bit light-headed.

'I tell you what,' she said, freeing herself, 'we could have a look for a table while everybody's dancing.' The trouble was the cape, she told herself. She hadn't risked leaving it at the bar, and it was much too hot.

'Good idea.' He kept an arm round her shoulders as they walked off the floor.

When they were making their way back to the bar Charlie spotted two vacant seats at one of the tables. 'These would be better than nothing,' he said. 'We'll grab them and maybe we'll get it to ourselves soon.' When they reached the table he said to the man and the girl already seated there, 'Do you mind?'

'Help yourself,' the man nodded; he was a corporal, red-faced and talkative. 'Great place this, eh? Bursting at the seams to-night.'

'Are you enjoying yourself?' Lisa said to the girl.

'Marvellous,' she said, 'but then everything's marvellous when you come up from the sticks.'

'Right bloody marvellous,' the corporal agreed.

'Came up to see him.' The girl slanted her head in his direction. 'Paid my fare an' all. Expect he'll get his money's worth later.'

The man roared with laughter. 'Last chance, eh?' He leered at Charlie. 'Here, let me get you both a drink.'

'No, please,' Lisa said, but he was away, weaving swiftly through the crowd.

'That's Ron for you,' the girl said, 'won't take no for an answer.' She giggled and raised her glass. 'Here's to the future, if there's any.'

Out of politeness they had to sip the beers the corporal brought back. Lisa could see Charlie was slightly embarrassed. The band struck up again, a slow foxtrot, and he said, 'Lisa?' She got up, thankful that she could leave the beer. To the couple he said, 'Aren't you dancing?'

'We're saving our energy,' the man said, 'eh, Sadie?' He lifted his glass to her.

Lisa took off her cape. 'Perhaps you wouldn't mind keeping an eye on this, then?' she said to the girl.

'Sure, ducks.' She was offhand.

'This is our favourite,' Charlie said to them, to be amiable.

'Is it?' Lisa said when they were dancing – if you could call it that, she thought. They had to inch their way through the crowds on the floor.

'What?' He looked entirely happy.

'Our favourite?'

'It is now.' He held her closely and loving-ly, and sang softly in her ear, 'Are you lonesome tonight...?'

She felt good now without the cape, happy to be near him, not delirious, but happy. The lights were lowered, violet searchlights played amongst the dancers, and the noise seemed to have quietened, as if the crowd had become thoughtful, a little sad. He came away from her, smiled down at her.

'Just wanted to see you. You have a Lady of Shallott look. Delicate, pale, beautiful...'

'It's the violet lights. I do feel...' she searched for a word, 'different, kind of ... floaty.'

'Floaty? I like that. Maybe you're tired?'

'I am a bit. I was up early and I have an

early start tomorrow.'

'You don't like my dancing, that's what it is.'

She laughed at him. 'Your dancing's great. We'll finish this one and then you can take me home – I mean, to my hotel.'

'OK.' They moved slowly together and this time he didn't speak. Did his leg hurt? she wondered, but he wouldn't like her to make any comment, she felt sure. She let herself be guided through the crowd, thought what a stoic he was, that she more than liked him, could even love him. The trembling sweetness would come, give it time.

When they got back to the table, the silver evening bag was there, but not the silver fox cape. Nor the corporal. Nor Sadie. They both stared.

'My God!' Charlie exploded. 'What a hell of a nerve!'

'Who would have thought it? They seemed so, well, nice...' She couldn't believe it.

'Nice! I've a different name for it. We'll report it to the manager right away. You were too trusting...'

'I never thought...'

'You look shaken. You sit there and I'll go...'

'No, Charlie.' She put a hand on his arm. 'Don't go.'

He looked at her. 'You're serious?'

'Yes. I've made up my mind. Don't go. I

never liked it anyhow.'

'It was lovely!' He looked astonished.

'No, it wasn't. It was too ... dressed up, too ... Kelvinside lady. Let's forget it.'

'If you're sure?'

'It belonged to my past,' she said.

A tip to the doorman got them a taxi, and they sped through the darkened streets. He put an arm round her.

'You're not mourning for your lovely cape?'

'No.' She shook her head. Doing that made her feel dizzy again. Despite her decision about it, had the loss really upset her? Or was she just tired? 'I've had a wonderful time,' she said, pushing all thoughts of the cape away; 'I feel I've seen the War at close quarters at last. I've always been guilty that I wasn't involved more.'

'Think of me as your war work,' he said. 'Seriously, Lisa, you've kept me going. I mean it.'

'Tush.' She felt embarrassed. 'I did nothing.'

'I depend on you. Will you keep replying to my letters? It's important to me.'

'They'll be important to me too. Don't worry.' She put her head on his shoulder and closed her eyes.

She stumbled going up the flight of steps to the hotel, and he laughed. 'Good thing I was here.'

'I don't know what's wrong with me. Maybe it's these high heels.' You know what it is, she told herself. Too much to drink. The penny had dropped.

When they reached the hotel foyer a waiter came towards them. 'Lift, madam? Follow me.' When he opened the doors Charlie stepped in beside her.

He pulled a face behind the waiter's back. 'Got to see you reach your room safely.' She gave him a wry smile. He was still there when she unlocked her bedroom door.

'Don't you think you're being a little over-protective?' she asked him. His eyes were on her, steadily, when she looked at him.

'No, not at all. I'm acting in a medical capacity.' He smiled.

'Oh, is that what it is?' She crossed the room and threw herself on the bed, hoping he wouldn't take it as a provocative gesture.

It was the excitement; first Mr Delmino, then Charlie, all the different places, the talk and the laughter... 'Utter bliss!' She stretched out. 'Absolutely lovely.'

But it was far from lovely. She felt the smile slipping from her face because the bed was swaying up and down. She knew she should lift her head off the pillow, but couldn't be bothered to make the effort. She put one foot behind the other one and levered off a shoe, then another. 'Bliss,' she said again, trying to smile.

She realised that Charlie was lying beside her, saw a pair of feet covered in blue-grey socks peeping out from blue-grey trousers. She looked again and saw the complete immobility of one foot compared with the other... 'Should you be here?' Her voice to her sounded strangled and far away.

He was propped up on one elbow, looking down at her. 'Lisa, are you all right? You look white.' His eyes were concerned.

She swallowed. 'I'm perfectly all right. It's this bed.' Not the immobile foot. She'd known, hadn't she? Or guessed; hadn't like to talk about it. 'Like being on the ferry from Gourock. A bit choppy, and the seagulls following you. And seeing Craigton across the water.' She knew he had lain down again.

'As long as you're all right. Do you still think of Craigton?'

'Yes; it's Neil to me, you see. Quiet, so peaceful, that ... untouched quality of his. I knew that wasn't right. But it's over now. I hope.'

'You'll go back when the War's over?'

'Oh, I don't know. I don't know...' She turned to him and he put his arms closely around her.

'Don't grieve,' he said. 'You made him very happy. You were the girl he would have liked to love.'

'If he hadn't died we could have been

friends, at least. I mustn't go on like this...'
To her horror she giggled suddenly. 'What's wrong with me? If only the bed would stop turning into a ferry boat!'

He laughed and hugged her. 'Lie still and see if it will help.'

But it didn't. She felt her stomach suddenly heave, and she flung herself out of bed and staggered towards the bathroom, letting the door bang behind her. She just made it to the lavatory bowl where she was violently sick.

Some time later, when she was throwing water over her face, she stopped and listened.

'Charlie!' she called.

'I'm here.' His voice was reassuring. 'How are you feeling?'

'I'm fine now. I feel so embarrassed.'

'I know. I felt the same the first time I threw up. After that you don't mind a bit.'

'Oh, Charlie!' she spluttered, and called, 'That's the first and last time *I'll* drink too much.' She combed her hair, examining her face in the mirror, summoning up her courage. 'I'm coming out now.'

'Good.'

He was sitting on the edge of the bed facing the bathroom door and he held out his arms to her, laughing. 'Poor wee soul. Come to Daddy!' She tottered towards him, putting it on a bit.

'My stomach feels like a hollow drum and my head's splitting.'

'Don't turn it into an illness,' he said, still laughing at her. She sat down beside him and he put a comforting arm round her shoulders. 'It's nothing to the hangover you'll have. It's partly my fault.'

'I'm old enough to know better. It was the mixture of drinks, and the excitement of being in London, Mr Delmino, then seeing you...' The foot. But you knew all along. Off at the knee. 'And my cape, but as I said, it's no great loss.'

'Look at me,' he said. She turned towards him and he took her hands.

'In spite of everything, my ... imperfections, d'you feel we could make a go of it?' She had never heard him so unsure of himself since she'd known him.

'What imperfections?' she said. 'And Neil will go. He wasn't perfect either, at least perfect for me...' She suddenly yawned widely in his face. 'Oh, Charlie,' she said, 'what a night, with everything! I'm *very* tired...'

'Poor you. I know when I'm being thrown out. Actually, there's a chap picking me up at the Officers' Club...' He looked at his watch. 'He'll be there now.'

'So this is it,' she said. 'Goodbye. That sounds like the Big Picture.' They laughed together. It was better than crying.

275

'*Au revoir* but not goodbye, as they say also in the Big Picture.' His face was suddenly solemn, and he drew her to him. He kissed her hard, then let her go. 'We'll get married when I come back?'

'That would be very nice.' It was no time for lingering doubts, with a man going off to the War. She put her hand to her mouth to stifle a yawn. 'Off you go before I fall asleep.'

'Such enthusiasm! Would you like me to help you undress?'

'No, I wouldn't, thank you very much.'

'A pleasure deferred, then.' He got up stiffly. 'Where did I put my cap and stick?'

'Beside your jacket. On that chair.'

'So they are.'

She watched him getting ready to go and thought, The sadness and the stupidity of it all. Was Tommy right?

'Thanks for a lovely evening. Good luck.'

'Thank *you*.' He saluted smartly, limped to the door and was gone.

She fell back and turned her head into the pillow. If she hadn't been so overwhelmingly sleepy she would have cried her eyes out, but sleep won. Tomorrow was time enough for tears.

Twenty-Six

Lisa came back from London feeling a changed woman, which seemed ridiculous since she had only been there for a weekend. It was Charlie, of course. She knew he loved her, and she was almost sure she loved him, or why else had she been so glad to see him, so impressed by his courage, and so distressed to think that, even disabled, he was choosing to get embroiled in the War again? Would he stay at base headquarters, she wondered, or would he wangle himself across the Channel when the invasion began?

Her daft behaviour, drinking and mixing drinks when she was unaccustomed to it, had precluded any love-making. The old doubt arose. Would she, could she, feel the same tremulousness as she had felt with Neil? 'In love with love', Charlie had said. Was that true, or would she never feel like that again, with anyone?

Her mind shifted to Tommy. She felt,

having been closer to the War in London, that she could better understand the isolation he must suffer, even in Glasgow, and better understand the strength of his convictions. Charlie had understood, and had been utterly generous in his attitude. Her thoughts were back with Charlie again.

She remembered their attempt at dancing in the crowded ballroom, especially when he had put his cheek against hers and sang, 'Are you lonesome tonight...?' His gaiety, which was part of his nature.

Had it all been a bit sentimental, a natural reaction to the general excitement, of being part of the Great Plan, being with others who were involved in it? Every man liked to have a girl to write to, to come home to; it was all part of the pattern which Tommy had turned his back on.

'Collected', Charlie had called her. Was she too cool, too detached, like her mother, who had lost the chance of a happy life by being too cautious and running away from Lionel Craig?

Enough of this, she thought, this ... dissection. She would go and see Tommy. For once she wouldn't go rushing back to Lyle's as if the place couldn't function without her. She'd leave it until tomorrow morning.

She quickly changed into more casual clothes and caught a tram in Woodlands Road going south. When they turned into

Sauchiehall Street, it rapidly filled up with chattering women laden with parcels, and she listened with more than the usual attention to the cadence of their voices after her brief time in London.

'A got a great bargain in Copland & Lye's, Mary. The last pair o' seamless stockings, in a sort o' buff. They were a small size, though. A'm lucky, aye, so a am. Ma feet are that small.'

The man in the clubhouse directed her to where some of the men were working. 'A don't approve of their principles,' he volunteered, 'but a'll say this. They give me a nice basket o' veg every Saturday. A've never been so well in wi' the wife fur years.'

She came across Tommy digging up potatoes, which he was dropping into a pail, and, looking at him before he was aware of her, she saw the change in him. His bent back gave him a dejected look, like a whipped horse. He was leaner. His hair was longer and had lost its sheen, and the thought came to her that any minority in a society wore its own badge.

'Hello, Tommy!' she said, stopping beside him. He looked up in surprise and she saw his face flush.

'Lisa! I thought you'd be working at this time.'

'Usually, but I've been in London for a

day or two. D'you think you could take a little time off? I'd like to have a chat.'

'Well...' He looked dubious. 'Is it important?'

'Not a matter of life and death, but there's something I'd like to discuss. I didn't know your address.'

'No ... I meant to give it to you. Hang on a minute.' He put down his spade and walked towards an older man a little distance away. She watched him talking, the man listening impassively. After a minute or two he came back.

'I can have half an hour. Come on.' He lifted a canvas haversack. 'There are some seats in front of the clubhouse.'

It was pleasant, sitting looking down the fairway, the rolling greensward no longer as pristine as it must have been before, the distant clump of trees. She imagined the men who used to congregate here, the businessfolk of Newlands and Gifnock, their jovial and liquid meetings at the nineteenth hole, their attire of plus-fours, tartan socks with green tabs, polished brogues. Would some never come back? Even Charlie was in danger as a non-combatant, had already been. She felt a sudden stab of fear for him. He's had enough, she thought.

'This OK for you?' Tommy's voice broke into her thoughts.

'Fine. Nice view.'

'I didn't fancy my lunch earlier, lucky for you.' He opened his haversack and produced a flask and a paper bag. 'My landlady isn't any great shakes at sandwiches, but she's cheap, at least. Three of us share a room.' The rough slices of bread, with the shiny pink edges of some unidentifiable meat showing, didn't look appetising.

'No, thanks. I'm up to here!' She put the edge of her hand to her forehead. 'I ate myself silly in London. You go ahead, but I'll pour myself a drink if that's all right. Is it tea?'

'Stewed.' He nodded, his cheek bulging with bread. 'What did you want to see me for?'

'Just to clap my eyes on you. I forget what you look like. And I wanted to tell you about London. I met Dr Cramond. Remember?'

'The squadron leader? The Highland bloke who knew Neil McLean?'

'That's it. London was brimming, bursting at the seams with soldiers, sailors and airmen. They're being gathered together for the landings in France. Everybody's quite sure it will be soon.' She hadn't meant to discuss the War.

'Yes, I've been following it. It will be any day now. The landing place is divided into beaches, American and British. Because I'm not fighting it doesn't mean I can't read about it.'

'Who's stopping you?'

'I thought I detected a surprised look.'

'Don't be touchy. Charlie thinks it's a pity they didn't let you go on at the university.'

'Such nobility from a maimed man! Sorry, Lisa, sorry!' He put a hand on her arm. 'Yes, I am touchy.'

'OK. I'll let you off.' She had seen the misery in his face. 'But get it straight. That role doesn't fit him. That's what makes him ... noble.'

'I'm eating dirt. God, I hate myself!' She saw the white, pinched look and felt sorry for him. 'Did he take you out?' She watched him shakily pouring out some tea from the flask. He'd left the sandwich half eaten.

'Yes. Dinner first, lots of booze, then an attempt at dancing. Then I lost my fur cape, remember it? I didn't mind. Then he took me back to the hotel, then I was sick.'

His face came up, grinning. 'Sick out loud, as we used to say?'

'Yeah, very much so.'

He was still grinning. 'A good enough test. What did you come for, Lisa?'

'To tell you how I got on in London.'

'With the squadron leader?'

'No, that's private. I saw Mr Delmino first, the art dealer Mother liked. I wanted to speak to him about the paintings. I showed him your photographs of them and he was impressed.'

He was buckling his haversack, his head down.

'And?'

'He thinks they'll be worth a great deal of money. He'd already seen another one I'd bought some time ago. He's very interested. He'll come and see them when the War's over.'

'He'll be right about their value. Mother thought a lot of his opinion.'

'She thought a great deal of your father's work.'

'I know.'

'You could well have some of his talent.'

'Not much sign of it.' His eyes lit up. 'But I'm really keen on photography.' He turned to her. 'I'm using that old Kodak quite a lot here, when the boss isn't looking. Well, I'm never anywhere else. And reading a lot. I get books from the library. Photogravure. Great word, isn't it?'

'You're helping a lot in Lyle's. That department is flourishing, and Bill is high in his praises.'

'Well, I'm glad I'm doing something right. Sorry, that's girny. There's nothing I'd like better than working there when the War's over.'

'What about Paris?'

'That's still my dream, but I've to work for that.' She met his eyes, saw the doubt there and knew the truth. He'd never been entirely sure about choosing not to fight, nor his reasons for that choice. Seventy-five per cent, possibly. Well, he'd have to live with that. He'd made his bed.

'I regard those paintings as yours, Tommy. I'm going to see old Cuthbertson about it.'

He blushed violently. 'No, no, Lisa! That makes me feel like a ... scab.'

'They're yours because they were done by your father. If we're ever short of cash at Lyle's one would pay easily for a year in Paris, and something left over.'

'I can't accept this.' The blush, now that it had receded, had left him looking paler and more pinched than ever.

'It's fixed. You may have a different father but I still think of you as my brother. We've been together too long.'

His head was down. It stayed down for a long time. When he looked up at last she thought he looked too fragile and longed to take him back to her flat and feed him up.

'You're a great sister,' he said. 'I'll work like the devil when I come to Lyle's.'

'That won't be long. The War will soon be over ... I hope.' Not long now till she saw Charlie again ... It was a surprisingly comforting thought.

Twenty-Seven

It had been brewing for a long time, the trouble, the snide remarks from Jenny's mother when they were having their evening meal. 'Some toffs think they can do anything and get away wi' it. Think folks like us are dirt.' She didn't look much these days, Tommy had thought. All the titivating at the cracked mirror in the scullery had stopped.

'Who's stole your scone, missus?' Jock had asked.

'You shut your gob,' she said to him. 'One wrong word frae you three and a can throw you out. You're only here on sufferance, thanks to ma kindness. No one else would take you in.'

'Don't annoy her, Jock,' Bert had bleated. All he wanted was peace, Bert, so that he could get through the day and crawl into bed and commune with his maker. Don't sneer, Tommy had told himself.

Jenny was no longer a worry to him. He had rebuffed her so often that she had stopped coming up to their room when she knew Bert and Jock weren't there. The final time had been when her mother had burst into the room and caught him standing at the bed where she was lying. He had been telling her to get up and get out, he had learnt his lesson, but her mother had shouted her head off.

'Whit are ye daein' to ma lassie, eh? I know you toffs. Want everything for nothing then blame it on the lassie. Aye, a know you lot!'

Jenny had lain on the bed, a smirk on her face which had infuriated him.

'This is my room!' he had shouted. 'Get out of it and take your daughter with you! I'm sick of her coming up here where she's not wanted. If she were the last woman on earth I still wouldn't want her here.'

There had been a stupefied silence. Jenny was the first to speak, spitting fire.

'D'you hear that, Maw? Puttin' aw the blame on me, and him askin' an' askin'...'

He thought he was going to burst with rage. He walked to the window and, looking out at the grey street, the children shouting and chasing each other, he thought, This is it. 'I'm waiting for you to get out,' he said, his back to them. He heard Jenny's wailing voice.

'He likes me, Maw. "Come up here, Jenny." Always askin'. When you came in he was jist...'

Her mother, who had been strangely silent, interrupted her.

'Get doon the stairs and get the dishes washed, you wee brat. A'm fed up wi' the lot o' ye, you included. Get doon the stairs!' He heard the door bang. When he looked round the room was empty. But he had known that was not the end of it.

He had told Bert and Jock when they came in but they weren't very sympathetic. 'You'll get us run out o' here and we'll never get another place,' Bert said.

'No, he won't,' Jock said, but his uncertain tone was a tacit assumption of Tommy's guilt. 'She needs the money. But you better watch your step, Tommy. She's got it in for you.'

Sundays were always bad days, but this particular one was one of the worst. The three of them stayed in bed most of the morning, glad of the rest. Mrs Doyle, who was a devout Catholic, never missed early-morning Mass, which seemed to give her a new supply of venom. When the three of them went down for their dinner her face was ugly.

'Are you goin' for a stroll in the park the day, missus?' Jock said, chancing his arm. She was in the scullery dishing up the food, and she came to the table with heaped plates in either hand, which she banged down in front of Jock and Bert. Tommy saw the unsavoury mess of potatoes running with watery gravy from the pile of mince and boiled cabbage, and thought of the meticulous attention to detail at Holland Street as practised by Lisa, and formerly their mother: the separate serving dishes, the serving spoons, the gravy boat, the cut glass water jug, Father sharpening the carving knife on the steel in front of the huge platter on which the side of roast beef rested. He could smell it now.

Nowadays he thought of himself more and more as Lionel Craig's son, noticing in himself little tricks of speech, a quick temper, an ability for ridicule, a joyful appreciation of form and line.

'None o' yer lip!' Mrs Doyle's raucous voice grated on his consciousness.

'I'm sorry, missus,' Jock said. 'A just thought...'

Jenny interrupted him. 'You're not paid to think. But a'll save you the trouble. Her fancy man has skedaddled off wi' another wumman, and she's fair boilin' wi' rage...'

Tommy looked at the girl. She was particularly unattractive today, her hair uncombed, slouching at the table, her petulant mouth twisted in a scowl.

'You keep your bliddy trap shut!' Her mother banged two further plates down on the table, one in front of Jenny, the other, the same unappetising mess, in front of Tommy.

'Oh, Gawd!' Jenny said. 'Will ye look at this! A'm gawn to be sick.'

'If the cap fits, wear it,' her mother said, standing glaring at her, arms akimbo. 'But, see, try to get anything oot o' that lyin' bitch...'

'Now, now,' Bert said, 'it's the Lord's day, missus. You've been to Mass, haven't you? A'm sure your priest wouldnae like you to speak like that to your daughter.'

'You keep out o' it, Holy Willie,' she interrupted. 'When a want your opinion a'll ask for it.' Her voice changed, became smarmy. 'But you're very quiet, aren't you, Mr Cowan? Are you listening, Mr Cowan? The toffs are famous for keepin' their traps shut. For taking advantage of a poor working-class lass and walking off, aren't they?' She gave Tommy a violent nudge in the back. 'Aren't they?'

'I don't know what you're talking about,' he said, angered by the pain of her nudging.

She mimicked him. '"I don't know what you're talking about." Too bad, don't ye know?' Bert and Jock were gaping. 'Don't ye know, then,' another nudge, 'that that poor fool is in the family way, thanks to you!'

He heard Jenny's weak snigger and looked at her, but she kept her head down.

'That's a load of rubbish!' He raised his

voice. 'Absolute rubbish!'

'Rubbish, is it, eh?' Her mother was enjoying the commotion round the table. Bert and Jock had stopped eating. 'Absolute rubbish! Dearie me! She's telt me. Said you held her down on your bed till she gave in.' Tommy laughed across at Bert and Jock, shaking his head. They didn't laugh.

'What next?' he said to the woman. 'What's next on the agenda?' The word seemed to infuriate her.

'What next?' she screamed. 'What's next is that you tell your folks and get enough money from them to make an honest woman out o' her, that's what's next! Gie that poor wee soul that's growing inside her belly a name!'

Tommy found himself on his feet. Was this Lionel Craig speaking? he wondered, as he shouted. The anger was like a flame running through him. 'Your daughter has kept coming up to our room trying to ... entice me. Jock and Bert can vouch for that. I did my best to stop her...' He saw Jenny sitting on top of him singing, 'Ride a cock horse...', but he'd have to forget that... 'You tell her, Jenny, tell her the truth. If you don't I'll get my father's lawyer to find out who is the real father of your child. It's certainly not me. I'll swear in court to that.'

'A want ma wean that's comin' to have a name...' Jenny was crying, her hair tumbling over her face. She looked pitiful, and Tommy thought, I have to get out. She's been put up to this.

'I'm not stopping in this house a minute longer,' he said, wondering where he would go.

'You'll not get the chance,' Jenny's mother said. She was brighter than her daughter. 'You'll pack up and get oot right away afore a murder ye, and good riddance to scum like you!'

'Now, now, missus,' Bert said. 'It's Sunday. The day of forgiveness. The lad has told you he's got nothing to do with your lass...'

She gave him a look of scorn, and addressed herself again to Tommy.

'Up you go and pack your things and get oot o' here!' She was beaten. Tommy looked round the table. Jenny was now eating, as if a wave which had nothing to do with her had washed over the table and receded; Jock looked at him sympathetically, but that was all he would get from Jock, or Bert. They didn't want to be landed in the street with him. The War would soon be over and they would be back to their holy pursuits.

'Right,' Tommy said, pushing back his chair. 'I'll be glad to get away...' He wondered if he should add, 'from your terrible cooking', but didn't want to chance his luck. He shut the door quietly behind him. After all, he was a toff.

While he was packing he asked himself where he would go. It would be ignominious to ask Betty and James to put him up, and he wouldn't go crying to Lisa when he'd been thrown out.

But he cheered up momentarily. Any place would be better than this ... And then he was in despair again. Mrs Doyle collected their lodging money on Saturday night. He put his hand in his pocket and brought out the few coins he had been left with. Until his next week's living allowance payment he had exactly three shillings and sixpence.

Maybe he would find a place that would take him in on tick for a week. He had his employment card, his ration book, he was in a job. But then the thought which he had been stifling jumped into the forefront of his mind. Who could he find who would be willing to take in a conscientious objector?

Don't look on the dark side, he told himself without much conviction. Something will turn up. He avoided glancing with regret at his bed which, however lumpy, he would never sleep in again, and where he had nearly ... Thank God he hadn't.

He wasn't able to say goodbye to Jock and Bert: they had stayed in the kitchen with their landlady until he left. Even Holy Gospellers knew which side their bread was buttered on.

He had been right about not being able to

find lodgings. He took a tram to Eglinton Street and trailed round the district, looking for likely places, but there were no notices on any of the tenement windows, and enquiries from the odd shawlie with her child in the crook of her arm always elicited the same reply: 'Naw, son, there's naebody roon here. Now, if you were lookin' for somebody who could help your lass – you ken whit a mean?' this said with a leer – 'a could gie you a good address and nae questions asked.' Abortions, knitting needles ... the stories he had picked up somehow lay there in his subconscious.

He ought to be at work by this time. Mr Robinson, the supervisor at the golf course, was strict. He didn't like 'conchies', he put up with them; and any request for addresses, he knew, would be met with a stony stare.

When he got to the allotments, the tonguing he got from Robinson made him greet Bert and Jock with an unconcerned air. 'Yes, I think I've got a place. I've to confirm it when I finish here.'

'A felt awful for not standin' up for you,' Jock said, 'but to tell you the truth, Tommy, if we were turfed oot, we'd have nowhere to go. The Mission's strict. But you're aw right. You've got rich relations...'

He had smiled and said yes, he was all right.

The worst part was wandering about the Trongate and High Street while it was light. He bought the *Citizen*, and spent some of his precious money on a cup of tea in a booth in an ice-cream shop.

'The first troops ashore,' he read, 'were those of the US Division, who landed at 6.30 a.m. on Utah Beach. Their beaches were cleared with few losses.' But what of Sword, the British one? What of Charlie Cramond? Was Lisa going to be unlucky for the second time? But they wouldn't allow him, especially non-combatant, near danger, surely? That would only apply to doctors who were fit. Yet he seemed to be fearless.

It's no good, he said to himself, bringing out the old argument that those who were fearless lacked imagination. That was an excuse thought up by a conchie, probably. He could taste the bitterness in his mouth, the self-disgust.

'Many men were lost wading ashore on the British beaches, where the surf was rougher. Good progress was made, but the British Division who landed on Sword failed to reach Caen...' The owner of the shop, swarthy, Italian, was at his side.

'We don't serve just teas, you know. You have to eat something. Would you like some pea-brae?'

'No, thanks.' He looked up into the man's

dark eyes. 'No, thanks.' Where did that horrible stuff originate? Not in Italy, surely. Pea-brae – peas boiled in water till they were mush, a generous dose of pepper and salt – on a June evening! Maybe they'd picked up the idea in Scotland, where broth was a favourite. But Lisa didn't make it like that. A good ham bone with plenty of meat adhering to it, every kind of vegetable ... Saliva ran into his mouth.

'That'll be tuppence, then.' It was a definite dismissal. He handed over the two coins and left.

He wandered about the lower end of Argyle Street for an hour or two, looking into shop windows, then, when he saw a policeman looking at him suspiciously, he made for the Trongate and walked up High Street until he came to the cathedral, backed by the huge bulk of the Royal Infirmary. Could he go in there and ask for a bed? He'd have to lose a limb first, like Charlie Cramond. What a thing to happen to an able-bodied man!

A knife screwed in his heart. Was he really, deep down, a coward? No, no, it was much more complex. You have worked it out, all the arguments. You were sure, sure, and here you are now, at the first sign of trouble, feeling again that niggling sense of doubt...

He should have liked to go into the cathedral for its peace and quiet, but he remembered the old regimental flags which hung in the side chapel, and knew they would only increase his guilt. And the minister might be there, might look on him suspiciously, see right into his soul.

He crossed the terrace in front of it and went through the gate to the Necropolis, looked around at the mausoleums to the worthy dead set on the hillside, and made for the obelisk of John Knox on its lofty pinnacle.

It was a great view. All Glasgow was there, its streets and squares, the Glasgow built by those men lying asleep here. Turning round towards the north, he could see the faraway bulk of the Campsies. A great city, worth fighting for. He'd sit here and wait till it faded into darkness.

Had his decision not to fight really originated from the sight of that nest of baby mice massacred by the dogs? But it hadn't been the dogs. They were animals. It was the lads behaving like animals that had done it. Blood lust.

And hadn't there always been young men like him, who had recognised the futility, the stupidity of war? Poets, scholars. And in the Great War, hadn't he heard of soldiers who were shot in the back as they ran away? *You avoided that by not joining up* ... No, no, it wasn't cowardice, it wasn't cowardice ... He put his head in his arms.

The great monuments around him became eerie as they faded into darkness, ghostly shadows containing the bones of the illustrious dead. He remembered Mr Blackie, the publisher, was buried there, whose house had been built by Mackintosh. And William Motherwell, the poet. 'Wee Willie Winkie runs roon the toon...'

Mother had not been one for bedtime stories, but Lisa had read to him. 'Are all you bairnies safe in bed...' She had been a second mother to him, gentle...

He sat in his corner against the stone plinth until it was completely dark, dozing for part of the night, but the cold woke him, and in his half-asleep state he thought also that it was the cold disapproval of John Knox seeping into him: a hard man, a man who wouldn't approve of conchies.

He got up wearily and walked down the hill until he came to a mausoleum with a vase on top. There was room at the entrance to lie down out of the wind, and the Egyptian feel of the edifice seemed to seep a little warmth into his bones.

He slept until light, then made his way further down the hill until he came to the Bridge of Sighs – what happened to the Molindar Burn? he thought – then walked down the High Street where he caught a southbound tram. It's a race between the War ending and me finding lodgings, he thought, as he climbed up to the top. If he were lucky, he'd find the clubhouse open – a woman cleaned there occasionally – and he could slip into the toilets and tidy himself up.

Twenty-Eight

1945

Lisa was sitting in the kitchen of her flat in Woodlands Road reading about the death of Goebbels and his wife and children. 'They poisoned first of all their six children, Helga, Hilda, Helmut, Holde, Hedda and little Helde, aged three.'

Were they laid out in a row when they had finished, all those children with names beginning with H? The tears were running down her cheeks, and she thought, Why not? I'm too self-contained, I've taught myself that. There was only one time I was able to relax, and that was with Charlie in London ... But it's strange that I should weep for six German children, and never once for Neil.

Or Charlie, for that matter, who must have been often in danger, in spite of what he implied, that he was at base headquarters most of the time. Once or twice there had been French postmarks on his letters, and she'd imagined him in field hospitals based not so far from the beaches. Whatever the case, he would be attending to the sick and the dying, in the early stages of the invasion, waves and waves of them. The death tolls had been high, if not so high as the Germans'.

Had he ever grown sick of the filth, the blood, the mess of war, wished he could keep his hands clean? If so he had never said.

His letters had been brief, but she had imagined him following the troops, plunging deep into France, living with the men, succouring them. His attitude had been the only one, Churchillian, get it over and done with. He had been consistently cheerful and loving. 'Can't wait to see you. I love you...'

And now it was over. He would soon be home.

'Then Goebbels and his wife, Magda, left the bunker and asked an SS orderly to shoot them in the back of the head...' She read the details deliberately to prolong her tears, a strange mixture of pity and yet relief, a feeling that they were good for her.

She put her head down on the table, cradled it in her arms and really let herself go. Oh, good, good, she thought, but felt ashamed that there would be thousands and thousands of women who would be crying for their dead or mutilated husbands and lovers, asking in their agony, 'What for?' or, if they accepted that, 'What now?'

Cup of tea, she said to herself through her tears, and was on the point of rising when she heard the doorbell ring. She quickly went to the small mirror at the side of the sink, looked in it at her face, grimaced and scrubbed it with her handkerchief, and ran her hand over her hair before going to the door. It was Tommy, a wan and dishevelled Tommy with a battered case in his hand.

'Tommy! Come in!' she said. 'What's happened?'

He shuffled at the doorstep. 'I don't want to interrupt anything...'

'Daftie! You're not interrupting anything except that I was having a good cry to myself because the War's over.'

'I thought you would have been out in the streets, cheering your head off.'

'I'm doing it in my own way.' She led him into the kitchen. 'I was just going to have a cup of tea. Would you like one?'

'Please. Are you sure...?'

'Of course I'm sure.' What's gone wrong? she thought. 'Put that case down and have a seat.' She remembered that she had a slab of Spam in the larder, and she brought out the oblong shape and began slicing it and making sandwiches with the loaf she took from the enamelled bread tin. She sprinkled the Spam with some HP Sauce before she

301

made the sandwiches. It needed something to improve its well-known tastelessness.

'You shouldn't have bothered if those are for me, Lisa.' He looked hungrily at the growing pile.

'Don't flatter yourself. They're for both of us. I like a sandwich at this time of night.' How white he was, the paleness showing through the stubble – no longer her little brother, a grown man. 'Supposing you tell me what you've been up to. You don't look as if you've come out of a bandbox.'

'Sleeping rough.' His grin was half-hearted. 'Climbed over the gates of the Necropolis at nights and had a kip on somebody's gravestone. First night I just walked in.'

'Oh, Tommy! Why on earth...?'

'Mrs Doyle threw me out. Accused me of "interfering" – her word – with her daughter.' He laughed. 'I'm not that desperate.' He was eyeing the plate of sandwiches and she pushed it towards him.

'Help yourself.'

'I was glad in a way. It was getting ... awkward.' His teeth made a crescent-shaped bite-mark in the bread. 'Nothing like Spam.'

'You can say that again. Was the girl bothering you?'

'Oh, don't put all the blame on Jenny. I wasn't entirely blameless ... once. A starving man doesn't turn up his lip at a crust.'

She laughed out loud. 'How you've grown!'

'Well, all I'm saying is ... well, I didn't. But maybe that was because I knew there was no lock on the door. I'm talking rot, really. Relief at seeing you. And those sandwiches.' He took another one. 'No, it wouldn't ever be Jenny.' Lisa was making the tea and she turned to him from the stove, hiding her surprise at this new Tommy.

'What happened to Bert and Jock?'

'Oh, they stayed on till the end, but they've now been welcomed back into the arms of Jehovah and thanked for their stand against the forces of evil.'

'You should have come here right away, or gone to Holland Street. You know Betty would always give you a bed.'

'Maybe you're right. Anyhow it didn't do me any harm. I could think things out. I didn't like to go to Holland Street. He's got Betty now.'

'He still loves you. He told you that. And she's fond of you.'

'Honestly? I thought she didn't, well, approve of me.'

'Far from it. She's more broad-minded than he is. She's doing him a world of good. She rules him with the velvet-glove technique, and he loves it.'

'That's good. I feel differently now, about everything...' He grinned unsteadily. 'Even about being a stepson. Good sandwiches, Lisa. Thanks.' He sat back, cup in hand. 'So, how are things at Lyle's? I've been living on a different planet. Nearer the stars.' He grinned. 'Sometimes it was not half bad.'

'In retrospect.' She smiled at him. 'Lyle's? I could do with some help, Tommy. I was beginning to wonder where you'd got to. And Mr Delmino may come up soon to see the paintings. He's had a bad time in London with those V bombs.'

'I'd be really glad to come to Lyle's as soon as I'm let out.'

'Great! So we'll see what he says about the paintings and you can ask him about Paris. He'll know all about it. According to him he was Picasso's right-hand man.'

'I'll leave that meantime. It's not that I don't want to, but I feel I have to *earn* Paris.'

'OK, for the time being, but don't forget we need a bit of European culture. I think Bill would like to bow out soon. He's not so well and he's beginning to feel his age.'

'He's been a great support to you.'

'The Photographic Department's picking up already, commemorative portraits before they all go back to Civvy Street,' said Lisa.

He looked shyly at her. 'When I came in you said you'd been having a good cry. I'm the one who feels like crying now. I don't deserve it. All this luck.'

'It's not being handed to you on a plate. That's Mother speaking...' She smiled at him. 'You've got the job of getting the photographic side going properly, maybe with the help of John and Peter, if they come back; if not, you'll have to get a new staff together. Then later there will be Paris, with only a limited amount of wine, women and song ... That's Mother speaking again, though she might say I have no right to lecture you since you're only my stepbrother.'

'In a way that's better. It makes us friends as well, and you—' His voice broke and he pushed back his chair, got up quickly and crossed to the window, where he stood with his back to her.

'You don't get much of a view there, Tommy: other tenements looking at you, a back yard with dustbins and wash-houses...' He didn't reply, and she went on speaking to give him time. 'The difference at Kilmacolm! Those fields sloping down to the Gryfe, the clean, fresh smell from the open window...' No reply. 'But I found it difficult travelling every day from there. And too much cosseting from Margaret ... For God's sake come and finish your tea!'

His laugh was strangled. 'Oh, hell!' He turned to face her, rubbing his eyes with a grubby handkerchief. 'You're too good to me.'

'You had your own war,' she said. 'I know

305

how difficult it must have been at times.'

'The thing was...' he had come back to the table and sat down, 'I began to *question*! Everything. My decision. Even the "Thou shalt not kill" concept. I listened to Bert and Jock. They were authorities on hell and damnation, which was an eye-for-an-eye thing when you come to think of it. With me to begin with it was an abhorrence for the act of war, the blindness of most of the people running it, their total disregard of the terrible carnage they were creating...'

'The end doesn't justify the means with you?'

'Not at the time I became a CO. I loathed any destruction of life.' He decided not to tell her of the baby mice.

'Maybe you would have quite liked Hitler striding about Loch Lomond?'

'Couldn't we all just have lived in peace and harmony together?'

'You're an idealist. We're not ready for it. You'll do your bit by living in Paris for a year or two, fraternising, becoming part of Europe. Maybe you'll be able to join some society where they think the same as you do. Look at the strength Bert and Jock get from theirs.'

'They're sure about themselves. That's the rub. I'm not.'

'That's your problem, lad. You've got all your life to work it out. I'll tell you how you should start.'

'How?'

'Have a good hot bath and then get into a bed for a treat.'

'You haven't room for me?'

'The divan in the sitting-room is quite comfortable.'

'I'll look for digs tomorrow.'

'You'll do no such thing. You'll settle in here for the time being, and we'll go and pay a visit to the newly-weds, give them your blessing.'

'I quite like the thought of that. Next to a hot bath.' He got up and she saw him sway, hold on to the table edge. 'You're quite right. You're like Mother. Hot baths, some-times mustard baths and all ... Pay no atten-tion. I'm raving.'

James and Betty received them with genuine pleasure.

'Come in, come in! This is how I like it,' she said, 'family dropping in.'

'Hello, Father!' He felt a rush of affection. James had filled out, probably because he was getting it ... He had learned that sort of talk from Jenny.

James sounded pleased to see him. 'Well, Tommy. Quite a stranger. You know you'll always be welcome here.'

'Thanks. In the mean time Lisa's given me a bed. And I'll be starting in Lyle's now.'

'Quite the businessman!' Betty clapped her hands, her eyes dancing. Lisa wondered if Tommy would be as quick as she was at recognising the swelling round her waist. Well, good for her, she thought. A late baby for Father. One of his very own. 'I always wanted to go to Paris, but James thought maybe in a year or so, the old fusspot.' She leant forward and patted his hand, and he smiled into her eyes. Anyone who can do this with my father, Lisa thought, is worth her weight in gold.

'Yes, plenty of time later, Betty,' she said, smiling sweetly, 'if you're not too busy.' She didn't meet the blackbird eyes.

'James!' the gracious hostess said, 'we must have a toast now that Tommy's back.'

'A good idea, my lovely.' James got up and went to the press in the corner of the room. Had Betty turned it into a modern cocktail cabinet instead of a store for old books? Lisa wondered.

'Here's to all the good folks who helped us win the War,' James said when he had poured out their tots of rich, dark sherry.

'And here's to Tommy who helped to feed us!' Betty said, raising her glass to him. She never missed a trick. 'And you looked fine in your tin hat too!' She raised her glass to James and they both burst out laughing. It must be a private joke: Father's face was as red as a turkey-cock's.

Twenty-Nine

'Well, we're all packed up,' Margaret Currie said. Lisa saw the tears in her eyes. She felt like crying as well.

'You'll enjoy your cottage, Margaret. It will be really nice, you and Alec together, retired.'

'It was good of you. We're right bowled over.'

'It was always my mother's wish. Alec will make a lovely garden there.'

'But he'll still come and do yours, don't you worry, and spring-cleaning – I'll help you.'

'You're retiring, remember! But you know I'll always be pleased to see you. And I'm looking forward to visiting you at Lochwinnoch Road.'

'You'll be making different arrangements as well, now that the War's over.' It was not in Margaret's capacity to look sly, but her eyes were sending messages, hinting at what she didn't like to say.

'Maybe, but I'll keep on the flat at Woodlands Road. Tommy will be living there meantime. Now, off you go. Alec'll be waiting for you.'

'Aye, so he will.' She threw her arms round Lisa. 'Now, you look after yourself. Mind and air the place to keep it fresh, and check the doors before you go to bed.'

'Yes, Margaret.' She returned the hug. 'And walk round any time to see that I'm carrying out your orders.'

'I'll do that. You'll get fed up with the sight of me.' She put her handkerchief to her eyes and turned away.

When Lisa had come to the Glebe this summer weekend, Margaret had agreed to give up working there. 'It's like fate, Lisa. You giving us that house, and the doctor telling Alec he must give up working at Baxter's farm. I doubt if he would have listened to him, but there was that nice wee place sitting waiting for us with a new garden to make, and he agreed without a murmur. We've never had a house of our own. I was in service to your Grandpa and Granny since I was fifteen. It's like a new lease of life and us both seventy ... starting again.' The Cottar's Saturday Night, in fact, except that there would be no bairnies running about the floor. So what? They were happy together.

The garden of the Glebe faced south, and

in the morning the porch at the front was flooded with sunshine. On the Sunday morning Lisa thought she would sit there and have her coffee and enjoy the sun. The church bells were pealing over the fields.

She should feel guilty about that, but her life had been centred on Glasgow, and she had lost her old contacts here. People grew away from a small place. Not enough scope. Perhaps when she was Margaret's age, or before, she would become one of the community again.

The peacefulness put her in a reflective mood, looking back to that year when the War started, when she had met Neil at Craigton. She felt different about it now, realising in a way that the encounter had petrified her, preventing her from fully developing her emotional maturity.

Beryl had been the sensible one. She had married Bruce first and then gone on to have children, ignoring the slackening of conventional morality because of the War. She, Lisa, had remained in a kind of stasis since that time, longing for Neil in spite of knowing that it had been impossible for him to love her as she had wanted to be loved.

And that state had been exacerbated by circumstances. There had been her mother's illness and death, which precluded everything else; the heavy load of running Lyle's single-handed, which had exhausted her often, although she had never admitted it. And as well there had been the care of her father and Tommy, and the flat ... Oh, there were plenty of excuses, but no real reasons. She had been holding on to a nebulous thing, a dream.

She was a poor bet for Charlie. He didn't need a stoic, a contained, frigid young woman. He needed a warm one, full of gaiety, who could help him forget some of the terrible sights of the War, help him forget his own infirmity. Comfort him. A little bit of Betty, in fact.

She had the door open, mindful of Margaret's instructions about airing the house, and the spicy smell of pinks came strongly to her. How many years had they bloomed there, backed by leafy rosettes from which airy pink florets were borne on slender scarlet stems? She had never looked up their proper names.

How this place was in her bones, she thought, hardly changed since her grandfather Lyle's day when it was a small village, much of the land taken up by the demesnes of the gentry. Her mother had known it then, when she had crossed the fields to the banks of the Gryfe to seek out Lionel Craig, her one and only love whom she hadn't had the courage to marry. That devotion to tradition, to work for its own sake, was in Lisa too.

There were a few changes. Motor cars, of course, road-widening here and there, the new houses for the city folk, but the church bells still pealed over the fields. A place of churches, Kilmacolm. You would have thought they didn't need them here, living in such peace.

And telephones. Most of the big houses near Strathgryffe had telephones, and now she had one here connecting her to Lyle's. And Betty would surely have one so that she could summon the doctor quickly when her time came ... oh, yes, Betty would have one. And Tommy had got a few orders for portraiture that way.

She idly watched a taxi stop at her gate, saw a tall, burly man in grey flannels and a sports jacket get stiffly out and lean forward to speak to the driver, put his hand in his pocket. Her interest was cursory, almost, certainly relaxed, sitting in the lambent sunshine of the porch.

The taxi drew away; the man put his hand on the swing gate, came through, walked a few steps, seemed to see her and stop. Their eyes met and she found herself propelled to her feet. What was she thinking of? It was Charlie! She ran to meet him, holding out her hands. They kissed. They were both slightly embarrassed and she felt it was her fault.

'I was sitting dreaming...' She rushed into

speech. 'Come in, come in! I'm just having a coffee.' She led him to the porch. 'Would you like one? Oh and please sit down.' Now that was tactless, as if she was too aware of his limp.

'I'd like that fine.' He was still standing.

'We'll have to go into the kitchen and I'll make some fresh.'

'OK. Lead on. Where's that wonderful Margaret who cosseted you?'

'She and Alec have gone to a home of their own. They've never had one, but it was Mother's wish. Can you believe it, she's been in service since she was fifteen! She's seventy now.'

'Service but not servitude.' He had sat down at the kitchen table. 'Where did I get that?'

She laughed. 'It's not like you.'

His eyes were steadily on her, warm and smiling.

'Don't look at me like that.' She felt she was blushing.

'I can't help it. I'd forgotten how gorgeous you were.'

'Gorgeous? Well, that's a new one...' He looked older, she thought. The glint in his hair was still there, but it was beginning to go grey at the temples, and there were lines round his mouth and eyes. His exuberance was muted.

'I thought of sending you a telegram.' He

314

sipped the coffee she had put down before him. 'I'm staying at the Grand Hotel at Charing Cross.'

'You could have telephoned me. We're quite up to date now.'

'I'll remember that. How are your folks?'

'Betty and my father are married and they're expecting their first child. They'll dote on it. Mother never allowed Father to dote on us.'

'I'll dote on you, if you'll give me the chance. Lisa...'

'Tommy is working at Lyle's. He's a dab hand at portraiture. He's finished being a CO. He and I had qualms. I regret that I didn't do more for the War, and I think he has a few misgivings about not doing anything except growing cabbages. Oh, and he shared a room with two Holy Gospellers. And was thrown out. And slept a few nights in the Necropolis.'

Why was she chattering on like this?

'All valuable experience,' he said solemnly, and then they were both laughing. She laughed so much that she choked on it and she had to take a sip of coffee. The strain was gone. She smiled across the table at him and said:

'Oh, Charlie, it's so good to see you!'

'I came straight away. Couldn't wait.'

'To think I was just sitting there, and didn't recognise you at first ... Tell me about *your* folks.'

'Quite chirpy, especially my mother. She's got a good seat on a horse, and he breeds Aberdeen Angus cattle, so you'll never be short of a juicy steak.' County, she registered. Well, well, she had always imagined a whitewashed cottage on the shore of a loch.

'That's an inducement.' She smiled at him. Yes, he was handsome, and there was a glint of gold also on his high cheekbones.

'Morag, my sister, is married to a lawyer in Arbroath and they have two children, Alison and Calum. Morag's always saying to me, "Come on in, the water's fine."' He moved in his kitchen chair.

'Would you like to go into the drawing-room? It's more comfortable. My mother always entertained there.'

'I'd be happy in a byre, as long as you were there.'

'We haven't got a byre, unfortunately.' And then they were talking naturally, and he was telling her a little about his experiences, how brave and cheerful the men had been under his care, and she told him about Lyle's and some of her worries, and about the paintings.

At tea-time she said, 'Supposing we start preparing a meal, and then we'll have it, and then we'll go for a walk by the river ... if you have the time to spare.'

He laughed at her over his teacup. 'All the

316

time in the world. Oh, and I didn't tell you, I've got a job in the Western. So handy for Kilmacolm!' His glance was impish. 'Assistant to a vascular surgeon. My superior officer in the Air Force was a vascular surgeon and I thought he was marvellous.' He looked solemnly at her. 'Once he performed an intricate operation when we had no anaesthetic, only brandy.' She put her hand to her mouth, appalled, and he said, 'Only teasing. You mustn't be squeamish if you're going to be a doctor's wife.' He was back on form.

'I'll murder you with this.' She was holding a kitchen knife in her hand. 'Supposing you peel some potatoes while I do the vegetables?' She had been busying herself at the sink.

'I'm a champion potato peeler. Can I look at you as well?'

'If you think I'm worth looking at.'

He got up and took her in his arms. This time it was no perfunctory kiss.

After supper they walked in the misty fields on the bank of the Gryfe. When they were leaning on an oak looking at the bottle-green water, she thought about Lionel Craig, and found herself talking about him.

'I feel his ghost is still here, and my mother's. Happy ghosts. It was a great love affair which nearly didn't happen. They were such opposites, he so easygoing, she so ... dedicated.'

'Opposites always attract. That's why you and I are made for each other.'

'You being easygoing?'

'Only if I get my own way.'

They walked back across the fields, with the occasional cry of a lonely peewit from the woods in their ears. She felt as if she had one foot in the past with her mother and Lionel Craig, and the other here with Charlie Cramond. Charlie's arm was comfortably round her shoulders but he didn't speak. She was glad he was sensitive to atmosphere.

They both accepted that he would stay. He did ask perfunctorily if there might be a hotel near, and she said she didn't know of any except the Hydro, and he said, 'God preserve me from that.' Besides, he had no luggage.

There was no question that he would occupy a separate room. This was it, the present, the fulcrum which had been reached. He didn't have any nightwear, no luggage, as he'd said, but he started off with white undershorts. 'Army issue,' he said. 'I'll have to give them up soon.' Which he did.

In bed she said, 'I have never, you know...'

'Well I have,' he said.

'Have you?' she asked. It was the first time the thought had occurred to her.

'I'm over thirty, for God's sake,' he said. 'I'm not a monk.'

'Well,' she said, cheekily, 'you'll know all the answers.'

'Not till I make love to you,' he said.

He took her in his arms, and instead of becoming passionate right away, he said, 'I want to savour this for a minute. You've been such a splendid hostess, welcoming me into your house, sharing your food with me, now your bed...'

'You've been a perfect guest.'

She knew he was trying to put her at ease. She relaxed, felt happy. She hardly noticed at first that he had stopped talking and was gently loving her, softly, tenderly, perhaps even expertly. Until she got impatient...

'Why had no one ever told me?' she said when they were having a rest. 'All this ... beauty I've been missing...'

'It's got to be with the right person.'

'Yes, I see that, but...' It took half an hour to completely convince her, or so she inferred.

'Would you like me to take you to Craigton for our honeymoon?' he asked.

She thought of that once quiet village, the torn-up shore-line because of the War, and halfway up the hill a deserted tennis court, overgrown, the wooden pavilion unpainted. No laughing voices. *Game to Miss Cowan and partner* ... Neil's voice came to her faintly; she remembered the dark eyes, the dark hair falling over his brow, the long-limbed, easy elegance of him ... the pity of it. And yet...

'I was worried at one stage if I should ever feel that ... tremulousness I felt with Neil.'

'Are you still?'

'No, I see it now. It was repression. Un-fulfilled desire on my part. And Neil's release came with death. The pity of it...'

'No, he had come to terms with himself. It was just damned bad luck.' It was like a requiem. They lay quietly.

'I tell you what,' she said after a time. 'Let's go to Paris!'

'Paris!' He sounded delighted, and sang a bar or two of Jean Sablon to prove it. All French songs were the same, made for love.

She turned to him again. Now it was *une révélation, le feu d'artifice, son-et-lumière, une cascade, une fontaine,* and then *un réengagement.* She surprised herself by her abandonment. She thought she surprised him too.

Stockton Borough Public Libraries